PRAISE FOR THE "SIZZLING"* ROMANCES

Susanna Carr

"The guys are hot, and the sexual tension is unbelievable!"
—*New York Times* bestselling author Sabrina Jeffries

"A must read for everyone." —Fresh Fiction

"Be sure not to miss out on this one, after all, being wicked and being in love can fall hand in hand. This is a keeper, definitely."
—The Romance Readers Connection

"I can't say that I have ever laughed so much while reading erotica, but Susanna Carr definitely delivered. I love this book. It was an enjoyment to read such a change from the average erotica." —Romance Reader at Heart

"Delightfully humorous, with sizzling chemistry between the characters, great secondary characters, and a love story that won't be soon forgotten. A definite recommend!" —*Love Romances

"A hilarious romantic read that will have you turning page after page . . . a must-read story." —*Romance Junkies*

"Carr's stories are full of well-matched characters, exhibitionist-style lovemaking and some wedding faux pas that are sure to entertain married and single women alike." —*Romantic Times*

"Witty and sexy . . . what a huge amount of fun!"
—Just Erotic Romance Reviews

"Sexy, sassy, delicious fun." —Shannon McKenna

"Delivers exactly what readers want." —TwoLips Reviews

THE YEAR OF LIVING
Shamelessly

Susanna Carr

A SIGNET ECLIPSE BOOK

SIGNET ECLIPSE
Published by New American Library, a division of
Penguin Group (USA) Inc., 375 Hudson Street,
New York, New York 10014, USA
Penguin Group (Canada), 90 Eglinton Avenue East, Suite 700, Toronto,
Ontario M4P 2Y3, Canada (a division of Pearson Penguin Canada Inc.)
Penguin Books Ltd., 80 Strand, London WC2R 0RL, England
Penguin Ireland, 25 St. Stephen's Green, Dublin 2,
Ireland (a division of Penguin Books Ltd.)
Penguin Group (Australia), 250 Camberwell Road, Camberwell, Victoria 3124,
Australia (a division of Pearson Australia Group Pty. Ltd.)
Penguin Books India Pvt. Ltd., 11 Community Centre, Panchsheel Park,
New Delhi - 110 017, India
Penguin Group (NZ), 67 Apollo Drive, Rosedale, North Shore 0632,
New Zealand (a division of Pearson New Zealand Ltd.)
Penguin Books (South Africa) (Pty.) Ltd., 24 Sturdee Avenue,
Rosebank, Johannesburg 2196, South Africa

Penguin Books Ltd., Registered Offices:
80 Strand, London WC2R 0RL, England

First published by Signet Eclipse, an imprint of New American Library,
a division of Penguin Group (USA) Inc.

First Printing, October 2009
10 9 8 7 6 5 4 3 2 1

SIGNET ECLIPSE and logo are trademarks of Penguin Group (USA) Inc.

Library of Congress Cataloging-in-Publication Data:

Carr, Susanna.
    The year of living shamelessly/Susanna Carr.
      p.   cm.
    ISBN 978-0-451-22516-0
  1. Man–woman relationships—Fiction.   I. Title.
    PS3603.A77435Y43 2009
    813'.6—dc22   2009022211

Set in Bembo
Designed by Jennifer Daddio

Printed in the United States of America

To my editor, Becky Vinter, with thanks.

PROLOGUE

❦

December 31

"Grab hold of your dates, ladies and gentlemen," the bandleader announced. "The countdown to the New Year will start in one minute."

It was time. Katie fluffed out her long black hair and smoothed her hands over her little black dress before pressing her palm over her nervous stomach. She was going to start her wild affair with Ryder Scott. Tonight.

Her skin stung with awareness at what she was about to do. She had never had the courage to really go after him until now. Well, what she currently had wasn't so much courage as it was imagining her regret if she never let him know how she felt. This unrequited crush was entering its eleventh year and no one was getting any younger. Katie gave a little sigh and fought her way through the crowd of shiny dresses and ill-fitting suits as she searched for Ryder.

Unfortunately, Ryder was best friends with her brother, Jake, and he still saw her as Jake's little sister. That was the downside of always having him around the house when they were growing up. Ryder's family life was sad and neglectful, but the Kramers had been happy to open their home to him.

In return, he was protective toward the family, Katie in particular, which was great when he wanted to check that her car had enough oil, but not so great when she wanted him to sweep her off her feet and make mad, passionate love to her.

Katie thought back to the one moment during the summer when she'd thought he might feel the same way. She had been hot and sweaty, wearing a threadbare tank top and Daisy Duke shorts while gardening. When Ryder had walked into the yard, he had folded his arms across his chest and run his eyes over her, giving her a certain look that suggested he was seriously considering pouncing and ripping her clothes off. But instead of pressing her against the dirt and doing some wicked and wonderful things, Ryder had clenched his fists, pivoted on his heel and walked away without looking back.

If he hadn't gotten the hint by now that she was a sensual woman ready for the taking, then it was time for her to make the first move.

"Ten . . . ," the crowd started to chant.

New Year's Eve was the perfect, symbolic night, Katie decided as she stood on the tips of her toes and looked over people's shoulders for Ryder. She thought she could see him in the far corner of the Women's Auxiliary Hall.

"Nine . . ."

Katie hurried toward him, her progress slow as she dodged and swerved around people. It was just her luck that she was on the other side of the hall for the countdown. She had to get to Ryder in time for her New Year's kiss!

"Eight . . ."

The specially ordered black velvet dress hadn't quite turned her into Cinderella for the night. She glanced down at it with a frown.

It was certainly feminine and elegant—but utterly the wrong choice for a seduction. The dress said sweet and demure when she needed naughty and sexy.

"Seven . . ."

The fitted bodice and full skirt didn't compete with the slinky dresses worn by Tatum and Sasha, Ryder's ex-girlfriends. Those two grabbed every man's attention with their scandalously short dresses in bold jeweled colors while Katie felt invisible. As usual.

"Six . . ."

It didn't help that Tatum had been all over Ryder all night like a leech, while Sasha had flitted around him, constantly readjusting her bra to draw his attention to her chest.

"Five . . ."

All night, Katie couldn't figure out how she was going to pry Tatum and Sasha off Ryder before the countdown. Ryder usually kept an eye on her, especially when the men were drunk and rowdy, but tonight he had only nodded and smiled at her once from across the room and that was it. Hilary and Melissa had kept nudging her to tell her he was looking at her, but every time she glanced his way, he was engaged in a new conversation.

"Four . . ."

The moment everyone shouted "Happy New Year," she was going to plant a long, wet and thorough kiss on Ryder Scott.

"Three . . ."

Then suddenly, she was in front of him. Her heart skipped a beat when she saw his dark brown eyes, high cheekbones and molded biceps. But it appeared that if she wanted her New Year's kiss, she was going to have to stand in line. Tatum wasn't waiting for any countdown.

"Two . . ."

The platinum blonde was kissing Ryder so deeply, she was probably tickling his spleen with her tongue. And Ryder certainly wasn't doing anything to stop her.

"One!"

Sasha stood on the other side of Ryder and grasped his chin with her hand. She determinedly pulled Ryder's face toward her and kissed him with enthusiasm.

"Happy New Year!"

Katie stood right in front of Ryder as everyone rang in the New Year. A shower of confetti drifted in front of her eyes, but she didn't blink. She wanted to yank Tatum away from Ryder and push Sasha aside. Then she would wipe the smears of red and pink lipstick from his mouth and claim him with a kiss that would make him forget everyone else in the room.

But she didn't make a move toward him. She felt her shoulders slump. Ryder could have his pick, and if the rumors were true, he might go home with both of them and enjoy a *ménage à trois* to start off the New Year. There just didn't seem to be any reason why Ryder would choose her.

Katie took a few steps back, turned and melded into the crowd. But something in her told her she couldn't let this setback get her down. She *would* have an affair with Ryder. She just needed to figure out a way to make him see her as someone other than meek and mild Katie. The girl he would rather undress than shove aside to get to the fridge.

It was time for a makeover. One just like in the movies. She had to become totally irresistible. A vixen. No one would dare give a noogie to a vixen. It would probably require some professional advice, and there was only one place in town where she could get it.

Katie squared her shoulders back and thrust her chin out. The journey to a new and improved Katie was going to start right this second.

Sex Goddess Secrets!

Katie wanted to know every one of them. She grabbed for the magazine, tucked it under her arm and kept searching.

21 Bad Girl Sex Tips!

And here she thought that sex was sex. She added the magazine to her pile.

10 Things That Will Make Him Beg for You!

Oh, yeah. She needed that one, too.

"Do we have to do this now?" Hilary complained. Melissa nodded in agreement.

Katie glanced at her friends, who were leaning tiredly on the magazine stand. Their party clothes were as limp as their hair, and the harsh fluorescent lights revealed that their makeup had melted off hours ago. Hilary shifted from one aching foot to the next while Melissa's eyes drifted shut.

"I need this stuff," Katie insisted, returning her attention to the magazine covers. She hoped there was something about seducing a sex god, because Ryder Scott was not just any man.

"It's two o'clock in the morning," Melissa complained with a whimper.

"And I don't want to start the year in a convenience store!" Hilary declared.

"Fine." Katie scanned the magazines and scooped up any that showed cleavage or used the word "sex" with a bunch of exclamation points on the cover. "I'll just take them all."

That jerked Melissa awake. "All of them? Why?"

"Because I totally blew my New Year's resolution one minute into the New Year!" Katie explained as she marched over to the counter.

"It's not the end of the world. You can kiss Ryder anytime you want," Hilary said as she trailed after Katie. "Start a hot and heavy affair tomorrow. You know, right after a good night's sleep."

"I wanted to kiss him at the stroke of midnight. But I couldn't. Why?" Katie dumped the magazines on the counter. "Because he was already being kissed. Not by one woman, but by two!" Ryder hadn't even noticed she was there. "I didn't stand a chance."

"And these magazines are going to push the women aside for you next time?" Hilary asked.

"It's time to show Ryder my wild side, and these magazines are going to help me unleash it. This year I'm going to be the sexiest woman Crystal Bend has ever seen." She caught the look of disbelief from the guy at the cash register. "I will!"

The cashier looked away and scanned the magazines as quickly as he could.

"I'm going to be a sex goddess that Ryder can't resist," she told her friends.

"Katie, have you been drinking?" Melissa asked, watching her with suspicion. "You're supposed to be the designated driver."

"I'm sober and I'm serious. This time next year I will be knee-deep in a wild affair with Ryder Scott."

CHAPTER ONE

❧

December 24
ONE YEAR LATER

She was here.

Ryder couldn't stop the tension from entering his body. He was surrounded by coworkers, who, thankfully, hadn't noticed his spine growing rigid. They were too busy singing along to "Santa Baby" so loudly that he bet the music pulsed through the walls of the Student Union Building. He was on the other side of the ballroom, far away from the entrance, with a sea of reindeer antlers, elves caps and Santa hats between them, but he still knew exactly where Katie Kramer stood.

He didn't like this sixth sense he had when it came to his best friend's little sister. It was probably developed from years of keeping his eye on her. Even when she was young, he'd wanted to protect her from the ugliness of the world, like when she was being bullied at school. He'd put a quick stop to that.

But now things were different from when they were younger. *Now*, he was painfully aware of her. He wanted to claim her body, her heart, and make her his in every way, but he knew it would be a huge mistake to act on his desires.

Ryder cautiously looked over his shoulder and instantly spotted her at the door. Tonight, Katie looked aggressively sexy. Dressed in all black from her figure-hugging turtleneck sweater to her leather skirt and dominatrix boots, she stood out in a crowd of red, green and gold.

She teetered slightly on those five-inch stilettos. Ryder automatically took a step in her direction, ready to catch her. He stopped just as she regained her balance. He watched as she flipped her long black hair over her shoulders and confidently strode into the crowd as if she owned the place.

He had hoped she wouldn't show up at the Christmas party. Yes, she worked as an administrative assistant for the college, but was a small reprieve too much to hope for?

Eight days, he reminded himself. He only had to be strong for eight more days.

He wasn't sure he would make it. He wanted her so much that it was turning him inside out. It didn't help that he was supposed to look out for her this year while she was house-sitting for her parents. They were very academic, but they were stupid not to realize how he felt about their daughter.

Ryder watched Katie greet some men from the biology department. Ryder gripped his drink tightly as he watched one of the men get overly familiar with a hug, his hands too close to Katie's pert ass. He wanted to go over there and break it up, but Katie skillfully disentangled herself. He closed his eyes and took a deep breath.

The sad thing was, he would like to hold Katie close, but he didn't trust himself. He was on guard every time she was near. It didn't used to be that way. When she was in high school, Katie was his favorite person to ski with. When she got older, they enjoyed playing pool together at the hall late into the night. He liked how things were before she changed, when she was sassy but never crossed the line. He remembered how much fun it had been teasing her. She gave as good as she got, but he stopped the minute the teasing held a sexual undertone.

Now she seemed to delight in provoking him by flaunting her confidence and independence. Not to mention her skimpy outfits. And just last week she'd informed him that she was going to use the small inheritance she'd received from her grandmother to buy the Merrill house. She was foolish to even consider it, as she well knew—that house was a death trap; it should have been condemned years ago. He wondered if she was trying to get a rise out of him with that outrageous plan, but he wasn't sure.

When it came to Katie, it was best not to get involved. He'd tried to follow that strategy for the past couple of months. He wanted to keep his distance, but it was difficult. As a carpenter for the college's Building Services, he had too many opportunities to drop by her office and see how she was doing. She was always around when he was hanging out with her brother, Jake. And no matter where he was after work, whether playing pool with friends or out on a date, he would see Katie strutting around in a cute little skirt and flirting with other guys. She had men drooling over her wherever she went and he couldn't take any more. His restraint was slipping.

Eight more days, he reminded himself again.

Katie turned her head and their gazes collided.

Shit. His heart began to gallop. She was going to come over. He might as well get this over with. He could handle this. He would just greet her as he always did, like old family friends, nothing more. . . . As long as Katie never realized how dangerous she was to his self-control, he could get through it.

———

Katie knew it was time to strut her stuff. She had been practicing all afternoon. She moved toward him, praying that she wouldn't trip. She enjoyed the aggressive feel of her new boots as she strode through the crowd, her hips swaying with every step.

She kept eye contact with Ryder, noticing not for the first time that he was all harsh lines and sharp angles. He watched her in tense silence, his brown eyes narrowing warily. She expected nothing less from him. One could tell by the crooked nose and the small white scars on his high cheekbones that he was familiar with the rough side of life.

Ryder was taller than most of the men at the party, but that wasn't what gave him a commanding presence. Tonight he wore a pair of snug faded jeans and a dark charcoal cashmere sweater, the sleeves casually pushed up. He was the kind of man who stood out in a crowd. He didn't have to do anything to garner attention, it was simply granted to him.

Katie was suddenly finding it difficult to keep her balance, especially with the way Ryder was looking at her. She had felt the same way when he helped her with her Christmas decorations earlier in the week. And there was an odd smirk on his face. That didn't bode well. She was almost breathless by the time she reached him. She gave him a slow smile, ready to toss some amazing pickup line when he gave her the look.

No, not the I'm-going-to-do-you-right-this-minute look. Wouldn't that have been nice? It was more like the you-have-to-be-kidding-me expression, complete with arched eyebrows and condescending amusement.

"Isn't it way past your bedtime?"

Her mouth dropped open. She felt the blush zooming up her neck. Her first instinct was to fold her arms and growl out *It's freaking ten o'clock*, but she knew, of course, no sexy siren would act that way. She might have been flaunting her newfound confidence for almost a year now, but it still didn't come naturally—at least not where Ryder was concerned. He knew how to hit all of her buttons.

Instead she tilted her head to one side and fluttered her eyelashes. "Is that an invitation to tuck me in?" she purred.

Ryder scowled, but she saw the hot flare in his eyes before he banked it. She couldn't tell if he was taken aback by her answer. Or did her suggestion tantalize some forbidden fantasy of his? That was probably wishful thinking.

"You better watch that mouth," he ordered in a brusque tone. "It's going to get you in trouble someday."

"Promise?" she asked, pursing her lips.

"Give it a rest, Katie." His voice was dangerously soft.

Unfazed by his warnings, she decided to throw caution to the wind and go after what she really wanted. Leaning forward, inhaling his delicious scent, Katie reached for the glass in his hand, making sure her breasts were visible as she moved toward him. "I thought you *liked* trouble," she said, with what she hoped was a sexy smile.

His jaw clenched and a ruddy color stained his cheekbones.

Feeling like she just scored a major point, Katie brazenly took his drink and gave a hefty swallow.

Oh, God. The man drank liquid fire. She braced herself as the alcohol melted her esophagus and ate a hole in her stomach. It took superhuman effort not to cough, wheeze or keel over.

Catching a drop at the corner of her mouth with the tip of her tongue, and ignoring the fact that it tasted worse than cold medicine, she returned the glass to him. "Here, Ryder," she said hoarsely, hoping it came across as husky, "you might need this tonight."

She wanted to stay with him, but the magazine articles she'd glanced over during the day warned her about crowding her man. The "Give Him Space" article promised that if she was the first to leave, he would follow.

Reluctantly, Katie started to move away, letting her hips roll as much as her precarious balance allowed. She sensed Ryder behind her and she hoped he was watching her sexy walk. She felt the tension radiating from him. *Follow me*, she silently urged. *Chase after me. You know you want to. . . .*

She counted to one hundred, probably quicker than she should have, and paused, pretending to look for someone. Ryder didn't collide into her. Then again, his reflexes were superior. Katie looked over her shoulder, her come-hither look withering to nothing.

Ryder was nowhere to be found. He wasn't behind her, and he wasn't watching her, stunned and gawking. He wasn't even where she had left him.

Damn, that "Give Him Space" writer had some explaining to do. She may have missed a golden opportunity by taking that advice. She looked around, not caring if she was obvious, but she couldn't find Ryder. Knowing her luck, he'd probably left. Double damn.

Craning her neck, she caught a glimpse of frizzy red hair. That had to be Hilary. Peering into the shadowy corner, she saw her friend sitting at a table wearing a beige thermal shirt and a light green cardigan sweater that dwarfed her petite frame. Next to Hilary was her other friend, Melissa. Melissa's long brown hair was pulled back into the usual ponytail and she wore a college football jersey over a white long-sleeved T-shirt.

Dressed casually, Melissa and Hilary could easily be overlooked among their festive and boisterous coworkers. Katie frowned when she realized they were huddled around a forgotten table, people watching. She hurried over, as quickly as her heels would allow, determined to get her friends in a party mood.

"Wow!" Melissa's eyes widened when she noticed the knee-high, laced-up black leather boots. "Did you get those boots around here?"

"No, I borrowed these from Winter." The goth student worker in her office had loaned Katie a couple of items that promised to make grown men weep. Winter forgot to mention that they would cause some weeping on Katie's part, too. She sat down gratefully next to her friends and gave a sigh of relief. "Why are you guys hiding in the corner?"

Hilary popped a Christmas cookie into her mouth. "Hiding is such a loaded word."

Katie wasn't deterred by Hilary's comment. Her friend was all about details, proof and rationalizing. "Remember why we're here?"

"Because you forced us to come?" Hilary responded.

"And you promised to be my designated driver for New Year's Eve if I came to this party." Melissa turned to Hilary. "Do you know how hard it is to find one for that night?"

"We are here," Katie replied, "because you, Hilary, want to make your move on Jake, remember?" Katie couldn't fathom why someone with a high IQ would want to date her brother, but there was no accounting for taste.

"I can make a move on Jake anytime, anywhere," Hilary said as she washed down the sugar cookie with a frothy, peppermint pink drink. "I don't need to do it today."

"But you do need to make the attempt someday, so why not tonight?" Katie argued. "And, Melissa, you wanted to meet someone special. You can't do that waiting in the shadows. No one will see you!"

"I know," Melissa said with a sigh and propped her chin on her hand. "It's just that . . . if he were Mr. Right, he would find me no matter what."

"Nice fairy tale," Hilary said, "but anecdotally speaking, it's not going to happen."

"I hate to say it, but I agree," Katie said. Although she would never use the word "anecdotally" like her research librarian friend. "Why else would I wear stiletto boots?" She lifted her leg to show off the five-inch heel. "It's to be seen, to be noticed. No, it's to make Ryder's head snap back and his tongue hang out."

"How's that working out for you?" Hilary asked as she brushed the cookie crumbs from her mouth with a napkin.

"Not well." Katie gave a huff of frustration and leaned back in her chair. "For the past year I have followed every article from every sexy magazine, and what do I have to show for it? Nothing."

"I wouldn't say that," Hilary said. "You have a new attitude, a killer wardrobe and plenty of dates."

"But I don't have Ryder," Katie pointed out. That was her mission. Anyone else was a distraction from her main goal.

"Don't give up," Melissa insisted, patting Katie's hand. "You and Ryder were made for each other. He's always been there for you. Nothing will ever change that."

"As much as I would like to believe that," Hilary said, crumpling her napkin, "Katie has basically served herself up on a silver platter and Ryder hasn't taken a nibble. I think we should take that as a sign and move on."

Katie shook her head. "No way. I'm not giving up yet. Just wait and see." She tapped her finger on the table. "This time next year I will be knee-deep in a wild affair with Ryder Scott."

Melissa and Hilary exchanged glances.

"What?" Katie asked.

"You have made Ryder Scott your New Year's resolution for the past two years," Hilary pointed out.

It was true. Two years in a row and she hadn't even had a kiss from the guy. . . . Ouch. "And I'll make it for next year." She tilted her chin up defiantly. "Who am I to break tradition?"

"Katie, maybe you need to cast your net a little wider," Melissa suggested.

Katie couldn't believe that Melissa, her love-will-conquer-all friend, had just said that to her. "You just told me that Ryder and I were destined for each other."

"I know, but that doesn't mean you need to wait around until he wises up," Melissa said. "Ever since your makeover, the men in town have been falling all over you. Why not go for one of them?"

"I've tried." She had purposely dated guys who didn't remind her of Ryder. That may have been her first mistake. Like Jason, the sexy banker who was the complete opposite of Ryder. Unfortunately, he was more interested in her credit rating than her body. Then there was Brian, the hot young history professor. Brian's idea of a good time was touring through cemeteries and making tombstone rubbings. "They bored me. But it wasn't all bad. Those guys must have gotten into a bragging contest because now they all want to date me. I seem to have gotten myself quite the reputation."

"Deservedly or undeservedly?" Hilary asked with a smile.

"Let's just say that reports of my bedroom activities were greatly exaggerated." There had been a couple of times this year when she'd thought she would never achieve her goal of getting Ryder into bed. She decided to "move on" with a man who knew how to treat and please a woman, but in the end the men she'd dated were just pale imitations of Ryder. "But I'm not wasting my time on those guys. I'm not going to settle for second best."

"Then you need to be aware of your competition," Hilary decided. "Take a look over there."

Katie turned around to where Hilary indicated with the tilt of her head. Her heart lurched, excitement tingling in her blood when she saw Ryder. He was talking to someone she couldn't see when he leaned back and laughed.

She had to smile in return. Katie loved watching Ryder, especially when his face lit up with pleasure. Who was he talking to? Most likely Jake. She shifted in her seat and her smile dimmed. Ryder was leaning in very closely to a stunning woman of Amazonian proportions.

A dull ache radiated from Katie's chest as the night's sparkle suddenly went out. Ryder was with Tatum, his ex, and they were so absorbed in each other they looked as if they existed in an intimate bubble that shielded them from the rest of the world. "That dress Tatum is wearing is very . . ."

"Nonexistent?" Hilary supplied the word. "If you want Ryder, go get him before he gets lost in that cleavage."

Katie took one look at Tatum's plunging neckline and regretted wearing a turtleneck sweater. She was writing a letter of complaint to that fashion magazine as soon as she got home. "I can't compete with that."

"Yes, you can," Melissa said fervently. But then, Melissa would say that. Not only did she work with the coaches in the athletic department, but she was a very loyal, and very blind to reality, friend.

"Oh, yeah, right," Katie said, letting the sarcasm seep into her voice. "After all, what does she have that I don't?"

"Besides an audacious body and vast sexual experience?" Hilary asked in her no-nonsense way.

Katie sighed. "Thanks." Hilary could never identify sarcasm. At least Katie could count on her friend to break it down in percentages and PowerPoint presentations, and without a hint of delicacy.

"There has to be something else," Hilary said, watching Ryder through a narrow gaze. "Those two qualities couldn't hold Ryder's interest for long. I could find out if there's a pattern in his mating habits."

"Mating?" Melissa groaned. "Please, Hilary, can you just call it dating like everyone else?"

"I could, but it would be inaccurate."

Katie tuned her friends out as she watched Tatum flirt with Ryder. The woman's sexy look was effortless. It just wasn't fair, Katie decided as she folded her arms across her chest. Compared to Tatum, Katie felt kind of stupid strutting around in an outfit that probably wasn't so sexy after all.

So what if most of the men at this party found Katie attractive? If there ever was a *Who Would You Rather Do?* contest, Tatum would win in a landslide. Why did Katie think she could catch Ryder's attention when he was used to dating the sexiest women around? It didn't matter if she had reinvented herself into the woman she needed to be; she still wasn't in the same league as Tatum.

Katie stared at Ryder and Tatum, hating how the woman could flirt as if she was born to do it. She'd bet Tatum never had to consult a magazine or expert for tips or tricks. Katie wanted to intervene, but why give Ryder side-by-side comparisons? She longed to escape and head home, but she was driven to watch. What should her next move be?

"Let's go," Hilary said, pushing her chair back.

"No, not yet," Katie said, still watching Ryder. She wasn't going to give up at the first sign of difficulty. "You just have to be patient. Something might happen tonight."

"Katie, have you made a move on him since you walked in?" Hilary asked. "Did you say anything suggestive? Flash a little skin?"

Flash Ryder? Katie smiled. Oh, yeah, that would get a response, but not the kind she would be hoping for. He'd probably throw a blanket over her and tell her she was going to catch a cold.

"There is a time for patience, and there's a time for action," Hilary said. "If you aren't ready to make a move, then why are we here?"

Katie was reluctant to inform Hilary that she had already made her move and it hadn't gone as planned. But that was just a warm-up and not her master stroke. Now all she had to do was work up the nerve to try again. If she really had transformed, she would stop being the mousy, invisible girl in the corner and instead be the brazen woman who went after her fantasies.

But her secret fantasy had Ryder going after *her*. Like a man possessed, a man unable to fight the desire she created in him. She would have to do nothing and he would break into a sweat simply thinking of her.

Men never acted like that with her. They wanted her, but they weren't going to be her sex slaves. These days the men noticed and flirted with her, but they were never going to make fools of themselves or make grand, expensive gestures or ruin their lives like they would for Tatum. Maybe Katie should just accept that her dreams about Ryder were too far out of reach.

She should, but she couldn't, Katie realized as she watched Tatum sit her perky little butt on the bar. Ryder wasn't looking too pleased with her. As he stood, hands on hips, glaring at Tatum, several men rushed to help her stand on the bar. It was quite a feat since she was wearing a skintight minidress and strappy heels.

Great, Katie thought with a groan as the rest of the guests turned to see what caused the commotion. Tatum was going to be the center of attention tonight. Was everyone going to be honored by a lame attempt at *Coyote Ugly*? Hilary's idea of leaving was sounding better and better.

"Okay, everyone," Tatum called out, motioning for them to quiet down, "as some of you already know, Ryder Scott is leaving town. . . ."

Katie jerked in surprise and sat straight up. Leaving? "Did she just say Ryder is *leaving*?"

"I think so," Melissa said.

Katie stared at Ryder, who continued to scowl at Tatum. Because Tatum had it wrong, of course. Ryder wasn't going anywhere. Katie would be the first to know about it. *Wouldn't she?*

"Ryder's moving?" someone yelled from the crowd. "When?"

Katie felt like her heart stopped beating. She didn't know why. She was overreacting. She took a deep breath. Ryder would set everything straight and the sudden ache in her chest would disappear.

"New Year's Day," Ryder reluctantly answered in his deep, gravelly voice.

Katie's world slowly stopped turning.

Ryder closed his eyes, resisting the instinct to seek Katie. He knew she was hurting right now. All because of him. Knowing that made it worse.

All hell was going to break loose, and there was not much he could do about it. He wished he had muzzled Tatum when he had the chance.

He felt a hand clasp his shoulder. "Sorry I spilled your secret, Ryder," Jake said. "I didn't know Tatum was standing right behind me. Can that girl keep her mouth shut about anything?"

Ryder faced his friend. Jake was as tall and lean as him. He also had short dark hair and always dressed casually, but that was where the similarities ended. Jake was the charmer, never without a smile. Sometimes Ryder wondered if the guy had a care in the world.

"The news was going to get out sooner or later," Ryder said. He let out a long sigh. Tatum had a knack for stirring up trouble, but Jake had no clue how badly she had just messed things up for Ryder.

"I still don't know why you swore me to secrecy," Jake said before he wandered away to follow a sexy blonde who walked past them.

If Ryder had his way, Jake never would find out the reason. How could he explain that he was sure Katie would pull out all the stops to bed him before he got away? Since the college was closed until the New Year, she would make it her full-time job to seduce him. She was like that whenever a deadline was approaching, whether it was doing her taxes or decorating her home for the holidays. And deep down inside, he wanted to see how far she would go. It wasn't very honorable of him, but he wasn't feeling very gentlemanly around Katie these days.

Not that he would confess that to Jake. There were some things you just couldn't say to your best friend about his little sister.

CHAPTER TWO

"You need a drink," Hilary decided. "A big one."

"No," Katie refused. Her voice sounded far away. She closed her eyes and took a weak gulp of air as the pain clawed at her. She felt like she was being torn into strips and bleeding from the inside.

She gasped for another breath, wanting to lay her head down on the table, but afraid she would never get back up. She needed to get home, in her bed, under the sheets, and have a good cry. One that lasted, oh, a month. "Why is this happening?"

"You didn't know about this?" Melissa asked, her voice rising with each word. "Didn't suspect it?"

Katie slowly shook her head. She barely had the strength to make the simple movement. All of her energy was spent on fighting off the pain and remaining upright.

"Don't you think she would have told us?" Hilary asked.

"True," Melissa said and looked at Katie with concern. "Katie is turning pale. Hilary, back up. I think she's going to throw up. You might want to move out of the line of fire."

"I'm okay," Katie said shakily. The numbness was beginning to spread through her body, from her core to her limbs.

"I don't get this," Melissa said, getting angry on her friend's behalf. "You guys used to be so close. He's always hanging out with Jake and he couldn't find thirty seconds to give you a heads-up? Why would he hide it from you?"

Hide? No, nothing like that, Katie thought, her mouth twisting with a bitter smile. He simply forgot to tell her.

"I can't believe he told Tatum and not me," Katie muttered viciously.

Hilary rolled her eyes. "You just got hit with bad news and *Tatum* is all you can think about?"

Melissa swatted Hilary's arm. "Shut up. She is obviously in shock." Melissa rose from her seat and walked over to Katie. "Tatum probably weaseled it out of him. And now it's your turn."

Katie frowned. "My turn for what?"

"Go over there and find out what's going on." Melissa grabbed Katie's arm and tried to pull her from her seat.

Katie shook her head and dug her heels into the carpeting. She couldn't face Ryder now. She might do something embarrassing, or show how hurt she was.

"Don't confront him," Melissa advised, yanking Katie out of her seat. "Simply ask him to dance."

Her stomach clenched at the thought. "In these boots?"

Melissa ignored the question as she stepped behind Katie and pushed her in Ryder's direction. "And congratulate him on the move."

Katie leaned back, her heels dragging on the carpet. "Oh, you mean *lie*."

"Do it now." Melissa gave a mighty push. "You have no time to waste."

Katie staggered forward, crashing into the crowd. She righted herself and looked back at the table, only to see Melissa and Hilary motioning for her to keep moving. Katie closed her eyes and felt like the party was swallowing her up. It was too hot, too crowded. The festive scent of cloves, cinnamon and citrus that she normally adored now overpowered her, and if her nerves weren't shredded enough, the DJ was playing the Chipmunks' Christmas song.

She wanted to run away as fast as she could. The old Katie would have done that, and the new Katie was heartily recommending it. She pivoted on her heel, looking for the exit, when Melissa's advice floated through her. *There was no time to waste.*

Wasn't that the truth? As much as she wanted to curl up into a ball and hibernate, that was a luxury she couldn't afford. Once she decided to rejoin the world, Ryder would be gone. She only had eight days. A little over a week to lure Ryder into her bed and seduce him into staying. And while she was convincing him, she had to get every one of her fantasies fulfilled. Katie groaned. Eight days wasn't going to be enough.

"Katie Kramer!" The deep, masculine voice boomed over the Chipmunks. "When did you get here?"

Katie cringed at the familiar sound. She didn't need this. Not now. She acted like she didn't hear the megaphone-strength voice and tried to sneak through a group of people wearing Santa hats. She thought she had made her escape just when she felt a thick arm around her waist tug her back.

Gritting her teeth, and reaching deep inside to find a polite smile, Katie turned around and faced Darwin Jones, her number-one fan. She wasn't sure what she had done to gain his admiration. She certainly didn't encourage it, although Darwin probably didn't see it that way.

Darwin thought he was a player. A tall, lanky guy who hadn't quite mastered control of his arms and feet, he wore his red hair slicked back because he believed that the chicks dug it, but all the style did was highlight the way his ears stuck out. He approached women with pickup lines in an obscure African language to demonstrate his worldly ways, but his pasty complexion indicated he rarely got out of his room. Darwin probably didn't realize how big he truly was, if the tight clothes that clung to his thin frame were anything to go by. His shirts were often an eyesore and the vulgar belt buckles were simply designed to draw a woman's eye to what he believed was his best attribute.

This time her gaze didn't make it all the way down to his waist. She couldn't stop staring at his red-and-green sweater. She blinked several times but it still looked like Mrs. Claus was doing something very suggestive with old Saint Nick.

"Like my sweater?" Darwin asked, placing his fists on his hips and thrusting out his bony chest.

Katie didn't have the heart to tell him what she really thought. She decided to avoid an answer altogether. "I've never seen anything quite like it."

"It's one of a kind," he said proudly.

Thank God. "Where did you get it?"

"The sex shop."

She knew he was talking about the small store just outside the city limits. "They sell sweaters?"

"They sell everything. You've never been there?" Darwin's wide blue eyes lit up and he curled his arm around her shoulders. "I would be happy to give you the guided tour."

"No, thank you," she replied. She always tried to be gentle with Darwin, sensing the vulnerabilities underneath his carefully crafted image. But nothing could ever provoke her into going out with him, even for a shopping expedition.

"You're sure? I know the owner. He'll let you use my frequent shopper discount." He gave her shoulder a squeeze.

"Gee, what an offer, but I have to refuse." She gradually unhooked his arm from her shoulders. "If you will excuse me, I need to speak to Ryder."

"Ryder?" He jerked his hand away from her and looked cautiously over his shoulder. "Oh, wow. I just saw someone I need to talk to."

Katie nodded. "I understand." And she really did. Darwin's self-preservation instinct was kicking in. He was afraid of Ryder. Which was really not necessary because Ryder didn't even acknowledge Darwin's existence.

Katie watched Darwin scurry away and then looked around for Ryder. She needed to find out what was going on, even though she knew she wasn't going to like the answer. Katie slowly made it through the crowd toward where she had last seen Ryder.

When she made it to the bar, she saw Ryder and Tatum together. Ryder was sitting on a bar stool and the buxom blonde was draped all over him, obviously begging for forgiveness for her impromptu announcement.

Katie looked away as jealousy streaked through her. She couldn't stand watching Tatum touch Ryder. Actually, she couldn't stand Tatum. She was just like all of Ryder's other women. Fortunately, Ryder didn't have a long string of ex-girlfriends. They were something of an exclusive club, but they all were brazen, sexy and possessed a dangerous edge. Simply put, Darwin wouldn't have the guts to flirt with any of Ryder's exes.

Katie never felt comfortable around those women, either, but then again, she had nothing in common with them. They were gorgeous blondes with street smarts. They could get any man they wanted, and they could get anything they wanted from those men.

What made her think she could break into that exclusive club?

No, *transcend* it. Why did she think she could have been the exception to the rule? Because she practically grew up with Ryder? They'd drifted so much since their teenage years that that hardly seemed to make a difference anymore. Now they rarely talked about anything meaningful. His work, life, girlfriends, all seemed more important to him than hanging out with Katie.

And here she thought she could get Ryder simply because she wanted him so much. Katie trudged forward, contemplating the depths of her delusions. She knew the world didn't work that way, but that hadn't stopped her. She had always thought that eventually Ryder would be hers, ever since that fateful night when she was ten years old. She had climbed a tree to spy on Jake and Ryder while they T.P.-ed a house. Jake had thrown a roll of toilet paper up in the tree to decorate it. It hit Katie and she had fallen out of the tree and broken her ankle. Ryder had carried her all the way home, with Jake at his side lecturing her. Katie hadn't listened to a word her brother said. All she knew was that Ryder was the man she wanted. Now she had to face the fact that her dream might never become a reality.

"Katie?" Tatum's little-girl voice broke into Katie's musings. She looked up and saw she was standing right next to Tatum and Ryder. "What are you doing here?"

Right. Like Katie was the intruder. "I was going to ask you the same thing," she said with a tight smile. "I work at the college. Why are you here?"

Tatum leaned forward and Katie was immediately enveloped in a spicy, exotic perfume. "I'm here with Ryder," she divulged with a catty smile.

Oooh. Katie tensed, bracing herself, as that information hit like a sucker punch. She hadn't expected that. Ryder brought Tatum here? As his date? Terrific. This just proved how far she and Ryder had grown apart—he hadn't even told her that he and Tatum were a couple again. How was she supposed to seduce the guy when he was with Bimbo Barbie?

She looked at Ryder and their gazes clashed. She paused, waiting to see if he had something to say, like an excuse or an apology. He said nothing.

"Congratulations on the move, Ryder." There. She said it. It didn't hurt. Much.

"Thanks."

"You didn't know?" Tatum asked with delight. She snuggled a little closer to Ryder, as if staking her territory.

Katie wasn't going to answer Tatum's question. She didn't even trust herself to look at the other woman. If she did, she would ruin her manicure clawing at Tatum's smile. And why wasn't Ryder shaking Tatum off?

Katie kept her gaze on Ryder, who was looking back intently, as if trying to predict her next move. Did he think she was going to make a scene? Considering how volatile her emotions were, it was a possibility.

"I guess Crystal Bend got too small for you," she said, hating the little hitch in her voice.

His expression was unreadable. "Something like that."

Katie felt Tatum's smugness and keen interest. It was seriously getting on her nerves. She needed to speak to Ryder privately.

"Ryder, let's dance." She reached out for him, and then froze. If he refused, she wouldn't be able to handle that kind of rejection, especially in front of Tatum.

He hesitated, and she felt the tears burn in the back of her eyes. Her heart pressed against her ribs as she waited. It was only at this moment when she realized Ryder had never directly refused her anything. Was he going to start now?

"Sure," he said and stood up, disentangling himself from Tatum. Ignoring the blonde's huff of protest, he didn't take Katie's hand, but grasped her elbow. It was an oddly gentlemanly gesture from him.

Ryder guided her to the dance floor, turned, and loosely held one of her hands as he placed his other hand firmly on her waist. The excitement fizzing in her veins went suddenly flat when she noticed that he was dictating how close they stood together—and they couldn't get much farther apart. She could get a whole conga line between them and still have room.

She wasn't going to push it, Katie decided as she placed her hand on his shoulder. For now, it was fine. She had other things on her mind.

The jazzy Christmas tune should have been soothing and romantic, but she was nervous. She had never danced with Ryder. Years ago, when he'd taken Tatum to the prom, she'd cried herself to sleep imagining the two of them holding each other on the dance floor. She had dreamed of being swept off her feet in Ryder's arms.

But this dance wasn't the stuff of her dreams. Ryder wasn't gathering her close and whispering softly in her ear. Instead, he felt stiff and tense. *He* couldn't be nervous. Was he wishing he was with Tatum instead?

"One dance," Katie promised, hating how her mouth trembled as she held back her emotions, "and I'll get you back to your date safe and sound."

"Tatum is not my date."

The relief rolled through Katie so violently that she wanted to sag against him. Instead she gave a quick look at where Tatum stood. The blonde glared at her before ordering another drink. Katie looked back at Ryder. "But she said she was here with you."

"She's crashing the party and walked in the same time I did. We're not dating, Katie. We're just friends."

Yeah, right. And how convenient. Tatum was probably hiding in the shrubbery until Ryder showed up. Was it evil to hope that Tatum had waited for hours and suffered frostbite? "Crashing this party? Now there's someone desperate for entertainment."

The edge of his mouth twitched in a smile. "Crystal Bend doesn't have a whole lot to offer."

Her stomach took another sickening dip. Was that why Ryder was leaving? There was nothing here to keep him? She wished she were enough. Katie lowered her eyes, shielding her hurt. "I didn't catch the whole announcement. Where are you moving to?"

There was an infinitesimal pause. "Dubai."

She jerked her head up and stared at him. "Dubai? As in . . . the other side of the world?"

"I have a friend there. He says the real estate market is booming and they could always use more carpenters."

Katie continued to stare at him. "Dubai?"

"It's in the U.A.E." He watched her, probably waiting for the comprehension to hit. "It's right next to Saudi Arabia. It'll be an adventure."

"I know where Dubai is," Katie claimed. Well, she had a vague idea where it was located. "When were you going to tell me? Were you planning to sneak out?"

Ryder frowned and a muscle bunched in his cheek. "No."

His gruff tone clearly indicated he didn't like her wording, but in Katie's view he was doing exactly that. "Then what?"

Ryder gave a long-suffering sigh. "I was going to tell everyone later this week, but Tatum overheard Jake saying something about it."

"Later this week?" He only had eight days before he left.

Unless . . . Katie narrowed her eyes in suspicion. "Like the *day before* you left?"

Ryder shrugged. "I just didn't want to make a big deal out of it. I hate good-byes."

Her heart galloped, as if she had dodged a bullet. As much as it pained her, she was thankful for Tatum's big mouth. Otherwise she wouldn't have found out until it was too late.

"How long are you going to be there?"

"I don't know. The way my friend talks about Dubai, I may never want to leave. He says the beaches are beautiful and parties there are out of this world."

He didn't think he was coming back? That idea shook her to the core. "So let me see if I've got this straight. You decided that you want to move to the other side of the world. For the *beaches* and the *parties*. And you might never come back? And this decision was all so sudden that you didn't have time to tell anyone. You're just leaving. What prompted all this?"

He looked straight at her. It was just a glance, but she got the feeling that there was a lot more behind his decision to move than he was telling her.

"The timing is right," he said in a low, rough voice. "That's all."

That's all. She exhaled sharply. It wasn't about her. That was wishful thinking on her part.

"Jake's going to miss you."

"He'll be fine."

So that plan of attack wasn't going to work. Katie tried again. "What about my mom and dad? They adore you."

She saw Ryder's expression tighten and knew her point made a direct hit.

"You're not going to wait until they get back?" she asked.

"Your parents are on a sabbatical in the middle of Africa," Ryder said. "They're not getting back until the end of the school year."

"They're going to be hurt to find you suddenly gone without any warning." Katie almost pouted her lips, but decided that might be overkill. "Can't you push back your move until June?"

"I'm not their son," he said gruffly.

"Come on"—Katie made a face at that argument—"you are just as much a Kramer as Jake and me."

Ryder ducked his head, and if she wasn't mistaken, that comment pleased him. Was he blushing? Ryder Scott blushing?

If being a part of the Kramer family was so important to him, why was he walking away from it all? When Ryder's own mother seemed disinterested in taking care of him, he became an unofficial member of the Kramer family. Ryder always had a place setting at the table during his teen years and was at Katie's house more often than his own. He and Jake were like brothers.

But maybe the ties he had with her family weren't enough to hold him. What was going on? Ryder had made it clear he was leaving immediately, but he wasn't telling her why. There was an unbridgeable gap between them, so different from the easy, teasing relationship they'd enjoyed when they were younger. His silence troubled her. She suddenly felt like she would never, ever see him again.

"Who's going to look after me when you're gone?" She didn't care if she sounded pitiful. Ryder had always been so protective of her and she was going to use that to her full advantage.

"You have a big brother," he reminded her.

"Puhleeze." Katie rolled her eyes. "I need protection *from* Jake. The guy is a terror."

Ryder stopped dancing but didn't let her go. He looked deep into her eyes. "If you really need me, I'll be there for you."

Her heart did a double flip. On some level, she'd always known that, but he had never said those words. Now they felt more like a brush-off. "Thanks, but how is that going to work when you are thousands of miles away?"

"I'm not disappearing off the face of the earth," he said with a hint of impatience.

"You might as well be." She gave a deep sigh. "I'm going to miss you."

"I know."

She waited. *I know?* That's all he had to say? She forgot how arrogant the man could be. Didn't he realize that this was the part where he should repeat those words and mean them?

She wanted to look away so he wouldn't see how she was handling this loss, but she also wanted to hold on to this moment. Katie needed to tell him how important he was to her. But they had practically grown up together—even if they weren't as close as they used to be, shouldn't he already know how much she needed him in her life? Saying it out loud would probably make it worse. But what did she have to lose?

Katie's hand tightened on his shoulder, the soft cashmere bunching under her fingertips. She didn't even know if she could explain how she felt. Katie knew she wasn't great with words. When she loved someone, she showed it by taking care of that person. Expressing it with words was much more difficult, and she usually mangled up the message. She couldn't risk that now.

"And," she strove to keep her tone light, "believe it or not, you're going to miss me."

Ryder gave a solemn nod. "I'll miss your bratty ways."

Katie's jaw dropped with outrage. "I'm not a brat!"

He raised an eyebrow.

A jumble of fragmented memories flashed through her mind.

Katie had followed him around like a shadow. No matter how hard Ryder and Jake had tried to get away, she would always find them and insist on tagging along for whatever they were doing.

Now that she thought about it, not much had changed. She'd like to think she was more clever and subtle in getting Ryder's attention. If not that, at least more successful. "Well, not anymore. I've grown up."

"That's true," he replied, his voice neutral. "You're no longer Jake's kid sister."

Katie smiled. Finally! It was as if the clouds parted and the sun shone down as the angels played the trumpets. It had taken him nearly a decade to realize that.

Her smile slowly drifted down as she wondered if there was a hidden meaning in those words. *You're no longer Jake's kid sister.*

Did that mean he no longer felt the need to protect her? As many times as his big-brother act irritated her, there were times when it pleased her. Her parents were big on freedom—at times a little too much—and she found the security she needed from Ryder.

Or did his comment mean something else? Maybe he didn't see her as too innocent anymore.

She suddenly looked up at Ryder and he cast his gaze to the floor, but he wasn't fast enough. She saw the sexual hunger in his dark brown eyes. Her body clenched as the heat poured through her.

Her breath caught in her throat. Was she imagining this heat between them or was it real? If there was ever a time to take action, this was the moment. All she had to do was step a little closer.

The move seemed monumental, and her legs shook, but she did it. Ryder's hand tightened around hers, but he didn't hold her back. Instead, he watched her silently, the flare in his eyes brightening.

Oh . . . wow. . . . Was Ryder letting her make a move? Now all she had to do was tilt her head just so. The stupid stiletto heels finally came into good use, lifting her to just the right height to kiss Ryder Scott. She could brush her lips against his and get the kiss she had longed for all these years.

But she couldn't do it. Katie felt the pulse at the base of her neck beating wildly. She was too scared. Not of him, not of getting one step closer to her fantasy.

She was afraid of ruining it. This moment. This friendship she enjoyed with Ryder. What if all she got was a kiss and had nothing—no friendship, no Ryder—to fall back on?

Those fears were already coming true, Katie reminded herself. It didn't matter what she did. In a week there would be no Ryder and their friendship would be something that belonged in the past. And if she didn't do something—anything—right now, she wouldn't even get the kiss!

Something close to panic washed over her. She had to make the first move. She quickly tilted her head up and brushed her mouth against his cheek.

Ryder's jaw felt rough against her lips and he smelled so good. Warm and masculine. He tensed but he didn't push her away. That had to be a good sign.

Her heart pounding in her chest, Katie grazed her soft mouth against his. She pressed her lips gently against Ryder's, waiting for him to take over.

But he seemed content with the gentle, almost chaste touch. That wasn't enough for Katie. She needed more. Darting the tip of her tongue past her lips, she outlined Ryder's bottom lip, silently asking for entry.

Ryder's mouth remained closed.

Katie slowly nibbled at Ryder's bottom lip. She felt, rather than heard, the groan vibrate deep in his chest. Encouraged, she slid her arms up his chest and linked her hands behind his neck, deepening the kiss.

She wanted to burrow into his heat and let it envelop her. His scent triggered something elemental inside. She needed to thrust her tongue deep in his mouth and devour him.

But Ryder wasn't gathering her closer. His hands were firmly on her waist. He wasn't pushing her away, but he wasn't drawing her in, either.

He might be letting her kiss him, but he wasn't allowing it to go any further. Impatience and something darker swept through Katie. She wanted, needed, *deserved* more. She sank her teeth into his bottom lip.

Ryder jerked back. Katie dropped her arms and tried to step away, but his hands clamped against her waist. Ryder didn't look mad, but a dangerous glow had leapt into his eyes. He slowly dragged his tongue along the swollen flesh of his bottom lip.

Katie realized she may have pushed her luck. How could she explain her actions? She tried to pull away, but Ryder contained her. His fingers dug into her hips as he stared at her.

"What the hell was that for?" he asked in a low tone.

She needed to brazen this out. "Ryder, I'm sure you know how to kiss. . . ."

"Katie, you're playing with fire," he warned.

He raised a hand and Katie didn't flinch. She knew he wouldn't hurt her, but she was surprised when he rubbed his thumb hard against her bottom lip. She noticed the slight tremor in his hand. His touch wasn't tender, but she could tell he was fighting hard to rein in what he really wanted to do. Katie felt breathless as she waited for his next move.

"You're still a brat, aren't you?"

Had she just ruined everything with that one action? She hoped not. "I'm not a brat, and I'm not an innocent little girl."

Ryder dropped his hold on her. "Wanna bet?"

He sounded almost regretful. "Yeah, I do." She poked a finger at his chest. "In fact, I have eight days to prove you wrong."

He caught her hand, his move fast as lightning. She should have known better—she was trapped.

Ryder leaned in close, his mouth right against her ear. "What are you planning? Whatever it is, I'm telling you right now to forget it."

"You can't tell me what to do." She wrestled for her release. "You have no claims on me." At least, not yet.

Ryder suddenly let go, as if he couldn't be bothered anymore. "I'm warning you, Katie."

"And I'm giving you some advance notice." Katie took a sharp breath, her body trembling with nervousness. "On New Year's Day, you are going to wake up in my bed."

Ryder held himself very, very still as she walked away, leaving him on the dance floor. Every primal instinct screamed through his body, begging him to chase Katie, haul her against him and kiss her senseless.

That would be a very stupid idea. Satisfying, but stupid. He shouldn't have let things get this far. He had weakened at that one crucial moment. He had truly believed his lack of response was the best defense against Katie's attentions, and would kill any fantasy she might have about them. Who would have thought Katie had a rough side? Damn, if that bite didn't give him a charge.

Ryder darted the tip of his tongue along his bottom lip. If he wasn't careful, he was going to wind up in bed with Katie *way* before New Year's Day. Once that happened, he wouldn't let her out until he had explored every fantasy he had about her. And she was way too innocent for that, so he had to make sure bedding her was never even a possibility.

CHAPTER THREE

December 25

"Mom." Katie held the cordless phone between her ear and her shoulder as she set the tray of crudités on the serving table, wondering if she had made too much food for a crowd of people who were probably already stuffed with Christmas dinner. She loved to cook and bake and sometimes she went overboard. "Did you know Ryder is leaving town?"

Katie had realized her strategic error the moment she had left the dance floor the night before. She shouldn't have informed Ryder of her intention. Now she had lost the element of surprise. Not that she was going to kamikaze the guy into bed, but she would have liked to keep her options open.

It had taken all of her self-control to make a retreat and leave Ryder after the dance. No doubt he was immediately caught in Tatum's clutches, but Katie couldn't spare the time to arm wrestle for Ryder.

Well, that's what she had told her friends when they asked her why she left so abruptly. The truth was that she was embarrassed. The kiss she shared with Ryder was supposed to be perfect, loving, romantic. She'd never imagined *biting* him to get a response. Now she needed to come up with a failure-proof plan to unleash the sexual hunger she saw in Ryder's eyes. But after tossing and turning in bed all night, she had come up with absolutely nothing.

She heard her mother's sigh on the other end of the phone. "I had a feeling he might leave one day."

"Really?" It was official: Katie was the absolute last person to know about Ryder's move. "What has he told you?"

"Honey," her mother's voice pierced through the static connection. "You know Ryder doesn't sit around and talk about his feelings. It was just a vibe that I had."

"He hasn't been unhappy," Katie insisted as she absently centered the nutcracker on a side table. The finishing touches were probably unnecessary, but she wanted her guests to experience a winter wonderland while they enjoyed cocktails and festive hors d'oeuvres. It was a Kramer tradition.

"You're right. I think he's leaving before his restraint crumbles."

Restraint? Katie stopped moving and tightly gripped the nutcracker. "What are you talking about?"

"I think . . ." Her mother paused, as if she was unsure to say anything. "I think he's leaving because of you."

"Me?" Katie closed her eyes and pumped her fist in the air. Yes! She hadn't been completely delusional last night. "Why do you think that? I haven't done anything."

"Sad, but true. Other than vamp it up."

"Mom!"

"Oh, that wasn't a complaint. I'm thrilled that you're finally getting out of your comfort zone."

Katie groaned with frustration. She felt a lecture coming on. Couldn't she get a reprieve? It was Christmas, after all.

"Even though you did it for a man," her mother continued. "That is not the greatest motivation for a personal sexual revolution. We need to talk about that."

"I didn't do it for a man," Katie said through clenched teeth.

"Riiight." Katie easily imagined her mom making a face. "Don't lie to your mother. You did it for Ryder. You changed your wardrobe, your style, even your hobbies, for goodness' sake. All for Ryder."

"How do you know that?" Only her mother would notice that this year Katie had stopped trying out the newest decorating techniques or making gifts from scratch. Katie knew bad girls didn't bake or decorate, but they *did* get Ryder Scott. It was a temporary sacrifice that she made willingly.

"What are you talking about?" her mother said over the crackling phone connection. "All of Crystal Bend knows how you feel about Ryder."

Katie felt a blush blooming over her skin. Her mother had to be exaggerating. "That's not true."

"Even your father can tell you have the hots for Ryder."

Katie cringed and the blush sizzled in her cheeks. Her father was the quintessential absentminded professor. If he could see it . . . Katie gasped. "Do you think Ryder knows?"

"He would have to be a very unobservant man to miss it."

"What?! And it never occurred to you to *tell* me? I think I'm going to die of embarrassment right now," Katie muttered as she headed for the kitchen. There was a tower of sugar-frosted cookies that would make her feel better. "You couldn't have pulled me aside at some point in the last year and told me that I was making a fool of myself?"

"A fool? Why? Because you let your desires be known?"

"Mom . . ." She grabbed for the top cookie and bit into it. The sweetness did nothing to coat her mood. She obviously needed more.

"Look, I figured you needed time to work things out in your own way. And if there is anything to be embarrassed about"—her mother's voice rose—"it should be the fact that you haven't done everything you could to achieve your goals."

"Now, that is not true," Katie said as she nibbled the cookie. "I have turned my world upside down in the past year. I have been very adventurous and opened myself up to new possibilities." She went on dates she would never have agreed to in the past, and created a sexy image that took more courage than she ever thought she had. "Oh, and let's not forget that I have logged more hours in the spa and gym than a normal person should."

"That's all great," her mother said, unimpressed, "but then what did you do to follow up? Nothing. You changed yourself and then you sat back and waited for Ryder to make the first move."

"What's wrong with that?" Katie shoved the rest of the cookie into her mouth. She wanted Ryder to take action. It was part of her fantasy that he would go wild with desire for her.

"Don't you get it?" Exasperation tinged her mother's voice. "It's pretty obvious at this point that Ryder will never make the first move. You're his best friend's little sister, for one. And maybe he thinks he's not good enough for you. Or maybe he thinks it would hurt his relationship with us. He might just be trying to be a gentleman."

Katie grabbed another cookie. *"Ryder?"* Sure, the guy had manners, but she always felt he was driven by primal instincts. He had a code of honor that might have been better suited to the Wild West. Ryder had gotten into a lot of fights at school, but he never swung first. Crime was rare in Crystal Bend, and when it happened,

Ryder was always the first suspect. Katie knew it was because of the vandalism and joyriding he'd done in his youth, but he had grown out of that phase quickly. And though one or two women had named Ryder as the father of their babies, Katie had known it wasn't true even before the DNA results confirmed her beliefs. Ryder knew what it was like to be abandoned by a parent. If he had been the father, he would have given his full support to the mother and child.

"I think Ryder's leaving before you tap into your power," her mother said.

"Tap into my *what*?" Katie rolled her eyes. "Mom, I'm not one of the witches in *Charmed*."

"Every woman is powerful."

Here we go. . . . Katie leaned her forehead on the refrigerator. She was going to need another cookie.

"And you, Katie Kramer, have power over Ryder," her mother declared. "He knows it and he's getting out of town before you figure it out."

She really wanted to believe it, but there was a problem with her mom's theory. "You make it sound like he doesn't want me."

"I think he doesn't *want* to want you. It's up to you to make something happen."

"And how am I supposed to do that?" She tossed her hands in the air. "I have seven days left."

"Hold on, I want to savor this moment when my daughter is finally asking for my advice."

Katie closed her eyes and took a deep breath. "Mom."

"This is what you should do," she said briskly. "Act like you are fully aware that you have power over him. Then *use* that power."

Sure, no problem. Nothing to it. *Why haven't I thought of that before? Oh, yeah, because it's too risky. Duh. How can I act powerful when*

Ryder and I both know that I'm the vulnerable one? Katie knew it would be a waste of breath to try to explain this, so she decided to point out an obvious flaw in her mom's plan. "Won't he avoid me, then?"

"Oh, not Ryder." Her mother sounded supremely confident. "He won't back down. Trust me on this."

Katie heard the back door open and a gust of icy-cold air swirled into the toasty kitchen. "Katie?" her brother called out. "Are you here?"

She moved away from the refrigerator and saw Jake stepping into the kitchen. Snow coated his black hair and winter coat. He shook his long, lean body, spraying the icy flakes. She took a hasty step to the side and saw Ryder standing on the back porch, stamping the snow off his boots. The sun was beginning to set, casting a soft light over him.

Katie felt her breath hitch as she laid eyes on Ryder and immediately looked away. There is no way she had power over this man. She returned her attention to Jake. It was safer and easier on her nerves. "I'm going to have to go, Mom." She hid a smile as her brother made the motion to keep his presence quiet. "Jake just came in."

"I've been trying to reach him all day," her mother said. "Put him on the phone."

"Okay, but don't expect too much. He looks really hungover." She handed the phone to her brother and smiled sweetly. "Mom wants to talk to you."

She ignored Jake's murderous look as he snatched the phone. He muttered something under his breath, squared his shoulders and placed the phone to his ear. "Mom? Merry Christmas!" Jake said in a bright, cheerful voice.

Katie cast a quick glance at Ryder and smoothed her formfitting tunic dress over her black leggings. She loved the long sleeves that left the shoulders bare while the rest of her was covered up. It was fun and flirty. The flash of skin made most men take a second look.

Ryder seemed to be the exception. He didn't even give her a first look as he walked into the kitchen. Was he still upset about the kiss on the dance floor? She wasn't sure how to approach him. Should she ignore him? Be on her best behavior? Or tease him about their kiss?

"Merry Christmas, Ryder," she said softly, almost shyly, and immediately wanted to kick herself. That was not how a brazen woman spoke. A powerful, sensual woman would remind him of their kiss and boldly claim his mouth again.

Ryder absently swiped his tongue along his bottom lip. Katie ducked her head to hide her smile, realizing she didn't have to refer to their kiss after all.

She tucked a strand of her long black hair behind her ear, drawing his attention to her bare shoulder. Her fingers brushed against the present she had opened that morning. "Thanks for the earrings. They're beautiful."

His gaze lingered on the jewelry made with red jasper and gold. "You're welcome."

Katie wanted to ask why he had broken tradition this year. Since celebrating their first Christmas together, Ryder had always given her a collectible ornament. She knew he probably chose it because it was the safest, least suggestive gift, but she treasured the collection.

So it was a big surprise this morning when she had opened the carefully wrapped gift under her tree and discovered the jasper earrings. Was this a sign that he didn't think of her as Jake's kid sister anymore?

"Hey, Mom," Jake said as he came back into the kitchen. His voice indicated his desire to get off the phone after only a few seconds. "Ryder just dropped in. Oh, you want to say hi to him?" Jake thrust the phone in Ryder's direction. "For you."

Ryder accepted the phone and sounded genuinely eager to wish her mother a merry Christmas. He also looked relieved to escape another awkward exchange with Katie. She leaned her hip against the kitchen table, remembering the first time Ryder had visited their house on Christmas Day. He hadn't even been a teenager when he dropped by, desperate for any excuse to get out of his own home. The moment he had stepped inside, he shuttered all expression from his face.

Ryder had been quiet and watched the Kramers from a distance, as if he had been afraid to remind anyone he was there and risk being sent away. From that moment, and every year since then, Katie gently guided Ryder into their celebrations. She liked how many Christmases ago his eyes brightened when he saw a stocking with his name on it at the fireplace. But this year he hadn't even looked at his presents. He was definitely avoiding her.

In past years, if Ryder had his way, he wouldn't have let anyone lift a finger so he could do all the planning and decorating himself. But Katie always wanted to create a perfect Christmas for him. It was torture to think that this would be their last holiday together.

She didn't have a chance to ask him about the earrings. The first guests arrived while Ryder was still on the phone with her mother. Soon the house was filled with neighbors and friends. But no matter how busy Katie was with her hostess duties, she couldn't shake her awareness of Ryder. She always knew where he was and what he was doing.

An hour into the open house, Melissa nudged Katie's shoulder.

Actually, it was more of a shove since Melissa didn't know her own strength.

"Merry Christmas, Melissa! I'm so glad you could make it." Melissa was dressed in her usual sporty style, the bright red tinsel ponytail scrunchie her nod to the season. "Have something to eat."

Melissa grabbed a carrot stick. "Katie, this is a fabulous party, but you need to circulate."

"Right after I take care of this." She held up the silver platter laden with fruits and vegetables.

"No, I don't think you understand." Melissa pointed the carrot stick at Katie. "You need to circulate now."

Katie got the hint and immediately looked to where she had last seen Ryder. He was in the front hall, next to the staircase decorated with garlands and miniature ornaments. And next to him was Sasha. The honey blonde stood very close to Ryder, jutting her hips to one side. At first glance it looked as if she was dressed down for the event in skinny jeans and a red sweater. It was like a flashback to the office party. Was there ever a moment when a beautiful woman *wasn't* monopolizing Ryder's attention?

But when Sasha shifted to the side, Katie's eyes bulged out. The sweater had a narrow slit in the front that plunged from her collarbone to her navel. It showed a thin strip of her bare skin and a hint of her breasts.

"And I thought *I* was showing skin," Katie said. And she thought she had a firm stomach until she got an eyeful of Sasha's rock-hard abs.

Melissa tilted her head to one side. "How does she wear that without flashing the world?"

"Double-sided tape," Katie murmured.

"Yikes, sounds painful," Melissa said as she munched on the carrot stick.

"I thought Sasha was after Jake."

"What better way to make Jake jealous than by flirting with his best friend?"

Katie made a face. "That's stupid."

"That's dating."

"Ryder's too smart to fall for that."

Melissa grabbed another carrot stick from the platter. "He doesn't seem to mind."

No, he didn't. Sasha was giving Ryder the full treatment: touching him, flipping her hair, licking her lips. It was flirting by numbers. Katie should know—she had read that article, too. She was grateful that Ryder wasn't encouraging Sasha to get closer, but he certainly wasn't shooing her away.

Melissa elbowed Katie in the ribs. "What are you going to do to get rid of her?"

What could she do? She needed to pick her battles and go for the ones she could win. "Nothing."

"Nothing?" Melissa coughed as the carrot went down the wrong way. "The woman is about to rub herself all over Ryder. If she were a cat, she'd be marking him with her scent to claim him."

Katie turned away reluctantly so her vision of the hall was blocked. "I have no claim on Ryder," she said quietly.

"I understand." Melissa looked back at Ryder. "But if the roles were reversed, Ryder would have none of it."

Katie frowned at her friend. "You've lost me."

"Let's say some guy was all over you. What would Ryder do?"

"Pull us apart." Melissa was right. Ryder's protective instincts used to irritate Katie no end, and he wouldn't heed her complaints.

Whether by intimidation or physically getting in between, Ryder made sure her dates didn't touch her too intimately.

He had made no claim on her, but Katie certainly felt like she belonged to him. Maybe it was time to give Ryder a taste of his own medicine.

"I'll take that tray," Melissa said, arms stretched out.

Katie relinquished the silver platter and marched into the hall, her ankle boots ringing on the wooden floor. Ryder saw her before Sasha did. He didn't step away from the blonde, but he watched Katie warily.

Katie knew she shouldn't just walk in with guns blazing. But she had no time to come up with an alternative strategy.

"Merry Christmas, Sasha," Katie said.

"You, too," Sasha replied without looking at Katie.

Katie figured she could go one of two ways: confrontation or sneak attack. But since she didn't truly have a claim on Ryder—well, not one he would recognize—perhaps a sneak attack was best.

"I love your sweater," Katie continued, wondering if a thunderbolt was going to strike her down for this bold lie. "That color is great on you."

That earned a fleeting look in her direction. "Thanks."

"And the split in the front. So edgy." Katie tried to inject some enthusiasm in her voice. "But I really love the split in the back. That must have been difficult. Who is the designer?"

"Split?" Sasha reared back and gave her full attention to Katie. "What split?"

"The one right down the back seam. You didn't notice when you put it on?"

Sasha twisted around, trying to see the back of her sweater. "You mean it's ripped?"

"You mean the designer didn't intend to do that?" she asked innocently. "Are you looking for a mirror? There's a full-length one in the bathroom. It's down the hall and to the left." She watched Sasha hurry toward the powder room. "Oh, that was too easy," she muttered to herself.

Ryder leaned against the banister. "When she figures out what you did, she's going to decapitate all those crystal snowmen in the bathroom."

"I'll take my chances," Katie responded coolly. A woman had to make sacrifices . . . although she really adored those snowmen.

"What was all that about?"

Katie folded her arms across her chest. "You tell me."

Ryder's eyebrow rose. "I don't respond to—"

Katie couldn't talk about this anymore. It was time for action. She put her hands on his shoulders and went up on her toes. Ryder hesitated and, as if he had found the discipline in the last second, tilted his head to the side to avoid her kiss.

But Katie had no intention of locking lips. When he moved his head, he gave her perfect access to his neck. She nuzzled against his throat, enjoying the warmth and scent of him. She placed an openmouth kiss below his ear. Licking his skin and feeling the pulse under her tongue, Katie caught the flesh between her teeth and sucked hard.

The breath hitched in Ryder's throat. She felt the hairs on his neck stand up. He lurched forward, his body slamming against hers. As he grabbed the back of her head, his fingers twisting in her long hair, Katie hoped he was going to draw her closer, or at least hold her captive. Instead, he pulled her away.

He stared into her eyes. Their faces were almost touching. She felt his warm breath waft over hers. The air between them shimmered.

He didn't say anything. The look in his eyes was feral. Red stained his cheekbones and she saw the muscle twitch in his jaw.

He looked like he was ready to pounce.

She waited, anticipation building inside her until she thought she'd burst. She loved the way his body trembled and eagerly watched the fire glow in his eyes. Ryder closed his eyes, and just when she thought he was going to make his move, he slowly unclenched her hair.

Katie watched almost in a daze as he stepped away. And then took another step for good measure. The crashing disappointment she felt was mingled with a hint of relief. As much as she hated to admit it, it was probably for the best. She wasn't sure what she had just unleashed.

Katie reached up and rubbed her finger over the love bite she'd left on his neck. Ryder jerked from the delicate touch.

"There." Her voice was heavy with satisfaction. "I've left my mark."

"What has gotten into you?" Ryder looked stunned as he reached up to touch the bruise.

"Now everyone knows you're mine," she announced. Katie turned and walked away with a swing in her step.

Finally, she was being outrageous. One might even say uncalled for. She didn't care. It felt good. It felt right. She was headed for the kitchen when she felt someone grab her arm.

At first she thought Ryder had caught up with her. But it was Hilary who was gripping her arm. Melissa stood behind Hilary, looking a little worried.

"Having fun?" Katie asked her friends. "Guess what just happened?"

"We have something to tell you first." Hilary looked very serious.

"Is something wrong?"

"Sort of," Melissa said as they guided her into a corner where no one could overhear. "It's about Ryder," she said in a hushed tone. She looked around and double-checked that no one was eavesdropping. "We've heard some disturbing rumors. He may not be the man you thought he was."

Katie laughed at the suggestion. "That's ridiculous. I've known him forever."

"Let me take a crack at this," Hilary told Melissa. "We might be asking the wrong question. Katie, what do you know about Ryder's exes?"

Katie shrugged. "Not much, other than they are blond, beautiful and bitchy."

"True," Hilary said. "And you're missing one more 'B' word. They are all into bondage."

Katie blinked. "Say what?"

"*Bondage*," Melissa enunciated. "Among other things. The guy you want is into the kinky stuff."

"How do you know that?" Katie asked in a scandalized whisper.

"I talked to a few people who would know. Apparently Tatum told Emily Jones that Ryder has seriously X-rated tastes. And remember when Ryder dated Jessica Wheeler back in college? You don't even *want* to know what they got up to together. I just forced Emily to give me all the juicy details," Hilary explained. "Maybe you should have done a little more research on your crush."

"I doubt Emily or Jessica would have told Katie anything," Melissa told Hilary. "Everyone knows how defensive she gets when people gossip about Ryder."

"True," Hilary agreed.

"Bondage," Katie repeated. She glanced in the hallway and studied Ryder, unable to banish the jittery feeling coursing through her body. Ryder was watching her as he dragged a shaky hand through his hair. He was changing before her eyes, as if she was looking at him through a different, sharper lens. He seemed mysterious, edgier, and even more fascinating than before.

"So this is probably why Ryder never touched you," Hilary said. "He knew you were far too innocent for him. He would have scared you off."

"Nah," Melissa said. "He's not touching her because she is Jake's little sister. That's my vote."

Katie couldn't pull her gaze away from Ryder. A dark wildness rolled through her. She wasn't sure why. She had never wanted to try bondage before, but she was open to the idea if Ryder would be her partner.

"What matters is that Katie did what she could," Hilary explained, "but this is why she never completed her New Year's resolution. It wasn't something she did or didn't do. These are extenuating circumstances."

Katie turned to face her friends. "Does he tie up his sex partner, or does he like to be tied down?"

"Uh-oh," Melissa said. "I know that look."

"And are we talking silk scarves or heavy-duty chains?" Katie was really hoping scarves, but she could be talked into a diamond-encrusted handcuff.

Hilary stared at her. "Katie, you might want to reconsider what you're planning. Ryder is way more out of your league than any of us realized."

"Unless you've been holding out on us," Melissa said. "What do you know about bondage?"

"Nothing. I don't remember a single magazine article on the

subject," Katie admitted. She gave another look at Ryder and her mouth curled up in a smile. "But I think I've just found a tutor."

Ryder dragged his attention away from Katie and turned around. He resisted the urge to rub at the love bite, but it seemed to burn brighter until he couldn't think of anything but the provocative mark. As much as he wanted to erase it from his skin, he felt a dark pride from knowing it was there.

What had made him think that Katie was innocent—too innocent for him? He was surprised that Katie knew exactly how to tempt him. One scrape of her teeth and he was ready to reciprocate. He longed to make a bold claim on her, something more permanent than a bite. The need burned violently in his veins and he didn't think it would disappear.

He wasn't familiar with this side of Katie. He'd never even seen a glimpse of this, or maybe he hadn't let himself see it. He liked knowing that he made her feel this way, that her intense hunger matched his. All this time he'd thought he would overpower and frighten Katie, but he might have to fight for dominance when they fell into bed.

No. They were not going to be anywhere near a bed. Ryder pushed the thought away. It was dangerous thinking. It was exactly what Katie wanted him to obsess over, and if he fell for it, it would be disaster. If he had sex with Katie, she would find out he was the rough, dirty and unlovable guy people said he was. Katie was the only person who looked at him with breathless adoration. He didn't deserve it, but he didn't want to lose it, either.

Ryder froze when he heard the click of heels over the hum of the party. He wasn't ready to deal with Katie yet. He started for the front door, deciding it was probably time to leave.

"I don't know how you put up with Katie," Sasha said, the clicking sound getting louder until she was suddenly between him and the door. "She's such a brat."

Ryder couldn't agree more. He refrained from rubbing the love bite and sidestepped Sasha. "I take it there was nothing wrong with your sweater."

"She lied about it." Sasha put her hands on her hips and the narrow slit in the front of the sweater gaped wider. "But I'll get even."

He gave her a sharp glance. "No, you won't."

Sasha heard the warning in his soft, rough voice and immediately backed down. "Fine, I won't," she said and linked her arms with his, nestling closer. "I don't know why you always feel the need to protect Katie. She doesn't deserve it."

That was where Sasha was wrong. Katie deserved everything the world had to offer. Why Katie had decided she wanted him didn't make a lot of sense when she could have her pick of men. It was in everyone's best interest if he removed himself from temptation. "It was good seeing you, Sasha," Ryder said as he reached for the coat closet.

"You're leaving? Already?"

"Yep." He put on his coat in record time and opened the door.

"I'll come with you," Sasha offered with a flirty lilt in her voice. "We can have our own fun."

Ryder didn't consider the invitation even for a moment. Sasha wasn't a good barrier when it came to Katie, and she wasn't going to be much better as a substitute. He opened the door and welcomed the cold, biting wind on his face. "Can't. Have stuff to do. Merry Christmas."

He stepped outside and closed the door before Sasha could follow. Before Katie spotted him and could stop him from leaving. He needed to leave. Retreat. Hell, he could be honest and call it what it truly was. He was escaping.

It was hard to believe that someone as sweet and delicate as Katie would have him running from just one touch. Actually, she was more powerful than that. Just the promise of something more with Katie Kramer had him running away to the other side of the world.

CHAPTER FOUR

December 26

Ryder stood in the center courtyard of Crystal Bend Community College for the final time. He'd just put his stuff in a small cardboard box and turned in his ID. He should head straight to his truck since he had a lot of things to do before he left town.

But something was holding him back. He ignored the freezing temperature and the wind whipping against him as he looked around. It was empty, thanks to winter break. The trees were covered in snow and the buildings looked cold and forlorn.

He had liked his job at the college, but he knew he was heading for something better, something more challenging. Yet he couldn't get very excited about it.

It didn't matter if he was excited or not, Ryder decided as he walked through the courtyard. He was getting far, far away from temptation. That was all that mattered.

"Ryder Scott, what are you doing here?"

Ryder turned around and saw Frank, one of the security guards, approaching him. The man was a retired police officer, and Ryder had had plenty of run-ins with him years ago. These days Frank greeted him with a nod or a wave and left him alone. Either Frank had gotten soft or Ryder no longer posed a threat to society. Ryder suspected Frank was simply too tired for the chase.

"And what's this about you leaving town?" Frank asked, his face red as he huffed from the exertion of walking in the bitter cold.

"News travels fast." Everywhere Ryder went, people stopped him to find out what was going on. The guys down at the pool hall made a point to track him down and get all the details. People had stopped their cars on Main Street to wish him luck and offer help. Early this morning he'd had to tell his neighbors a going-away party wasn't necessary. Ryder was surprised that this many people cared about him and what he was doing.

"So it is true." Frank clucked his tongue. "Well, that's too bad."

This from the police officer who had logged many hours trailing him in his squad car, waiting for Ryder to do something stupid. And there were times Ryder obliged, just for the hell of it.

Ryder lifted an eyebrow. "I'm sure some people will be celebrating once I'm gone."

Frank wasn't going to argue. "That may have been the case ten years ago."

Ryder gave him a look.

"Okay, a couple of years ago. Maybe even last year," Frank amended, "but you've changed. You're not looking for trouble anymore."

"It finds me on its own. Believe me."

"And you're not the only one who has changed. The town has mellowed out about you."

"If you say so." There were still quite a few people who walked the other way when they saw him coming.

"If it was so bad, then why'd you stay?" the older man asked as he stomped his feet to ward off the cold.

"Force of habit," Ryder said, but he didn't think that was totally true. He could have left years ago, start over where no one knew him or his wild past. But for every ten people who gave him grief, there was one person who made up for it.

"What's the place you're moving to?" Frank asked. "Dubai? Never heard of it."

The way the guy butchered the pronunciation, Ryder would believe it. "Think beaches and parties."

"You're not interested in that stuff," Frank said, surprising Ryder with his insight. "You'd give up all this for a bunch of sand?"

Ryder was willing to give up a lot for peace of mind and a Katie Kramer–free zone. "Spoken like a man who has never lived anywhere else."

"Why would I want to?" Frank looked genuinely puzzled. "Crystal Bend has everything a man needs."

It was true. He loved it up here. He liked testing himself against nature, whether it was skiing or rock climbing. He looked forward to fishing in the cold mountain streams with his friends or watching the autumn storm clouds roll in at his favorite lookout point.

But it was more than that. Crystal Bend was isolated from the rest of the world, and the neighbors looked after each other. Sometimes he felt like he was butting heads with the other residents, and sometimes the sense of community was suffocating, but Ryder always felt like he belonged here.

"I know there's going to be quite a few ladies who will be disappointed to see you go," Frank said with a twinkle in his eyes.

"I'm sure you'll be there to offer them a shoulder to lean on," Ryder replied with a straight face, knowing that Frank didn't have eyes for anyone other than his sweet little wife.

"It's the least I can do. But there's one girl who's heart will be broken." Frank shook his head. "Katie Kramer isn't going to handle the news well. Not at all."

Ryder tensed. He didn't like the idea of anyone gossiping about Katie, not even Frank. "I don't know what you're talking about."

"I could always tell when you're lying, Ryder."

"I'm never going to date Katie," Ryder insisted. "The sooner she realizes it, the better."

"Too late," Frank said with a smile. "Everyone in Crystal Bend knows that Katie loves you to distraction."

Ryder's frown deepened as the words pierced him. Loved him to distraction? That he had the ability to make someone love him so strongly, so unconditionally, nothing could break it. If only. "That's an exaggeration."

"Hah. She's been your shadow from the moment she laid eyes on you."

"Are we talking about the same Katie who's been flirting outrageously with every guy in town this year?" He'd hated seeing Katie out with other men.

"That's the one." Frank nodded. "She isn't going to let you go without a fight. Mark my words."

That was what he was afraid of. "Frank, you're forgetting who you're talking to. Nothing and no one is going to hold me back."

Katie couldn't believe she was doing this. She had never shopped at a Day After Christmas sale, and if she survived today, she wouldn't do it again. This was clearly a sign of how far she would go, or how far she had fallen, to get Ryder into her bed.

She had braved the darkness and the frigid cold. She battled the ice and snowbanks. She tossed and turned in bed all night, and her spirits were already flagging. But she was on a mission. A quest. Probably an impossible one, but she couldn't stop now.

The oversized sales sign promising drastic discounts wobbled and threatened to topple on her aching head. She ducked and the sharp corner bounced off her shoulder before falling onto the floor with a clatter. Katie rested her forehead on the cool metal rack. If she'd known there would be so much pushing and shoving at a Day After Christmas sale, she would have worn the leather stiletto boots and used them for self-defense.

She quickly sorted through the circular rack, the colors whirling in front of her like a rainbow spiraling out of control. Katie wasn't sure what kind of outfit would best convey the message that Ryder needed to tie her down to the nearest bed right away. She hadn't found any outfits with chains or straps, and she tried on a purple bandage dress that made her look more like a lumpy mummy than a sleek, sexy woman.

She had memorized articles like "Heating Up Your Holiday Look" and "Naughty New Year Dresses." But the selection on offer in Crystal Bend was nothing like in the magazines. She needed what Beyoncé would call a freakum dress. It was time to impress. No, time to get her man under control. And nothing on this rack would do.

As she wondered if a freakum dress was an urban legend, in the corner of her eye Katie spotted a scarlet red dress hanging on a rack. She lunged for it, snatched it from the hanger and fought her way to the dressing room. Checking the label, she noted that it was a size too small, but she wouldn't let that stop her. She was on an urgent mission. She was going to find the knockout dress before the day was over.

She waited in the long, winding line, impatiently tapping her toe to the beat of "Jingle Bell Rock" that played on the loudspeakers. How much longer would she have to wait? She was down to six days to seduce Ryder and every second was crucial. She peered over the shoulders of the women in front of her and glanced down the corridor of dressing rooms.

One of the doors opened and a tall, gorgeous woman stepped out of a dressing room. Katie's stomach did a pitch and roll as she recognized that shade of peroxide blonde. It was Tatum. Katie watched with reluctant admiration as the woman whirled around in the mythical freakum dress.

Where had she found that dress? Did she know someone? Did she live under a lucky shopping star, or had she simply sold her soul to the devil? The snug gold dress looked like it was tailored just for Tatum.

She looked like a sex goddess. Someone who could tame Zeus himself. She was going to turn heads wherever she went in that dress that clung to her like a second skin. No other woman could compete with that vision.

Katie hid behind the customer in front of her as Tatum called out for her friend Sasha. Sasha appeared, wearing a bold orange halter dress that barely skimmed the top of her toned, skinny thighs. Sasha wasn't in the sex goddess league, but she was still a threat to the mere mortals of Crystal Bend.

"What do you think?" Tatum asked her friend as she twirled around in front of the big three-way mirror. "Ryder won't be able to say no to me if I'm wearing this."

As Sasha wholeheartedly agreed, Katie looked up at the ceiling. Why? Why must Tatum go after Ryder? Katie knew she was going to have enough problems getting that man into her bed without this kind of in-your-face competition.

Katie looked down at the red dress clutched in her hands and knew it wasn't going to be enough ammunition for her manhunt. She needed something wild. Breathtaking.

She suddenly knew what she had to do. Katie quietly stepped

out of the line and tossed the dress on the rack of unwanted clothes. The kind of outfit she needed wasn't going to be found in a department store. She needed to think out of the box and out of the city limits.

Katie kicked the shopping bags to the side and stared at her reflection in her closet mirror. It wasn't quite the freakum dress she had planned, it was something a little bit more unexpected. Outrageous. And quite possibly an expensive mistake. Katie frowned and looked at herself from every possible angle.

PVC was a heartless bitch. It was a good thing she went to the gym five times a week. And that she had been waxed and buffed to within an inch of her life before the holiday celebrations. The black polyvinyl vest and pants were smooth and shiny. The vest lifted, hugged and molded her breasts, exaggerating her curves. The pants fitted so snugly that it looked as if oil was painted onto her legs.

The outfit definitely met her requirements. It was wild— although not as wild as other things she could have selected from the sex shop—and the PVC was doing its best to take her breath away. She grabbed a vintage black leather jacket from her closet and put it on. She tugged at the lapels and studied her reflection. She looked tough in the outfit. Hard-bitten. And, yet, oddly familiar.

She shifted from one leg to the other, pouting her red lips. She had seen someone wearing this before. Who did it remind her of? Katie's eyes widened when it suddenly hit her.

Oh. My. God. She looked like Sandy in *Grease*. All she needed to do was fluff up her hair and sing "You're the One That I Want" to complete the picture.

Katie whipped off the jacket and tossed it onto her bed. She looked back into the full-length mirror and studied the black vest. Now she just looked like a biker chick. Or maybe a groupie for a hard rock band.

Had she gone from Sandy to slut? Not that it was necessarily a bad thing. . . . Should she play it safe and grab a T-shirt, or should she play it shamelessly?

She heard the knock on the kitchen door. The pounding was fierce. Katie glanced at the clock as her heart started to gallop. Her plan was already in action. She wasn't ready!

Katie gave one last look in the mirror before she left her bedroom. It looked like shamelessly was going to win. At least she was embracing her daring side.

She strolled to the kitchen as best she could in the PVC pants. Her bare feet were cold on the linoleum floor. Goose bumps prickled her bare arms, but she knew that wasn't from the cold as much as it was from anticipation.

Katie opened the back door without checking in the window. She had a strong feeling Ryder was on the other side because she had made sure he would hear a piece of gossip he couldn't ignore. She looked up and Ryder immediately towered over her. His hands clutched the sides of the door frame as he leaned in. She felt surrounded by him.

Oh, sweet mother of . . . Ryder's mind fizzled to a blank. He blinked hard and stared at Katie. His cock stirred as he took in every inch of the black outfit that coated her sexy body.

He didn't think he was going to be able to keep his hands off her for long. He'd struggled enough with his self-control years ago when she'd worn dresses in soft, feminine colors that accented her curves. When she had the grace and beauty of a princess and he wouldn't dare touch her.

Those were the good old days. He hadn't been able to take his eyes off her, but he had been able to keep his distance. Then she gave herself a makeover. The skin-tight jeans raised his temperature and the sexy outfits begged for his touch. He'd fought hard not to accept the silent invitation, and there were moments when he'd almost surrendered, but he'd always managed to hold himself in check.

But this outfit . . . oh, God. It was going to be his downfall. The shiny fabric had him mesmerized. Her breasts were thrust out, demanding his attention. It was Katie at her most aggressive, most brazen. She was shamelessly advertising her body and her need for hot and dirty sex.

His hands clenched the door frame while his blood roared through his veins. The lust was so strong he was surprised his knees didn't buckle from the impact. He clenched his teeth and a muscle in his jaw bunched. He was afraid to speak, knowing that his tongue was going to hang out, or worse, that he would say something he could never take back.

"Hi, Ryder," he heard her say over the buzzing in his ears. Katie swung the door open wider. "I didn't expect to see you."

"Right." His gaze traveled down the length of her body and he watched her nipples tighten in response. His skin was hot and prickly, his clothes suddenly constricting. He had to get out of here, get far away from Katie, but he couldn't leave. Not yet.

He gestured at her and immediately stuffed his hands in his coat pockets. He didn't trust his ability to keep his hands off her. "What are you wearing?" His voice was rough and low.

She placed one hand on the door frame and the other on her jutted hip. "Just something I picked up at the mall. Oh, like you've never seen PVC clothing before."

Ryder felt his throat tighten. "Not on you," he said hoarsely.

"What do you think?" she asked as she twirled around, sliding her hands over her chest and waist before gliding them over her hips.

She looked ready for a bondage club. Damn, the rumor was true. It was only a half hour ago that Jake was laughing his ass off over nothing while they were packing up Ryder's apartment. Jake thought it was hysterical that Katie had asked for directions to the bondage club in Seattle. The thought of Katie in that place had Jake rolling on the floor with rib-cracking laughter.

Ryder didn't find it funny at all. One minute he was staring at Jake in horror, and the next he found himself banging his fist on Katie's door. He wanted to believe it was all a joke, but he knew Katie, and seeing her in that outfit confirmed his worst fears.

Unlike Jake, he could imagine Katie walking into the club looking like that. She would have to beat off the men with a stick. But that wouldn't stop them. They would be crazed with lust like he was right now, promising her anything just to fulfill one fantasy with her. Katie would be in over her head and deep in trouble, but wouldn't discover it until she was trapped, chained to the wall.

Hell, he wasn't in the club and he was tempted to make some impossible promise just to fulfill one fantasy. In fact, he wanted to skip the negotiation part and tie Katie down onto the kitchen floor right here, right now, peel off her clothes and explore every inch of her.

Nothing was stopping him. She sure wouldn't. And that knowledge cut through the fog of lust like nothing else. If he wasn't careful, he would take her like an animal. He would overpower her, seduce her into something she didn't understand and couldn't control. She would hate him for it, and that was one thing he couldn't live with.

"You're not wearing that outside this house," he ordered in a low growl and clamped his mouth shut. The less he said about her outfit, the better.

That's it? Katie frowned. That's all he had to say? She was sure this outfit would provoke a bigger reaction. "We'll see about that," she said, hiding her disappointment, and took a step to the side to let him enter the house. "Come on in, Ryder. What brings you here? Did you forget something?"

Ryder stepped inside and pushed the door closed behind him. "I know what you're planning and you can forget about it."

"Hmmm . . ." She strolled to the kitchen table. "Could you be more specific?"

"A bondage club?" His voice echoed in the small kitchen. "You want to go to a bondage club?"

"Where did you hear that?" she asked as she sat on the corner of the table.

"What did you expect when you asked your brother for directions to the closest bondage club? Or was that the point?" He moved closer to her. "Give it to me straight: Were you teasing him?"

She shrugged one shoulder. "Maybe." She needed to keep Ryder guessing.

Ryder frowned and stood right in front of her. He placed his hands on either side of her legs and leaned forward. "Katie, I'm trying to look out for you, that's all. You are not going to any club."

"Ryder, you can't tell me what to do." She couldn't let his intimidation tactics work on her.

"Yes, I can," he replied. "I've been doing it for years."

"Yes, and there were times when I actually appreciated it." She tilted her face up and looked straight into his eyes. "But those days are gone. You're moving soon, remember? And you weren't even planning to tell me about it."

"What does that have to do with anything? You don't belong in those nasty places."

"How would you know?" she asked and then faked a surprised look. "Have you been to one?"

Ryder stared into her eyes and suddenly looked away.

"You have," she said in a whisper and leaned forward eagerly. "What's it like?"

Ryder straightened to his full height. "Who told you?"

"Told me what?" Katie batted her eyelashes. She hoped she appeared innocent and flirty, but his answer was confirmation. He really was into bondage, and if she wanted him she needed to explore that world, too. She just hoped she had it in her.

"What have you heard about me?" he asked quietly.

"Was it a secret?"

"To you."

"Huh." Now that was a strange answer. Why did he need to hide anything from her? "Do you often find it necessary to keep secrets from me? Am I that intimidating?"

That made him smile, the lines bracketing his mouth and fanning his eyes deepening. "Try innocent."

She scoffed at his answer. Why did he keep insisting that she was innocent? She wasn't a virgin. Not even close! "I won't be that innocent once I find a club."

"Katie . . ." The warning in his tone was unmistakable.

She leaned closer, ignoring how her vest squeaked from the movement. "Why did you keep it from me?" she asked gently.

He glared at her. "It didn't concern you. It still doesn't."

"Did you think I wouldn't be able to handle it?" He might have a case there. A couple of years ago she might have been a little wary. "Or that I might find it too intriguing? Haven't you considered the possibility that I'm a little kinky?"

He closed his eyes and curled his hands into fists. "You are playing with fire."

Katie smiled. She knew that, and she was hoping that it would be his self-control that would go up in flames.

"Well, if you aren't going to tell me where the club is, I'll find out from someone else," she taunted.

He opened his eyes and she saw he was back to being firmly in control. "No one will tell you. I'll make sure of it," he promised and headed for the door.

"That's not fair. It's a free country," she called after him.

"I don't care," he said over his shoulder.

"Of course, there are other . . . clubs around," she said, swinging her legs casually, as if she had no idea she was pushing her luck. "I'll find them on my own. I can easily look them up online. I hear there's a swingers'—"

Ryder whirled around and the savage look on his face made her shut her mouth. He marched over to her before she could say another word. "Forget it. You are never going to that place."

She silently agreed with him. She was a one-man woman, and once she got Ryder in her bed—*if* she got Ryder into bed—she was never going to share. But he didn't need to know that information right now. Katie blinked innocently at him. "Don't tell me you've been there, too."

"Cut the act. You're throwing these outrageous plans around because you know how I'll react." He gripped her chin between his thumb and forefingers and made her look at him. "You can threaten all you want, but I know deep down you're a good girl."

Good girl? Katie made a face. Had the guy been in a coma for the past year? She was doing everything she could to remove that label. She didn't want to be a good girl. She wanted to be the kind of woman who could catch Ryder. "What makes you think they are just threats?"

"I know you." He let go of her chin, sounding very confident. "You won't act on them."

She leaned back, resting her elbows on the table. "In case you haven't noticed, I've changed over the past year. I'm going to live it up. Experiment. Have fun."

He stared at her as if he couldn't help it. Her breasts felt heavy, her nipples tight, under his gaze. He jerked his head, shaking off the seductive spell she was trying to weave. "I swear, you will say anything to get my attention. You're pushing me, Katie. Are you trying to punish me for leaving town?"

"Don't flatter yourself," she muttered. Ryder was getting too close to the truth. She had the uncomfortable feeling that he understood her as well as she understood him.

He avoided looking at any part of her body from the chin down. "Katie," he said very seriously, "I want you to promise me you won't go to these clubs."

Katie held his gaze. "No."

His eyes narrowed. *"Katie."*

"I can't make that promise." She paused to gather her courage. "My first choice is to explore them with you."

"No way." His voice was cold and brutal.

His immediate, automatic reaction hurt. "Then I have to go with my second option," she said huskily. "I'll just wait until you're gone and explore this subculture all by myself."

"Think again."

"There is nothing you can do about it once you're gone," she pointed out, wanting him to know he didn't have as much power over her as he'd like to believe. "Anyway, I don't know why you think this concerns you. You have no reason to get all weird about it."

"I'm trying to protect you!" Frustration threaded his voice, making it husky.

She knew that, and a part of her adored it, but did it mean he had to keep his hands to himself? "Is what I'm suggesting really that dangerous?"

"Yes! It depends on the partner."

"Hmm." She swung her legs again as she gave it some thought. "Interesting. Who is considered a good partner?"

He rubbed his hands over his face. "I can't believe I'm having this conversation with you."

She sat up and watched him closely. "Is that your way of saying you don't know?"

He dropped his hands and met her gaze. "A good dominant treats his submissive like a rare treasure," he answered with obvious reluctance. "He has to respect and adore his partner, but most of all, he needs to master self-control over himself."

"You're assuming I'm submissive," Katie was quick to point out. "I'll have you know that I can be very aggressive in bed."

He took a deep breath but the tension seemed to build inside him. "And a bad dominant will try to break your spirit."

"So I need to find a dominant who has amazing self-control." She reached out and flattened her hand on his chest. He flinched but stood still. "Someone who has my best interest at heart. Someone who will protect me and have firm boundaries."

He looked at her hand as she claimed him as her dominant. "No way, Katie."

"Come on, Ryder." She hooked her fingers into his shirt. You know you want me."

He removed her hand from his chest. "I said *no*."

"Look, I'll even compromise. You don't have to initiate me"— she ignored his groan—"at a club. We can do it in the privacy of my own home."

"I can't believe you are offering me sex," Ryder said slowly, as if he were in a daze. "Are you insane? We've been dancing around this issue for far too long. It's never going to happen. Not now, not ever, and especially not in your parents' house."

Katie rolled her eyes. "Wow, Ryder, I had no idea you were that conservative."

"I don't know why we're discussing it."

And yet he made no move to walk away.

He held his hands up and shook his head. "You would make a horrible submissive."

She wasn't going to argue that. "I never said I was submissive."

"Then we would never work," he decided as triumph glittered in his dark eyes. "A dominant doesn't take a dominant."

Terrific. Katie inwardly winced as she recognized her mistake. She had walked right into that one. "Then again, I could be submissive with the right encouragement."

He crossed his arms and braced his legs. "You wouldn't do what you were told."

"Isn't that the whole point?" she asked sweetly. "So you could punish me when I'm bad?"

"If I punished you, you wouldn't be able to sit down for a week."

Katie purred and stretched, rolling her spine and shoulders. "That's big talk coming from someone who swears he's only trying to protect me."

Ryder thrust his hands into his hair. "You drive me crazy."

"Good to know." And it was good to hear she had *some* power over him. "So, are you going to tutor me in bondage or not?"

"No," he said sharply. "Why would I do that when I've managed to keep my hands off you all this time?"

CHAPTER FIVE

He cringed, his heartbeat stuttering to a stop as his words replayed in his head. *I've managed to keep my hands off you all this time.* Now Katie knew how much power she had—had always had—over him. Why didn't he just save himself some time and hand all the control over to Katie?

"Really?" Katie drew the word out. "All this time?"

He sliced a hand in the air as if he could erase the past few moments. If only. "That's not what I meant," he said, not sure how he was going to recover from this mistake.

The victory dancing in Katie's wide eyes clearly indicated that she didn't believe him. He could tell that she wanted every hot, delicious detail. But he wasn't going to give in. He needed to convince her that nothing would ever have happened in the past, and nothing ever would in the future.

"How long have you wanted me?" she asked carefully.

Ryder didn't trust himself to say anything. He was already feeling shattered. But Katie's question poked at him. He couldn't remember when he first desired her. Maybe it was the time years ago when he had seen her come out of the bathroom after a shower.

He had been in the upstairs hallway in their house, waiting for Jake, when Katie walked past him wearing only a towel and a flirty smile. His desire for her had come hard and fast, and Ryder had immediately pushed the idea out of his head, but it came back every once in a while. He didn't like the feelings, didn't like himself for desiring her, but he'd thought he could control it.

Instead of his desire dying out quickly, it had bloomed into something stronger. Soon his need for Katie was something that he was always aware of. At first it colored his day, and he was careful not to be left alone with Katie. Then it began to influence his life, when he realized he was making decisions on where he lived based on Katie. He tried to hold himself in check, but he was always afraid that one day it would rage out of his control.

And then this year, it had become clear that he had to entirely remove himself from temptation. She'd transformed into a sensual, confident woman, and if she chose to go after him, he knew he couldn't fight it. Not anymore.

"Huh. That long?" she asked softly when his silence dragged.

He still didn't answer.

"And you never went after me?"

He looked straight in her eyes. He needed to regain control of this situation before Katie took advantage. Before she realized that his self-control was not as strong as he'd led her to believe. "I have my reasons." Ryder hoped his low and steady voice hid the chaos that was swirling inside him.

She nodded her head with mock solemnity. "And I'm sure they are very honorable. I'm too sheltered," she said, ticking off the list on her fingers. "I'm too innocent, I'm Jake's sister, blah, blah, blah. . . ."

Ryder narrowed his eyes, not appreciating her lighthearted take on his concerns. "None of that has changed."

She pressed her lips together for a moment to hold back her irritation. "One major thing has changed. You're leaving. But we shouldn't see this as a problem. This offers us an opportunity."

She hadn't said anything explicit, but Ryder's stomach tightened into knots. "What are you talking about?"

"Don't you see?" She spread her arms wide open. "We can have a wild affair with no consequences."

A wild affair? Ryder didn't trust himself to move as the words pierced his heart. He was a mess because of how he felt about Katie. He was ready to toss away everything he'd made of his life and start over again with nothing on the other side of the world because of her. She had the power to destroy him, and the power to turn him into the man he wanted to become. But all she wanted was an affair.

Wow. He had never thought Katie would see him the same way other women did. But was it really any surprise that she was turning out to be just like every other woman in Crystal Bend? They all saw him as a sexual adventure. He'd hoped Katie saw something more, especially since she knew him better than anyone else. If Katie didn't want a relationship with him, then his worst fear about himself must be true. He was the guy you screwed, but not someone you could love.

"You are more naïve than I realized," Ryder said with a humorless laugh, refusing to show how much her offer hurt. "There are always consequences."

Katie scowled. "Think about it. You and I are alone and we can do anything we want to each other. *Anything*."

Anything. Interest flared deep inside him, cutting through the pain. She wanted to do anything with him. Well, anything except love him or promise him forever.

"We live out every fantasy we've ever had about each other," she continued, apparently taking his silence as a good sign. "Keep at it for the next five or six days until we're satisfied."

Five or six days? His eyes widened. He could have her, exclusively, in his bed, for all that time. It wasn't nearly enough, but it was more than he ever allowed himself to consider before.

No. Ryder cleared his throat. After all these years of holding back, he wasn't going to give in for the promise of six days. He had to be strong.

"And then it'll be over on New Year's Day," she said with a casual flourish of her hand. "We walk away with no regrets and no strings attached."

Walk away. She could walk away from him just like that? Why was he holding out, trying to be honorable? Why was he making a sacrifice when it obviously didn't mean anything to her?

Ryder glared at Katie. "You want me to treat you like a no-name one-night stand?" His voice was low and roughened with anger. "What do you take me for?"

She held her hands up in surrender. "Think about it, Ryder. There is no messy breakup, no awkwardness the next time we see each other. No one even has to find out about the two of us."

He crossed his arms. "Now I'm a shameful secret?" He should have known.

"No! I didn't say that! I can't wait to take you to my bed," she blurted out in naked honesty, "and I don't care who knows it."

Ryder reared back, surprised by her frankness. It broke down his defenses easily. If something as simple as that statement made him want to forget all of his noble intentions, then he was in danger of giving up the fight in the next few minutes.

He uncrossed his arms. "I gotta leave," he muttered and walked toward the door.

"Before you do something you regret?" she mocked.

"Yes!" he said without a break in his stride. She knew the effect she had on him. He had to get out now.

"Do you know what you're going to regret the most?" she called out to him. "Not having an affair with me!"

His hand was on the doorknob. He hesitated and his shoulders sagged. He knew he was going to have that regret. It would eat at him until he couldn't think straight. "Katie." Her name dragged out of his throat.

"I will be the submissive of your dreams," she said with absolute certainty. "I will do anything you say."

A tremor swept him. "Promise?"

He was surrendering. He couldn't fight it anymore. Katie was offering him his greatest fantasy, the one thing he wanted most. He was no prince, no good guy, and he sure as hell wasn't a saint.

He was no good for Katie, and accepting this offer was proof of that. But he couldn't pass it up. Having Katie submit to him? That already made her the submissive of his dreams.

Would Katie really do anything he said? The power, the promise of pure pleasure, flooded through his veins with such force, it made him dizzy.

"Is that a yes?" she asked.

Oh, yeah. Now she wasn't sounding so sure of herself. She shouldn't have given this level of power to him. To any man, but especially to him. He was weak when it came to Katie, and once he got a taste of her, he wouldn't be able to control himself.

It was time for her to find out what kind of deal she was suggesting. He wrestled back a portion of self-control. He would show her the consequences of her desires, let her know what it was like to really be submissive, and then let her escape unscathed. *Then* he would leave town. It wouldn't be a wild affair. It would be a simple tuition in the art of bondage—he'd teach her just enough to be sure she wouldn't do anything stupid once he was no longer around to keep an eye on her.

He pivoted on his heel and his gaze collided with hers. "For a trial run," he declared.

Katie's hopeful expression collapsed into disappointment, and for a moment she looked like the innocent schoolgirl he remembered from years ago. "No way. We don't have time for that."

"I'm going to start you off with something easy," Ryder promised as he strode back to the kitchen table.

Katie watched him approach. She wasn't as eager as he had expected. If anything, she was suspicious about his sudden and easy capitulation. She was smart, because he wasn't going to let things go too far. Not today anyway. "What's the catch?" she asked.

"If you can't handle it, then that's it," he said with a shrug. "We stop right then and there and we never mention it again."

"And it's going to be something easy. Right. You don't want me to understand this lifestyle, but you're going to give me a gentle introduction? Sure, you are. How do I know you're not setting me up for a fall?"

"Trust is the most important element in the relationship between a submissive and a dominant. If you can't trust me"—Ryder flinched from the unexpected jab of pain as he considered the possibility—"there is no reason to start."

Katie swallowed roughly, and he saw the struggle in her eyes. He wished her trust in him was absolute and automatic, but it was better that she thought this through. She had no idea how difficult it would be to have no control in the situation and give him her trust completely.

Ryder waited patiently, watching her face intently. He wasn't going to make the choice for her, and he wasn't going to wait indefinitely. Either she knew that he was going to take care of her or she didn't.

"I trust you," she said quietly, then tilted her chin up. "I always have."

Her words pleased him, but the claim sounded uncomfortably like a vow. "And I leave on New Year's Day," he said, reminding himself not to get too comfortable with her. "It ends then, no matter what."

"Of course," she said steadily, but was quick to add, "if you can drag yourself away from me."

Ryder felt a bittersweet smile tug the corner of his mouth. "I'll do my best."

"When do you want to start?" She rubbed her hands together. "Are we going to the bondage club?"

"No club!" he ordered harshly. "Ever!" The image of her, dressed like this and unprotected, was enough to make him lose his cool.

"Okay, okay!" She lifted her shoulders and held up her hands. "I got it. No club."

"We start now." He unzipped his winter coat, but that was all he was removing. The more clothes he had on, the less likely he was to crawl on top of Katie and dominate her until he satisfied his intense hunger—and ruined his relationship with her forever.

"Now?" Her gaze was transfixed on Ryder's dark green hoodie. "As in right here and now?"

"Do you have a problem with that?" he asked as he slung his coat on the back of a chair.

"Not at all." Katie's voice was high as her heart rolled over and over. "I'm all yours."

She reached for him eagerly, and licked her lips. Ryder got the sense that she was preparing to give him a long, wet, hard kiss that would grab at his very soul. He held out his hands, ready to lay down the law. "No, you can't touch me."

"I can't what?"

He pushed her back gently, ready to shock her. "Keep your hands flat on the tabletop." He held her hands and put them in position before letting go. "Imagine that your wrists are chained down."

"I'm not that imaginative. Hey, I have some leftover gift-wrapping ribbon. I can . . ." Katie started to move away from the table, but he stopped her.

"No," Ryder said as he guided her back to her original position and stood between her legs. "I want to see how good your control is if you aren't relying on something holding you down."

Katie frowned, and Ryder could tell she wasn't too sure about this. "What's my reward?"

Ryder gave her a quick glance. "Excuse me?" Wasn't this reward enough?

"Let's say I pass this trial run. Then what? What's my reward?"

"Interesting." She wasn't accepting this opportunity without asking for something more. Now that was the Katie he knew and adored. "Then we meet for a true bondage scene," he promised rashly.

"Tonight," she decided.

Ryder shook his head. "You don't get to pick the time." Not that it would matter. She wouldn't pass this test. He would make sure of it.

"Yes, I do. You're leaving soon and I'm not taking any rain checks. If I pass this trial run, we meet tonight."

"Okay, tonight." He pointed at her hands. "Flat on the table."

She did as he asked. "What are you going to do?"

"You'll find out soon enough. Stay perfectly still."

Her eyes widened. Was he serious? She couldn't touch him and she had to remain still?

No matter how much she tried to keep them still, her legs, dangling off the edge of the table, brushed against his thighs. He didn't call her on it and Katie allowed her legs to rest against his as he reached for her. She sighed when his fingertips glided from her hair to her forehead. He then caressed the bridge of her nose and her cheeks, before smoothing his fingers along her jaw. His touch was light and teasing. By the time he reached her chin, she was gritting her teeth. She wanted to lean into his hand, but she wouldn't move. She had a lot riding on this test.

Ryder drew a line around her mouth with his finger. Katie parted her lips and froze. Did that count as moving? Maybe he hadn't noticed. Please don't let him have noticed!

"I feel you trembling," he said with a knowing smile. "I don't think you will hold out."

"I will," she promised.

He continued to circle his finger around her mouth. Her lips tingled and they felt fuller. Was it her imagination or were the circles he drew getting smaller?

Ryder's finger was now on her plush bottom lip. She wanted to pucker her mouth. Okay, that wasn't true. She really wanted to flick her tongue out and lick him before curling her tongue around his finger and drawing him into her mouth.

But that might be considered moving.

Ryder watched her mouth with unnerving intensity. She

wondered if he would notice if she moved another part of her body, but she wasn't going to take the chance. He dragged his finger along her red lips, smearing the lipstick. Still she didn't move.

He dipped the tip of his finger into her mouth. Katie tried to control the tremor in her jaw. She wanted to give him a little nip. Catch him with the edge of her tooth. She longed to swirl her tongue around his finger and mimic what she could do with his cock.

And while her imagination ran wild, mostly with the idea of slurping his finger, she remained perfectly still. She wasn't sure if she could keep it up much longer, when her body longed to pounce. Her hand pressed hard against the table and she sat ramrod straight. She was not going to mess this up.

Ryder withdrew his finger and Katie tried not to follow. She bet Ryder had expected her to crack by now. He didn't get how much she wanted this. How much she wanted *him*.

Ryder covered her hands with his. Katie almost flinched from the unexpected touch, but caught herself just in time. She liked the feel of his warm, big hands. She felt small and delicate, but protected.

Ryder leaned closer until his mouth hovered above hers. He was going to kiss her—and she wasn't allowed to kiss back! That was incredibly unfair.

His mouth was so close to hers. She felt his warm breath on her lips. He didn't move any farther. She wanted to scream. This was the kiss she had been waiting for. The one *he* instigated. The one that was supposed to devour her, take her breath away and leave her swollen and limp, but begging for more.

He still didn't move. She got the feeling he was fighting with himself. That he wanted to take the last step. That he only needed a little more encouragement.

His lips were right there, waiting. She could claim them now. This might be her last chance. . . .

Ryder lifted his hand and brushed his fingertips along her throat. She remained still as he softly rubbed his thumb against the fluttering pulse at the base of her throat. He said nothing but she saw the primal satisfaction in his eyes. She didn't care what he claimed; he liked having this sexual power over her. He wanted to explore it as much as she did.

His hand glided down the slope of her breast, as if he couldn't help himself. Katie's breath hitched in her throat. Her skin tingled at the intimate touch, her nipples tightening with anticipation.

Katie felt like her entire body was wound tight, ready to spring wildly at the most gentle touch. Ryder lightly caressed the curve of her breast, the slick, clingy material of her vest the only barrier between them. Her soft, choppy panting echoed in her head while he drew lazy circles around the tip of her breast. A tremor swept through her as the circles grew tighter and closer. Her nipples were puckered and stinging for his touch. He was almost there . . . almost. . . .

Ryder pulled back abruptly. He rubbed his hands over his face, breaking the spell that bound them. Grabbing his coat from the back of the chair, he walked to the door.

"Are we done?" she asked without moving her lips.

"Yes," he replied roughly. He grabbed for the door as if it were his lifeline.

The tension released from her in one giant wave. She punched her fist in the air. "Yes! I passed."

Ryder stopped in his tracks.

"I will see you here tonight." She was tempted to jump off the table and do a little victory dance, but that would ruin her sophisticated image.

His face was expressionless. "I'll be here at eight."

Eight? She couldn't wait that long! She had thousands of fantasies to explore with him. "Can you come earlier?"

"No," he answered in a strangled voice. "I'm moving, remember? I have stuff to do."

She didn't appreciate the reminder. "Fine, but I'll be ready if you want to come around earlier," she offered.

He kept looking straight ahead of him. "And don't wear that outfit."

She stroked her shiny vest, wondering what he had against it. "If you insist." She would give in just a little. "What would you prefer? A negligee? Plastic wrap?"

His spine stiffened. "Something the old Katie would wear," he said in a low growl as he closed the door behind him.

Something from her old wardrobe? Katie wrinkled her nose. Now what was the fun in that?

Ryder threw a bunch of old clothes in the charity box and slowly straightened to his full height, working out the stiff muscles in his back. He'd never really had much stuff to begin with, although Katie, who was addicted to those home improvement and decorating shows, made sure he had the basic necessities when he'd first moved in.

He looked around his small apartment. Legs braced with hands on his hips, his muscles shook in the aftermath of nonstop work. He was hot and sweaty, wearing nothing but a ripped pair of jeans, but the lust was still screeching through him, and he was desperate for relief. It didn't matter how hard he worked his body. It was no use. He couldn't get the image of Katie out of his mind.

And she expected him to follow through on their agreement tonight and he couldn't let her down. He should never have tested her. As much as he didn't want her to pass, so he could leave town with a clean conscience, a secret, dark part of him wanted Katie to succeed, to prove that she trusted him. In truth, he was desperate for another excuse to touch her, kiss her.

He never could leave well enough alone, could he? Ryder thought with disgust. He only had to endure a few more days of Katie torturing him and he would have been home free. And what had he done? Screwed it up. He wanted to keep Katie ignorant of his sexual tastes, but at the same time, he wanted to initiate her. Tutor her. Because deep down he knew they would be amazing together.

Ryder heard a knock on his door. He tensed, his muscles quivering. *Please don't let it be Katie,* he prayed as he went to answer it. He didn't have much armor left to ward her off. He wanted her so badly right now that he wouldn't put up even a pretense of a fight.

He opened the door reluctantly and frowned when he saw Tatum. She stood in front of him wearing bright red heels, a skimpy black raincoat, and a big smile.

"Tatum," he greeted her warily. "What are you doing here?" It sure wasn't to help him pack.

"I thought I'd come by and reminisce about the old times." Her hands curled along the lapels of her raincoat, drawing his attention to the fact that she wore nothing underneath.

Ryder paused. He and Tatum had shared a good thing a year ago. It was kinky and dirty, but after a while he broke it off. No matter how creative Tatum could be, when he was with her, he felt empty inside.

"We were really great together." She reached out and flattened her hand on his bare chest. Tatum smiled when she felt his strong heartbeat under her palm.

Did she think she had him hot and ready? That all she needed to do was show up and he would want to jump her? No, he wasn't interested in Tatum like that anymore. Now, if it had been Katie knocking on his door dressed up like that . . .

"This morning I went past the drive-in movie and I remembered the night we . . ." Her voice trailed off and she glided her hand along his sweat-slick abdomen.

He remembered. It had been in the summer, but it wasn't the heat wave or raunchy movie that had set him off. He had seen Katie on a date at the drive-in. It was bad enough watching a guy have his hands all over her while they stood in line for popcorn, but she had looked incredibly sexy in a white lace cami and tiny denim shorts. Right then and there he wanted to grab Katie by her long ponytail, throw her into his truck, rip off her clothes and make love to her until the fierce lust drained from his body.

Instead he kept his distance. Did everything he could not to look at Katie while the white-hot need tore through him. And before that movie was over, he and Tatum had enjoyed some rough and wild sex in the cab of his truck. He immediately regretted it, and not because he gave most of the customers at the drive-in something more interesting than the movie to watch. He had felt restless, and guilty, which had made no sense.

Tatum palmed his rock-hard cock through his jeans and cupped his balls with her other hand. "Oh, you do remember," she crooned. She reached for his zipper and slowly dragged it down. "This time it'll be better than ever," she promised.

Ryder wrapped his fingers around Tatum's wrist, stopping her. "I'm sorry, Tatum," he said in a cold tone. "It's not a good idea."

She appeared stunned by his refusal. "Why not?" she asked as she stepped closer until her breasts pressed against his chest and her hands were trapped between their bodies as she dragged his zipper all the way down.

Ryder wasn't sure how to answer. A rough, fast screw with Tatum might take the edge off the lust that was eating at him. It had in the past, and there was no reason why it wouldn't work now. Why not have a meaningless quickie with an ex-girlfriend who knew the score?

But he already knew the answer. Katie Kramer had gotten under his skin and wormed a place in his heart. He would only find peace and satisfaction with her, and there could be no substitute.

Ryder grabbed both of Tatum's wrists and lifted her hands away from his pants. He guided her a step away from his door before he let go.

"Good-bye, Tatum. Next time call before you drop by," he suggested as he closed the door. He turned the lock and rested his head against the wall. He didn't regret his choice, but Tatum must be wondering what had gotten into him.

Katie had, along with the promise of something better, something sweeter. She really had turned his life upside down, and there was nothing he could do about it. He couldn't deny that something was about to happen between them. She obviously wanted it as much as he did.

Hilary set down her coffee cup with a clatter, the confusion apparent on her face. "So, let me see if I've got this straight," she said to Melissa and Katie as they sat around a tiny table in the quaint coffeehouse later that afternoon. "Ryder laid down the law and told you what you can and cannot do." She paused. "And we're excited about this?"

"He accepted my offer," Katie explained. She spoke very calmly as her pulse tripped and skipped. Leaning back in her chair, she tried to look as if she fully expected every one of her fantasies to come true. She wasn't freaking out. Not at all.

"He *sort of* accepted your offer," Hilary pointed out, "as long as you do everything he says."

"Hey, don't knock it," Melissa said, as she wrapped a protective arm around Katie's shoulders. "This is a major development. It's a step in the right direction."

"True." Hilary nodded. "But how many steps are involved before you actually get to have sex with him?"

"I don't know," Katie admitted. It was something that worried her.

"I think he's playing you," Hilary said under her breath.

Katie bristled at her friend's opinion about Ryder. "Ryder won't jerk me around. He's not like that."

"If you say so." Hilary's thoughtful gaze wandered down Katie's long-sleeved blue T-shirt, black PVC pants, and black ankle boots. "You know, it's weird. You look like a kick-ass, take-no-prisoners woman, but you're acting like—"

"So," Melissa interrupted quickly. "When do you see him again?"

"Tonight," Katie answered, dragging her gaze away from Hilary. She knew what her friend was saying. How could she be a confident and sensual woman if she had essentially agreed to be a sex slave? "At my place."

"Interesting," Hilary commented. "He meets you on your territory. Then again, he's free to leave when he wants." She flinched and groaned as Melissa kicked her under the table.

"Don't listen to her," Melissa advised Katie. "What are you going to wear tonight? I recommend those stiletto boots."

"Forget that," Hilary said, leaning down to rub her injured shin. "The important question is how are you going to go after what you want if you're tied up?"

"I'm after Ryder," Katie clarified. "And the beauty is that I don't have to do anything but lie there and take it."

"You're taking whatever you can get. If I had Jake in my hands"—Hilary tilted her face up as she let her imagination run wild—"I'd have him naked and shaking and I wouldn't let him walk away."

Katie held up her hand. "Okay, first off, please don't use my brother as an example. It's going to traumatize me. Second, I had agreed to follow the parameters. If I had ignored them, the deal would have been off."

"You'll find a way to fulfill your fantasies. I know you will." Melissa patted Katie's arm. "You're being very patient for someone who only has a few days left to get her man. I'm impressed."

"Unless . . ." Hilary leaned back in her chair and studied Katie as she took another sip of coffee. "Unless you're hoping for more than a couple days."

Katie looked away guiltily. Her friends knew her well. They knew how much she loved Ryder, and she wanted more than one night or a week. She wanted Ryder to stay and be with her forever. And if her plan worked, he would discover that she was his dream lover and he wouldn't consider leaving. At least, she hoped so.

Melissa frowned. "What are you talking about? Ryder is leaving on New Year's Day."

"If Katie doesn't give him a reason to stay." Hilary gave Katie a knowing look. "That's what you're hoping for, isn't it?"

Katie fiddled with the neckline of her shirt. "I'm just offering him a taste of what he'll be missing."

"Oh!" Melissa blinked as she suddenly caught on. "Hey, it's possible," she told Hilary. "Ryder has feelings for Katie and they are entering a relationship."

"It's not a relationship; it's sex," Hilary said. "And they haven't even had that yet." She cast a suspicious look at Katie. "Are you hoping to drag it out and prevent him from leaving, even though he specifically told you it would end on New Year's Day? I'm just worried about you getting your heart broken, Katie."

"No, I'm not going to drag it out." She wanted him hot, hungry and wild in her bed. She wanted to take him in so deeply, her legs tightly wrapped around his hips, well and truly caught, that he didn't ever want to break free. "But I can't lie. I hope he considers staying."

Hilary pursed her lips. "After your whole no-consequences speech?"

Katie fiddled with her hair. She wasn't a hypocrite. If Ryder really wanted to walk away, she would put up a very sophisticated front and wouldn't give him any drama. "Actually, he seemed kind of offended when I said that."

"Katie, sweetie, don't get your hopes up," Hilary pleaded, her eyes filled with concern. "I don't want to hurt your feelings . . ."

"I hate when people say that," Katie muttered. "It means they're going to lay it on me."

"Ryder Scott is what you would call a lone wolf. He isn't going to stay because he's in your bed. It doesn't matter if you had the best sex ever, or never got around to having sex. You've seen how he treats his ex-girlfriends. He has a short attention span and he breaks things off fast and clean. There is no guarantee that he will treat you differently. I expect that he's going to leave you without a backward glance. Nothing you do or say will keep him here."

"Ow," Katie said dryly as the shaft of pain went through her heart. She liked to think she was a little more important to Ryder than that. She was different than the other women in his life. But, then, maybe she wasn't.

"Not necessarily," Melissa argued. "Ryder is teaching Katie about being a submissive. Hey, here's an idea. What if she's the worst submissive? I mean, really, truly horrible. He's not going to leave her if she's not ready to handle the bondage scene without him."

Katie tilted her head as she thought Melissa's idea over. She would rather be the best submissive Ryder ever had, but if she was good at it, he'd have nothing to worry about. "That might work."

Hilary groaned and covered her face with her hands. "No, it won't."

"Think about it," Melissa urged, leaning forward, her eyes bright with enthusiasm. "Ryder is very protective about her, and will see her through a rite of passage. Remember when he taught her how to drive because her dad basically gave up?"

Hilary dropped her hands. "Operating heavy machinery is way different from experimenting with kinky sex."

"Well, I guess that depends on the guy you're with," Melissa said, "but my point is, Ryder isn't going to leave until he knows Katie is going to be okay."

Hilary shook her head. "I want it on record that I disagree with this plan. Vehemently."

Melissa gave a sharp nod. "Noted."

Katie pressed her fingertips against her forehead. "Okay, guys, I get what you're saying. Basically, I shouldn't get my hopes up."

"Exactly," Hilary replied. "You are in way over your head with Ryder."

"Play it dumb," Melissa said with a smile. "Give him a reason to spend lots of time tutoring you."

"My advice is to play it smart," Hilary said. "Change the rules on him. Grab for your dreams with both hands and don't think you can come back for seconds!"

Katie whimpered. She liked both ideas, but each had its problems. She didn't know what to do. Why did she think having a wild love affair was going to be simple and straightforward?

CHAPTER SIX

He was late.

Katie stared at the kitchen clock, willing it to slow down. Freeze. Not move until Ryder got there. He had said he would be there by eight o'clock and she had believed him. Ryder Scott always kept his promises. If he said he would be there at eight, he would be there at eight.

It was 8:15.

She gnawed on her bottom lip and peered out the window over the sink. Had he changed his mind? Or was this his plan all along? Had he set her up to trick her into staying at home, believing it was for her own good?

Now it was 8:16. Katie smoothed her damp palms over her hips. The burgundy wool dress felt warm and soft under her touch. This old wraparound dress was one of her favorites. She always felt good in it and wore it whenever she needed an extra boost of confidence. And she needed it desperately tonight.

But now she wondered if she was overdressed. That was the problem with Ryder being sixteen minutes late. She was second-guessing everything. Maybe she should throw on a pair of jeans and a sloppy sweater. That was probably what he'd meant when he asked her to wear something the "old Katie" would wear.

She didn't know why he'd made that request. Katie knew he liked her new, sexy style. She could see it in his eyes. *Maybe he liked it too much,* she thought with a smile. Did he think he could control the "old Katie" any better? He was in for a surprise.

Her heart gave a violent lurch when she heard the doorbell. Ryder was here. She was not ready for this.

What? What was she thinking? She was so ready for this. She was going to follow Ryder's sexual demands and throw in a few challenges for him. She would exceed his fantasies and live out each and every one of her own.

Katie strode to the front door as if she hadn't been pacing frantically for the past fifteen minutes. Her kitten heels echoed loudly as she crossed the hallway to reach the door. She saw Ryder's silhouette framed in the window. He was looking away toward the street. Was he seeing if the coast was clear, or was he wondering if he should make a run for it?

It was strange that he was at the front door. The guy always came around back, enjoying a casual, open invitation to drop by at any time. Why was he using the doorbell and waiting at the front? It was so formal, and the change threw her off balance. Her nervousness ratcheted up.

Taking a deep breath, she unlocked the safety chain and opened the door. Ryder turned around and locked eyes with her. She couldn't read his expression.

"Here," she said, unsure what to say as she reached for him. Her movements were awkward and jerky and her spine was still pressed against the door. "Let me take your coat."

Ryder was silent as he shrugged out of his winter coat. Katie was also aware that he hadn't dressed any differently for this night.

He wore a brown long-sleeved shirt, faded jeans and boots. She felt overdressed, but she had followed his request.

"How do you like my dress?" she ventured bravely as she took his coat. "Is this what you had in mind?"

His long, thorough appraisal felt like a caress as his gaze lingered on her curves. "Yes," he answered gruffly.

"Yes?" That's it? That's all he had to say? She'd spent a long time getting ready for him. No detail was ignored. She hid her impatience as she hung his coat in the entry hall closet. "I don't know why you have a problem with my new look."

She didn't hear him move, but suddenly his hands were flattened on the closet door, caging her in. Katie's eyes widened, her heart pumping hard. He crowded, surrounded her, and she didn't want to break free.

"I hate the rubber outfit because it's not you."

She scoffed at the idea. "It's PVC and it's totally me."

"I hate the leather boots," he continued as he trailed his hand along her arm to her shoulder. "They are for someone hard and tough."

"I'm tough," she protested. Okay, maybe not right now when she was melting at his touch.

"I like this dress because it's you." His hands were light and gentle as he stroked her hair before tucking it to one side. "Warm and soft."

"That makes me sound very weak," she said in a whisper, closing her eyes as she enjoyed his scent enveloping her. "I want to be powerful."

"You have no idea," he murmured, his warm breath wafting onto her neck. "And that's probably for the best."

Katie frowned at his cryptic answer. She opened her mouth to ask for clarification when Ryder pressed his mouth below her ear.

His touch was possessive. She gasped as a fiery shower of sensations set off in her blood.

Ryder moved his lips along her earlobe. His tongue flicked the red jasper earring. "You're wearing my Christmas present," he whispered. There was no mistaking the satisfaction in his gruff voice.

"Of course." Didn't he know that she treasured every one of his gifts? She still had the first Christmas ornament he had ever given her. It was flaking with age, but it held a special, prominent place on the tree every year.

"Take me into the living room," he told her softly as he tenderly kissed her cheek.

Katie tilted her head. Had she heard that correctly? She always had imagined him saying "take me to bed." "Why the living room?"

"Katie"—ooh, how she loved the way he said her name. It was rough and low.

"Yes, Ryder," she replied in a purr.

"A good submissive doesn't question her master's choices."

Katie's spine went rigid. "Wait a second. Did you just call yourself *master*?"

"Tonight I am your master," he whispered in her ear.

Master? That wasn't agreed on. She knew he would be dominant, and she was looking forward to that part, but there was no freaking way she would call him Master!

"Do you have a problem with that?" He slowly turned her around until she faced him. He was so close, his forehead resting against hers, his big hands cupping her face. "I need to know now before we begin."

Her brain was yelling that even though she was relinquishing control for a short time, no man would ever be her *master*. Her heart was a little uncertain. But when she opened her mouth, she replied weakly, "No. No problem."

She couldn't tell if Ryder was surprised by her answer. She sure was! Katie wasn't sure what she had planned to say, but she knew that if she didn't sound one hundred percent sure, Ryder would leave and the opportunity would be lost.

"Take me to the living room," Ryder repeated.

Katie licked her lips as she hesitated. She had a feeling he wouldn't tell her again. She reached for his hand, sliding her fingertips over his callused palm. Threading her fingers with his, Katie led him into the living room.

Once she stepped inside the room, she understood his request. The lights were on in most rooms except this one. She kept them off to showcase the colorful, twinkling lights of the Christmas tree. Small, white lights woven in garlands hung from every window and doorway. A blaze crackled and glowed in the stone fireplace.

Katie went to stand in front of the huge Christmas tree and reluctantly let go of Ryder's hand. She faced him and held her hands behind her back, hoping she appeared to be a good submissive. But she refused to bow her head or look down. She maintained eye contact as she waited for Ryder's next move.

Ryder didn't seem to be in a hurry, which bothered Katie to no end. Why wasn't he eager? That wasn't to say he was unaffected. She could tell by the rise and fall of his chest, the tension humming in the air, even the way he held himself apart from her, that he wanted to surge forward and grab her. But his self-control was stronger than hers.

Finally he took a step closer, his movement swift and sure. Her breath caught in her throat as she anticipated being swept up in his arms. Instead, he cupped her face with his hands again and pressed his lips against hers.

Katie closed her eyes, hiding the gathering tears that threatened to spill over her lashes. She had waited a long time for Ryder Scott to kiss her and it was worth the wait. Her skin heated as joy and desire flooded through her. Her knees bent and she struggled not to sag into him.

She greedily accepted his kiss, but Ryder wasn't prepared to devour her. He kissed her slowly, savoring the touch, the moment. He tasted every inch of her lips before delving his tongue into her eager mouth.

Katie grabbed at Ryder's shirt and felt the heavy thud of his heart. She tried to draw him closer, but he didn't move. She wiggled against him in a silent plea. *Faster. Deeper. More.*

Ryder's kisses were unhurried and deliberate, his lips lingering on hers. Her mouth clung to his. He was driving her crazy. Were his kisses designed to make her beg? If she was this hot and bothered over a kiss, what could she expect once they were in bed? She shivered as excitement swirled deep in her stomach.

Ryder suddenly took a step back and Katie clutched at his shirt. He gently lowered her hands and firmly let go. As he put his hand in his back pocket, Katie noticed that he wasn't so immune to the kisses he controlled. His breathing was harsh and heavy, and his hard cock pressed against his jeans.

She was smiling proudly when Ryder pulled out a piece of black cloth. "What's that?" she asked.

He held it out for her to inspect. "A blindfold."

"Blindfold!" Katie took a step back, bumping into the tree. She spread her arms out to keep her balance and the ornaments jangled as the branches swayed. "That wasn't part of the plan."

"What's the matter?" Ryder asked innocently. A little too innocently in Katie's opinion.

"I agreed to being tied up. I never said anything about being"—she gestured at the black strip of cloth—"blindfolded."

"You're not ready for bondage," Ryder decided. "The blindfold is a good introduction. You'll still follow my lead, but you'll have the freedom to move if it gets too intense."

Ha. Freedom. Nice choice of words. "I don't think so." She could handle being tied up. She had geared herself up for that. And more important, the chances were that if she was tied up or down, she could still see what was coming at her.

"Okay. That's fine. It's your choice," Ryder said, as if her decision didn't surprise him.

So much for being the sophisticated lover. Katie belatedly realized the fir tree was poking into her butt and she hastily stepped away, searching her mind for a way to erase her unworldly reaction from Ryder's mind.

"Obviously, the stupid bondage club is not for you." He tucked the dark strip of fabric in his front jeans pocket. "I'm glad you found out before you walked in there."

What? Katie's jaw dropped at his statement. That was it? He was calling it quits because she said no to the first thing he threw at her. "This isn't fair. You knew how I was going to react about the blindfold."

Ryder shrugged. "The problem is, *you* didn't know."

Katie didn't like the sound of that. She folded her arms across her chest as her eyes narrowed with growing resentment. "So all of this was to protect me from myself?" Disappointment welled in her chest. Maybe he didn't want her.

Ryder rubbed his hand against the back of his neck as he wrestled for the right words. "No," he answered reluctantly. "Not all of it."

That was all she needed to hear. She held out her hand. "Give me the blindfold."

That surprised Ryder. "No, it's not necessary."

Maybe not for him, but she wanted to prove something to herself. That she didn't have to be in charge of her environment every moment. That she didn't have to be in total control to live out her fantasy. And she could be safe and wild if Ryder was part of the fantasy. She could surrender to him and know he would take care of her.

She could have her fantasy if she stopped trying to push things and allowed this affair to unfold on its own course. The time limit, the urgency, was making her focus on what she was about to lose. If she wasn't careful, she wouldn't enjoy what she had until it was over.

Katie quickly tugged the blindfold from his pocket, but Ryder grabbed the other end. He wouldn't let go.

"Come on, Ryder, let me have it." She refused to get in a tug-of-war. That would cement the unsophisticated image. "I want to know how it feels."

"No, you don't. You were against it a minute ago."

She could understand his disbelief, and knew she had to explain as honestly as she could. "And then I reminded myself that nothing could go wrong. I'm safe with you."

His mouth pressed into a firm, unyielding line. She could tell he was fighting the attraction that sizzled between them. Ryder slowly let go and gave a sigh of surrender. "You're the one who doesn't play fair."

"Ryder, when are you going to realize that I'm not playing?" She held the black fabric against her eyes. Wow, it really blocked out everything. She had hoped for some light to filter through. But there was something very erotic knowing that she couldn't see Ryder, but he could see everything about her. She trembled as dark excitement swirled around her.

She wasn't going to back down now. She meant what she had said: Ryder would guide her through this rite of passage. He would satisfy her and keep her safe. Katie tried to knot it at the back of her head. Her fingers fumbled along the blindfold, betraying the nervousness that she hid in her voice.

"Here, let me." She felt Ryder's hands on her shoulders before he turned her around and grabbed the ends of the blindfold. She knew the Christmas tree was now in front of her, but she couldn't see the twinkling lights or the gleam of the metallic ornaments.

"Not too tightly," she said, her voice higher than she liked.

"It has to be tight or you'll see," Ryder said as he pulled the blindfold snugly. "We wouldn't want that, now would we?"

"I don't want you mad while I'm blindfolded, either," she muttered. Was he pissed because she'd called his bluff?

Ryder paused and pressed his mouth to the top of her head. "I'm not mad," he said, her hair muffling his voice. "Just not sure what I'm doing."

"What are you talking about?" She straightened up, her hands flattening against the blindfold, ready to whip it off. "I thought you did this all the time."

"Not with you," he said as he placed his hands on her shoulders and turned her around.

Katie frowned and lowered her hands, slightly disoriented. "I'm not delicate or fragile."

"You are to me." His words were barely audible as he kissed a trail from her cheek, along her jaw and finally to her lips.

Once again, his kisses were controlled and fleeting. Only this time, trapped under the blindfold, Katie felt his touch differently. It was almost as if he didn't trust himself. As if deepening his kiss would trigger something uncontrollable inside him.

Katie wasn't sure if the blindfold offered a skewed reality. All sensations were heightened, but with a strange dreamlike quality. The evergreen scent was stronger, the crackle of the fire louder. That didn't mean that Ryder's touches held more meaning.

Ryder slid his mouth to her throat as his hands skimmed her shoulders. He glided his fingers along the deep V of her neckline. Katie held her breath in anticipation as his fingertips brushed along the tops of her breasts. She couldn't wait for him to pull her dress down and reveal her curves.

Her nipples stung as they hardened. She waited for his touch of skin on skin. Ryder slid his hands under her breasts, growling in the back of his throat as he felt their full heaviness before skimming his hands down to her waist.

His mouth was following a slow, meandering journey along her collarbone. Did he realize that his lazy touch was her anchor in a darkened world? She didn't think she could take much more of this. Curling her fingers in his short hair, Katie was about to thrust her breast in his face when she felt Ryder give a decisive, almost savage yank of her sash.

Her wraparound dress billowed open. Katie sensed Ryder stepping away. Her dress flapped and it was almost as if she could feel his gaze. Her breasts felt full and heavy as her skin heated. A naughty thrill zipped through her veins before pooling in her hips. It was exciting being almost naked while he was still fully clothed. She was on display for his pleasure and she wanted him to take a good look. She was tempted to pose for him. Arch her spine, adjust her hip or thrust her breasts. But she didn't move, unsure of his reaction. She really was beginning to hate the blindfold.

"It's like unwrapping a present," he said softly.

She bit her bottom lip as a wave of shyness swept through her. She was thrilled at the pleasure in his voice, but, damn, she wished she could see his face. Was he merely smiling, or did he look like he'd been run over by a truck?

Still, he didn't touch her. Maybe she should thrust her breasts, but she was feeling a little vulnerable. Did he like what she was wearing underneath her dress? Could he see it? It wasn't what the "old Katie" would have worn, but he didn't need to know that. Let him think she always wore sheer, frothy lingerie that would make a man blush.

She hoped he was blushing. No, she hoped he was on his knees and thanking the stars for his incredible luck.

"Ryder?" She tilted her head to one side, listening intently, but the only thing she could hear was the fire.

Oh, my God. Had he left? She slowly moved her head as if she could scan the room, but the blindfold revealed nothing. She didn't hear his breathing, but her heart was pounding loudly in her ears. "Ryder?"

He didn't answer. She brought her hands to the blindfold and hesitated. Should she risk taking a peek?

CHAPTER SEVEN

Katie wavered, her fingertips clenching the blindfold. Did she really need to take it off? If she was completely honest, no, she didn't. Not now. Deep down she knew that Ryder wouldn't leave her. He wouldn't do that. She was curious and vulnerable, but she wasn't scared.

Wouldn't she have heard Ryder leave? He must still be standing in front of her. She lowered her hands in front of her and her fingers collided with Ryder's rock-hard chest.

"There you are," Katie said softly with a smile of relief.

"I thought you were going to take off your blindfold."

"You didn't give me permission," she answered primly, as she pressed her fingers into his chest, enjoying the warmth and strength of him.

"But you wanted to," Ryder said.

"Because you didn't answer," she defended herself. "Why didn't you? Were you testing me?"

"Yes," he answered. "I wanted to see if you would take off your blindfold without permission."

"No more tests," Katie told him.

"No more tests," Ryder agreed as he brushed a knuckle along her cheek. She frowned, almost certain that his hand was trembling.

Ryder let his hand drift down her throat until he reached the collar. He gently pushed her dress off her shoulders and it fell from her and landed softly at her feet.

Katie clenched her hands at her sides, but she didn't move. She tried to imagine how she must look. She hoped her appearance was sexy instead of out of place, standing in front of the Christmas tree wearing nothing but a pair of black heels, a teeny pair of panties, a demi-cup bra and a blindfold.

"You are so beautiful," Ryder said in a hushed breath.

"Thank you," Katie shyly replied as the adrenaline rushed through her veins. She reached for him. "Now it's your turn."

He caught her hands. "No, not yet."

"But . . ." Wasn't he eager to get naked with her?

"I'm in charge," he reminded her. "And you don't get to touch me yet."

She didn't like the sound of that. "Why not?"

"You have to earn it."

Who did Ryder think he was?

"I'm your master," he said with supreme confidence.

Had she said that out loud? "I didn't agree to that."

"You will by the end of tonight." His husky voice was full of promise.

Oh, she really hoped he would try to make that bold statement a reality. He wasn't going to succeed, but finding out how he would try to convince her would be fun. "You haven't done anything that would make me agree," she taunted.

She felt his large, callused hand on her collarbone. He slid a finger under her bra strap and pushed it over her shoulder. Katie couldn't see it, but she felt her bra falling from the curve of her breast. Could he see her light pink nipple puckering, waiting for his touch? Katie tried to calm her short, choppy breath as Ryder trailed his fingertips down the slope of her breast.

He didn't delve into the demi cup like she had expected. Instead he traced the luxurious edge of her bra. His touch was light and teasing, part on the lace, part on her hot skin. Katie swallowed back a moan, her body shivering with anticipation as her nipples stung for attention.

She heard Ryder's knowing chuckle. She really wished she could see his face. "Stop teasing me," she said with a smile.

"Why? You teased me all these years."

So he knew. Her skin flushed from the knowledge. She hadn't been as clever or as sneaky as she thought.

Ryder covered the front closure of her bra with his large hand. She felt the expert flick of his fingers, and suddenly her bra was undone. She held her breath as he peeled the lace and silk away from her curves. She didn't exhale until the straps fell from her arms.

Katie took a step forward, wanting to share his body heat, enjoy the contrast of her soft curves against his hard chest. She didn't get very far. Ryder held her upper arms, preventing her from moving.

He said nothing, but she sensed his hot gaze on her breasts. Her nipples were hard tips and she was desperate for him to touch them with his hands and mouth. She wanted to feel the edges of his teeth and the rasp of his tongue.

Why was he just looking? What was holding him back? Her self-confidence took a little dip. She needed to regain some control, and she would play nice if that was required. "May I take off my blindfold?"

"No."

She tried not to pout. "I asked nicely."

"You could ask with your mouth around my cock, but that doesn't mean you're going to get your way."

She pursed her lips with frustration before saying, "At this rate, I'm not going to get anywhere near your cock."

"Is that a complaint?" he asked, and she heard a thread of amusement in his voice.

Whether or not he was amused, Katie knew it was not a good move to criticize a guy when you were half-naked and blindfolded. "Take it any way you want."

"Oh, I will," Ryder said, his voice dropped low. "I'll take you any and every way I want."

If Ryder meant it as a sensual threat and hoped she would call this whole thing off, then he wouldn't get the response he was looking for. She wobbled, her knees caving at the dark, delicious promise. She would have tumbled back into the Christmas tree if Ryder hadn't taken her into his arms.

She felt warm and protected as he gathered her close. His jeans were rough against her bare legs and his belt buckle rested on her stomach. But all she was aware of was his thick and hard cock pressing against her. Her core was slick and hot as she anticipated Ryder driving deep inside her.

Ryder walked her away from the Christmas tree. As the heat of the fireplace receded, Katie knew they were moving toward the doorway. He was heading for the bedroom. She wiggled impatiently, not sure she could wait that long.

Katie flinched when she felt the solid wall against her spine. She frowned with confusion. Had he missed the doorway? How was that possible? She was the one wearing the blindfold.

Ryder didn't guide her away from the wall. She felt him leaning

into her, his hands gripping the edge of her panties. "Where—
where are you taking me?" she asked.

"I'm going to take you right here," he whispered in her ear.

Their first time would be against a wall. The idea, the possibilities, uncovered the primal side of her. She didn't want anything
fancy or all the seductive trappings. She wanted Ryder to take her
like she was in heat. It was the only way to quiet the sexual excitement and hunger that gnawed at her.

He cupped her sex. The move was bold and possessive. Katie
bucked against his hand, silently asking for more. But he did the
opposite and removed his hand. She growled in the back of her
throat, only to feel his fingers curl along the lace band of her panties. Ryder shoved the fragile fabric down her hips and stripped
them off her legs.

Her shoes came off with a clatter. She was now totally stripped.
Nothing shielded her from his eyes but the blindfold. She was hot
and eager for more.

He clasped her breasts with his hands, his fingers splayed and
digging into her flesh. That was her first indication that he didn't
want to—couldn't—go slow anymore. He rubbed his rough palms
against her hard nipples. She felt the circular motion deep inside her
and twitched her hips to alleviate the growing need. Katie gave a
low groan of pleasure and almost grabbed for him, but stopped
herself in the nick of time.

Ryder played with her breasts, squeezing and molding her flesh.
She felt his warm breath gust over her nipple before he took it in
his mouth. He pulled hard and a fierce cry of rapture escaped from
Katie before she could stop it.

As he licked and nibbled, she realized her hands were tangled in
Ryder's hair, guiding him closer. She dropped her hands and flat-

tened them on the wall before he stopped everything, but something didn't feel right. She needed to take action.

If she couldn't touch him, she would touch herself. She cupped her breasts and offered them to Ryder. In her mind's eye, she looked shameless and inviting as she presented the wet and rosy peaks to his mouth. It didn't matter that he could take whatever he wanted. She was offering herself to him.

Katie heard him mutter something low and raw. She felt the violent shaking of his body before he plunged his mouth onto one of her breasts, taking all she had to offer. His stubble scratched her skin, his teeth scoring her nipple. Katie loved it. This was what she wanted, she thought as she felt the bruising grip of his fingers on her hips. Ryder, rough and almost out of control. She wished she could see it.

"Do you want to take off my blindfold?" she asked.

His fingers stilled on her waist. "Not yet," he answered in a rough and unsteady voice.

Katie gritted her teeth with frustration. As much as she enjoyed having his full attention, and all the focus on pleasing her, she wanted to watch Ryder. She needed to see the pleasure and desire in his eyes.

She jerked when she felt Ryder's mouth against her stomach and inhaled sharply as he kissed a trail down to her navel. The breath hissed through her teeth when Ryder flicked his tongue along the indentation, but the air stilled in her lungs when he placed his hand over her sex.

The gesture was blatantly possessive, and just as effective as if he had shouted "Mine" for the world to hear. And who was she to disagree? Katie wondered as he stroked her.

She felt Ryder stand up to his full height while seeking her clit with his hand. She didn't expect him to claim her mouth with his, but he thrust his tongue past her lips. Katie immediately surrendered. She widened her legs, wanting him to explore while he continued to rub her clit.

Katie moaned against Ryder's mouth. Pleasure, hot and intense, swirled and twisted inside her. It sparkled and flickered under her skin before blooming into a heavy pressure that wanted to burst through and spring wildly free.

The climax took her by surprise and she lurched forward as she gave a very primal grunt. She never came that quickly. Katie shuddered, riding out the sensations, her muscles clenching as the ecstasy rolled and crashed inside her.

Ryder held her up, supporting her with his hand on her waist. His shoulder pinned hers to the wall. She appreciated his strength more than ever. She would have melted into a puddle on the floor otherwise.

Ryder didn't stop stroking her clit. She shifted her hips, his delicate touch almost too much to bear. She bit her bottom lip, trying not to say or do anything uncivilized, when he slid his fingertips along the wet slit. Katie couldn't smother the moan once he sank his finger inside her.

Her flesh gripped him hungrily and drew him deeper. She heard Ryder's murmur of satisfaction before he pumped her faster. Katie arched against him, wanting so much more.

She was breathing hard, her nails scraping the wall, as he set a fast, unpredictable pace. Katie couldn't refrain from widening her legs even more. She never knew when to expect a shallow thrust or a deep plunge. Her groans and guttural cries echoed in the room. Fragmented words spilled from her mouth as she rode his hand.

When he inserted another finger, Katie rolled her head back and slowly stretched her legs. She wanted the exquisite pleasure to stream and heat her from the inside out. She gasped as he curled his fingers, moving them in a come-hither gesture. Even in her fuzzy mind, she knew he was seeking her elusive G-spot.

She couldn't take much more of this. She felt like she was going to explode. Shatter into a million pieces so there would be no way to put her back together whole. Katie wanted to see Ryder's face. Was he ready to die of pleasure, too?

Katie reached for her blindfold and pushed it up and over her head. She blinked her eyes open, stunned to see his face so close to hers. Ryder's features were harsh and rigid, but even in the shadowy room with the twinkling Christmas lights behind him, she could see his eyes glittering with desire.

The intimacy was too much for Katie. She almost looked away, but there was something about the way Ryder held her gaze that made her keep her eyes on his. She didn't feel the need to speak, to touch him, as long as she could see his face.

Her panting breath sounded harsh to her ears as he continued to tap her G-spot. The pleasure was so extreme that it was almost painful. And yet she wanted more. She wanted everything Ryder could give her.

Katie hooked her leg over his hip and his fingers sank in deeper. She pressed her lips together, feeling incredibly emotional as tears welled up in her eyes. If Ryder saw the sheen of tears, he didn't comment as he gave a wicked curl to his fingers.

He glided his other hand down her breast and pinched her nipple hard. Katie gasped as the hot sensations forked through her veins before pooling in her hips. Ryder let his hand slide down to her thigh. He rubbed her leg hard, obviously enjoying the smooth, silky skin as he pumped his fingers inside her.

Ryder continued to explore the length of her leg, then ran his hand over the curve of her hip before cupping her ass. When he gave her buttocks an unrelenting squeeze, it added to her heightened pleasure. She was so close to coming again. If only he would give his full attention to her clit while he filled her with his hand.

But he didn't, even though he must have known that was what she wanted. Instead he ran his finger along the cleft of her buttocks. Katie's eyes widened, surprised by his audacity, while at the same time delighted by his naughty move.

No man had ever done that to her before. And when Ryder pressed his finger hard against her rosebud, it was like a trigger. Her hips vaulted and she ground against his cock as the swift, savage climax took over. She stared at Ryder, his eyes her only anchor as she shook and trembled.

Ryder gathered her in his arms when she went limp. With the wall behind her and Ryder in front, there was no chance of her falling. She yielded to the explosive sensations until her body quieted.

Katie continued to stare silently at Ryder. If she responded like this to his mere touch, she couldn't wait for the moment when he would tumble into her bed. Her hand was still a little shaky as she flattened it against his chest. She was pleased to feel the thunderous beat of his heart, knowing that it matched her own.

Katie let her hand drift down to Ryder's lean waist and she tugged at his shirt. Ryder held her hand still. "No."

"No?" Maybe she hadn't heard him correctly. Her heart was pounding hard in her ears. "Don't you think you're overdressed?"

He shook his head. "You took off your blindfold."

Oh, yeah. He noticed that. "It . . . fell?"

A wry smile pulled at his mouth. "You pushed it off."

She wouldn't be able to talk her way out of that. "So?"

"You didn't follow instructions, so it stops here." Ryder let his arms drop.

She stared at him in astonishment. "You want to stop? *Now?*" How could he suggest such a thing when her body was clamoring for more?

"You knew the consequences," he said in all seriousness.

"But . . . but . . ." Her mind whirled as she tried to come up with a good comeback. "But why should *you* be punished?"

He smiled, the grooves by his mouth deepening. "I'm not going to fall for that line of reasoning."

"Why didn't you stop the moment the blindfold was off?" she asked as she closed in on him and linked her arms over his strong shoulders.

He looked down at her eyes and the smile vanished. "Because that would have been cruel."

"That's not why," she said as she slid her hand through his tousled hair. "You were caught up in the moment, too. Come on, Ryder. It's cruel to stop now."

"No." He lifted his hands up. "You can't follow the rules."

Screw the rules! she wanted to say. Scream it until the walls came tumbling down. But she had agreed to the rules, and followed them up to a point.

"I wore the blindfold most of the time," she pointed out, rubbing her naked body against him in hopes of distracting him. "That should count for something."

The doorbell rang. Three short staccato rings that made Katie jump. Damn, who could that be? "Ignore it," she urged.

Ryder reluctantly dragged his gaze from her and toward the hallway. "It's your brother."

She took an instinctive step back into the darkness, knowing she couldn't be seen through the window if she stood in this corner of the room. "How can you tell that from here?"

"I just can." Ryder turned away, walked stiffly to the Christmas tree and scooped up her discarded dress and practically threw it at her. "Here, put this on before Jake remembers he has a key."

"We don't have to answer," she whispered as she clasped the dress to her chest. "He'll go away soon."

"I parked out front," he reminded her and went to the door.

Katie squeezed her eyes shut. Why did Jake have to drop by the day Ryder parked in front of the house? She shoved her arms in the sleeves with more violence than she intended. Life was so unfair, she decided as she heard the front door open.

"Hey, Ryder," Jake's voice carried into the living room. "Sorry I'm late."

Katie stopped tying her sash around her waist. Late? Ryder made plans with Jake? She couldn't hear Ryder's response.

"Why did I have to come by here and knock if I saw your car?" Jake asked. "Is Katie bugging you again?"

Katie bit her bottom lip and she sagged against the wall. Ryder had planned everything so they wouldn't have sex. The hurt, the disappointment gnawed at her stomach, but she remained perfectly still. She wanted to hide, but she bet Ryder was counting on that.

"No, I'm not bugging Ryder," she called out, hoping she sounded normal as the hurt clawed inside. Her throat felt raw as she fought to act nonchalant. Katie shoved her feet in her shoes and saw the blindfold on the floor. She grabbed it before she strode into the hallway.

"He may be a carpenter," Jake said as he stamped the snow from his feet and blew on his cold hands, "but he is not your personal handyman."

"I'll keep that in mind," Katie said, refusing to look at Ryder. "Don't let me keep you, Ryder. Let me get your coat."

"I'm sorry, Katie."

Sorry for what? she wondered as she opened the closet door. For stopping? For setting up an elaborate plan to prevent them from having sex?

Every move he made had been working toward this moment. Parking in front. The slow, deliberate lovemaking. He hadn't taken off one article of his own clothing, doing his best to fend her off until her brother interrupted.

She felt like such a fool. She handed Ryder his coat when she really wanted to throw it at him.

"Are you feeling okay, Katie?" Jake asked.

"I'm fine," she said with her hands on her hips. And she would be until they walked out that door. Then she would stuff her face with the last of the Christmas candy.

Jake scrunched up his face as he gave her an odd look. "You seem kind of out of it. And you look . . ."

"I'm just tired. I *was* planning to go to bed." She gave a pointed look at Ryder.

"We'll be out of your way," Ryder said as he zipped up his coat. "Ready, Jake?"

As Jake stepped outside, a devilish urge tickled Katie. "Oh, Ryder," she said sweetly. "I think you forgot this." She held out the blindfold.

Ryder gave her a warning look. "Keep it. It's yours."

"Because I earned it?"

"No," he answered as he reached for the door, a flash of regret in his eyes. "Because that is all you're going to get from me."

She stared as the door closed and she heard Ryder's and Jake's feet shuffling in the slushy snow. Katie bunched up the blindfold and threw it at the door. It floated to the floor. Was this supposed to be some kind of souvenir? Of what might have been? Well, she didn't want it. And if Ryder thought they were done, then he didn't know her at all.

She whirled around and marched into the kitchen, determined to polish off the last of the peppermint bark and come up with Plan B.

Whatever that might be.

He should have stood her up.

Ryder kept his head down, staring at the snow as he headed for his truck. He always tried to keep his promises, but this time he should have made an exception. Instead of giving Katie a taste of something special, he had hurt her.

But there was no way he could have given Katie the whole night. He was supposed to be initiating her into the art of submission, nothing more. He hadn't trusted himself, and he'd done the one thing he never thought he'd have to do: he called Jake for reinforcement. It was a sign that his self-control was not what it used to be.

Ryder had staged the interruption for Katie's own good. So why did he feel like scum? He wanted to go back into the house, gather her in his arms and apologize. And then he wanted to start all over and not finish until Katie exhausted her imagination. That would take some time.

"You never can say no to Katie."

Ryder jerked his head up. "Huh?" Something close to panic kicked him in the gut. Had Jake caught on to the vibes that sizzled between Katie and him? It was bound to happen sooner or later. He just wished it could have happened when he was already halfway across the world.

"What is it with you two?" Jake gestured at the house. "She asks you for a favor and you always give in."

Relief flooded through Ryder's veins. Jake had no idea what had just happened. If he had, Ryder would be dead meat.

Ryder scowled at his friend. "I don't always give in." But he did. Each and every time. He liked being wanted. Needed. Most of all, he wanted to take care of Katie. He didn't expect anything in return or any kind of acknowledgment. Just looking after Katie brought him satisfaction.

Ryder noticed that Katie took care of him, too, in a thousand different ways, big and small. She didn't ask for anything when she made him a home-cooked meal or did something to make his life easier. He enjoyed the attention. It made him feel important and loved.

"Well, she'll learn her lesson," Jake muttered as he trudged through the snow to his truck. "She can't rely on you anymore."

Ryder's lips twisted in self-disgust. Katie had already learned that tonight. She'd discovered that he broke his promise, and that she couldn't trust his word. Not exactly the lesson he wanted to give her, but there was nothing he could do about it now.

"Once you leave, who is she going to call for help?" Jake asked as he continued his rant.

"Uh, you," Ryder said as he walked to the driver's door of his truck.

Jake snorted at the idea. "Think again."

Ryder's hand stilled on the door. "You're her brother."

"Let's face it, Katie is a brat. Always has been, because she knows she has you wrapped around her finger."

So it was his fault? Fine. He'd take the blame. He kind of liked the idea that he'd had some influence in shaping the woman Katie had become.

"Good thing I'm leaving, then," Ryder said, yanking the truck door open. It wouldn't be long before Katie realized the full extent of her power over him.

"Tell me about it. I don't trust her around you."

Ryder froze as Jake's words cut through him like a sharp knife. "What's that supposed to mean?"

"I get that, as an only child, you find the idea of a little sister fascinating. I would have thought that by now you would have realized it's not like in the sitcoms. Little sisters are hell."

"Thanks for the insight."

"Katie is not the sweet girl you think she is. If she wants something, nothing will stand in her way until she gets it. And if she thinks you have a soft spot for her, the power will go to her head. You will be her exclusive handyman and be at her beck and call."

"I think I can handle Katie."

"Yeah? Then why did you call me to interfere tonight?"

Ryder's scowl deepened. They both knew the answer to that. He was already in Katie's power.

Jake laughed. "Come on, let's go find some girls. Tatum was looking for you a while ago."

Ryder didn't want to be around Tatum and her friends. He would rather be alone. No, that was a lie. He would rather be with Katie right now, finishing what they'd started. Ryder looked at the house. It was warm, inviting, and beckoning him to go back inside.

But he couldn't. He only had a few more days left and then he could let his guard down. Until then, he wouldn't be alone for any length of time. He would stick to Jake's side as much as he could. That would keep him away from Katie.

She had probably washed her hands of him already. Either that or she was going to do something drastic to get him into her bed. He had a feeling it was going to be something daring and stupid.

"Let's go play pool," Ryder told Jake. He got in his truck and revved the engine, forcing himself to leave Katie when every instinct screamed for him to stay.

CHAPTER EIGHT

December 27

Katie stood in front of the Merrill house early in the morning, stuffing her gloved hands into her coat pockets and hunching her shoulders as the arctic air tugged her long black hair. She usually visited the abandoned and neglected house when she needed to think or to recharge. There was something about the yellow two-story farmhouse that usually brought her comfort, but today she found no peace.

Katie walked along the outside of the wraparound porch, not really noticing the missing rails or the boarded-up windows. The white paint on the trim was peeling in chunks and the wood railings were streaked with green moss. This house needed attention, and fast.

Her friends and family couldn't see the beauty of this house. They called it an eyesore or a money pit, and they thought she was only interested in it because it would be the ultimate renovation project, the ultimate challenge.

It wasn't true. Katie slowly walked around the house, carefully stepping on the cracked sidewalk that was still covered in snow. When she looked at the Merrill house, she wasn't thinking about color combinations or interior decorations. She thought in words and emotions like *cozy, safe, love* and *family*.

In her mind, that family included Ryder and maybe a few kids. She was kind of hazy on the children part. All that mattered was that she and Ryder were the strong center. And she would do whatever it took to protect that idea of family.

But she didn't think she would have to struggle so early. How could Ryder have walked away from her? Worse, he had planned it from the beginning. He wanted her, but he wouldn't take her.

It must be true that Ryder thought she was too innocent for the likes of him. He spent years protecting her from the hormone-crazed guys of Crystal Bend, unaware that Katie was able to handle them before her reinvention. If there was anyone a "good girl" shouldn't have, it was Ryder, so of course Ryder had to protect her from himself!

She had to break through Ryder's misplaced chivalry, but she only had five days left. If only she knew how to hold his attention . . . but that required having some kinky knowledge. How was she going to become an expert in bondage in that short amount of time?

Well, she knew how, Katie thought as she strolled around the back of the house. She just didn't think she had the courage to follow through with it. How far was she willing to go to get the man and the life she wanted?

She knew she wasn't very brave or bold. Hilary had pointed out that Katie dressed like a kick-ass woman but would give up all her power to fall into bed with the right guy. Ryder thought her beauty and strength came from being soft and sweet. Her mother thought anything traditionally female was a sign of weakness.

Katie knew that, compared to most women her age, her goal and her beliefs were unpopular. Was she the only one who thought a powerful woman was someone who took care of those around her and protected her relationships no matter the cost? Even if it meant surrendering or making a sacrifice.

Or did that mean she was simply weak? Sometimes relinquishing control could be the most powerful act, but only in certain cases. Was it the best course of action for her?

Katie gnawed on her bottom lip as she gave the Merrill house one last look before walking to the pitted, unkempt driveway. She knew what she wanted in life and she had the ability to get it if she could work up the courage. How far she was willing to go would determine her success. She rolled her shoulders back and there was a spring in her step. She *was* prepared to go all the way.

Katie retrieved her cell phone from her coat pocket and hit speed dial. Within moments she heard her friend's voice.

"Hilary, how would you like to go to a bondage club tonight?"

There was a pause before Hilary responded. "I don't think I have anything appropriate to wear for the occasion."

Katie was surprised that Hilary would worry about that. "You can borrow my PVC pants," she offered. "So how about it?"

"Sure, why not? I'm always up for an anthropological field trip."

"Ryder, it's your turn."

He was going to stay far away from her. It was the only way to handle Katie Kramer. He was willing to admit it, now that he had pulled back from the brink of disaster. Now that he had gotten her hot, wet and willing. He could not be trusted around that woman. He'd known it all along, but now he had proof.

"Ryder?"

Avoidance was the only way to go. Sure, it sounded cowardly, but now it was a matter of self-preservation. If he saw her again, or even heard her voice, there was no telling what he would do.

"Ryder!"

He blinked and looked around the pool hall. It seemed darker than a moment ago. Louder, too. He rubbed his eyes and looked at Art, his former coworker. "What?"

"I won," Art proclaimed.

"You did?" How the hell did that happen? Art never won. Ryder glanced at the pool table and noticed the game was over. He'd barely even had a turn.

The pool table was a dark green, just like Katie's Christmas tree. The one she'd stood in front of as she took off her dress. . . .

"You are so out of it." Art slapped him on the back. "Dreaming about Dubai, aren't you? Those beautiful beaches."

"That's right," Ryder lied. He was thinking about Katie. Hadn't stopped thinking about her since he walked out of her house. He couldn't sleep, couldn't eat, and obviously couldn't play pool. Pretty soon he wasn't going to be able to function. He had to snap out of it. "Another game?"

Art hesitated and shook his head. "Nah, too easy."

Ryder's eyebrows went up, but he didn't rise to the challenge. He knew he wasn't at the top of his game. He was too busy wondering what Katie was up to. Ryder grabbed his cell phone and looked to see if there were any incoming calls.

Nothing.

"You keep looking at that phone. What's up with that?"

Ryder shrugged. He had called Katie a couple of times to check—and he'd left a message—but she hadn't returned his call. That was unprecedented.

Either he'd really hurt her feelings last night to the extent that now she couldn't stand the sight of him or she was shaking things up to keep him on his toes. Whatever she was doing, it was effective. He thought about her all day. He'd been distracted and grumpy, which more than one person had been happy to point out.

Five more days. He only had to avoid her for five more days. That was less than a week. It should be easy. Except for when he closed his eyes and remembered what she looked like, blindfolded and wearing next to nothing, waiting for his touch. . . .

Ryder jerked out of the daydream and stifled a groan. He didn't think he was going to survive.

He slid his cell phone back into his pocket. If he didn't hear from Katie soon, he might break down and go back to her house. He was kind of hoping to avoid that.

"Hey, Art. Have you seen Katie Kramer today?"

"Yeah," he said and grinned.

"What's with the smile?"

Art's smile widened. "She was wearing this very sexy outfit."

Ryder glared at his friend and tried not to growl. "What's the big deal about that?" She had been wearing very sexy outfits every day for the past year. Although his favorite was the soft burgundy dress that could come undone with the pull of . . .

"It was all leather. Or it looked like it was all leather." Art's eyes started to twinkle. "You should have seen those boots."

"I've seen the boots." Ryder hated the boots. If he could rip them off her without touching Katie, he would have done so already.

"My wife calls them dominatrix boots. I think she asked Katie where she got them."

He didn't want to know if Art's wife was getting in touch with her inner dominatrix. "Where did you see Katie?"

"At the gas station."

That didn't sound good. It was probably no big deal. It could mean anything, like her tank was empty. It could also mean that she was filling up for a road trip to Seattle. "Who was she with?"

"I didn't notice," Art answer dryly. "What's with all these questions?"

Ryder reached for his cell phone again and hit redial. "I think Katie is doing exactly what I told her not to do," he said as he put the phone to his ear. If she didn't pick up, he was going to hunt her down.

"Knowing Katie, she's probably doing just that."

Ryder scowled at Art just as his call went straight to voice mail. He closed his eyes and slowly put the phone back into his pocket. He was going to find Katie and, if she was smart, she would be safely tucked away in her own bed.

Ryder didn't find Katie, but he did find Jake at the Crystal Bend Café. His friend was enjoying the slice of hot apple pie in front of him and flirting with the honey blonde at his side. Ryder slid into the booth across from the couple. He gave a curt nod to the woman toying with a diet soda and his gaze narrowed on Jake. "Have you heard from your sister today?"

"No, and it's been nice and quiet," Jake said with a big, relaxed smile. "Just the way I like it."

It was too quiet in Ryder's opinion.

Jake dragged his attention from the blonde when he realized Ryder wasn't leaving. "Something the matter?"

Yeah, a lot of things were wrong, but he couldn't reveal all. Ryder drummed his fingers on the tabletop. "You didn't give her the address for the bondage club, right?" He ignored the blonde's jerk of surprise and the way she inched away from him.

Jake made a face. "I'm not stupid. Why would I want to help my little sister get into bondage? Anyway, you know what Katie's like. She's just asking these questions for attention."

"I got a bad feeling she found the place." And he couldn't shake off the sense of impending doom. Katie was going to push back hard, any way she could.

Jake dismissed Ryder's concern with a wave of his fork. "Even if she got the address, she wouldn't use it. She's not the type. She's just teasing you. You know how she likes to push your buttons. She's been doing it for years. Remember when she stole your leather jacket and wouldn't give it back until you promised to drive her to school every day for a whole semester?"

"I'm not so sure." He had given her a taste of kink last night. She may want more, with or without him.

"Trust me, Katie asked for shock value. It's the way she gets attention." Jake ate another big chunk of pie. Ryder glared at him. His best friend was obviously more concerned about his stomach than his sister.

"Then where is she?" Ryder demanded. He was used to worrying about Katie, but this was different. He would feel a whole lot better knowing she wasn't doing something stupid just to prove a point with him. "Why isn't she answering her phone?"

Jake paused, his fork in midair. "You checking up on her?"

"Call it a hunch."

"If you're so worried, why don't you talk to Melissa?" He pointed his fork in the direction of the counter next to the kitchen. Ryder looked and saw Katie's friend.

"Don't you find it odd that she's not with Katie?" Ryder asked as he rose from his seat.

"No, I find it normal," Jake muttered.

"I'm going to find out what's going on." Ryder moved swiftly and cornered Melissa before she saw him coming. "Hey, Melissa. Do you know where Katie is?"

Melissa gave a little yelp of surprise when Ryder spoke. "Uh, hi, Ryder," she squeaked as her gaze shifted away.

"Melissa?" he asked with a hint of warning.

"Well"—she lowered her voice—"if anyone asks, you tricked it out of me, okay?"

A knot formed in the pit of his stomach. This couldn't be good. "It wouldn't be the bondage club in Seattle, would it?" he asked, his voice clipped with cold anger.

Melissa slowly nodded her head. "She and Hilary just left. How did you know?"

"I know Katie." And she had gone too far this time. He was going after her, just like she wanted. Only this time she would reap what she sowed.

"Okay . . ." Hilary looked around the bondage club. "This isn't what I was expecting."

Katie nodded slowly. The club was a renovated hotel in downtown Seattle. It was decorated in the Regency period, with a lot of wood paneling, settees and delicate chairs, and gold-framed portraits of fox-hunting scenes.

She wasn't sure what she had expected. Maybe a little dance music, a strobe light or two, and plenty of booze. "It looks like a gentleman's club," she muttered from the side of her mouth. "The kind you see in those Jane Austen–type movies."

"Do me a favor," Hilary said in a whisper, "and don't ever use the words 'Jane Austen' when you talk about bondage."

"I'll try my best." She clapped her mouth closed when she saw a woman in a designer dress guide a man out of the room using a leash. They walked to the elevators as if nothing was unusual. "Do you think we're dressed wrong?"

"I think we have newbie written all over us," Hilary said. "Let's hope they don't have any initiation rites."

Panic bloomed in Katie's chest. She hadn't thought of that. "If anyone asks, we're doing research."

Hilary rolled her eyes. "Yeah, that'll go over well. Face it, Katie. This was not one of your better ideas. Melissa was smart to stay back in Crystal Bend."

Katie clucked her tongue. She hadn't been able to convince Melissa to join them on this grand adventure, no matter how much she begged and bribed. "What could possibly go wrong?"

"Do you want me to list it alphabetically or chronologically?"

There was no way they would face that many problems. "We have to give consent for anything to happen," Katie reminded her friend.

"In theory." Hilary stepped in front of a mirror with an ornate frame and checked her hair. She had straightened her red mop and it hung past her shoulders like silk, and she'd gone for broke with the black eyeliner and red lipstick. The snug black T-shirt, PVC pants and heels completed the transformation. Hilary looked less like a research librarian and more like a tough dominatrix.

"Well, I understand your concerns," Katie said as she watched Hilary dab her finger along the edge of her full red mouth. "But I'm not leaving until I know what Ryder wants in a relationship where he is dominant and I'm submissive."

"I did a little bit of fact-checking on this before we left." Hilary puckered her lips at her reflection. "BDSM is a sexual game based on fantasy."

Katie was all for fantasy. She had too many fantasies and knew what it felt like wanting each and every one of them to come true. "I can totally be his fantasy girl."

"It's considered an art, and . . ." Her eyes widened as she looked in the mirror, and then she cast a quick glance over her shoulder. "Someone is coming over here. Let's go."

Katie was tempted to make a run for it as a very tall, large, muscular man approached them. "It's probably the, uh, bouncer."

"No, I think that was the shirtless guy with the executioner's mask that we passed when we came in."

"Welcome to the center," the man said. He was dressed in a pinstriped suit and wore a red carnation boutonniere. "Your first visit?"

"How could you tell?" Hilary muttered, stepping closer to Katie. Katie couldn't tell if Hilary was offering protection or using her as a shield.

The man smiled. "I know all the members."

"Members? Oh, you mean you need a membership to be here? Shucks." Hilary snapped her fingers. "I guess we have to leave."

"Not at all." He motioned at the double doors the one couple had walked out of. "There are some meeting rooms here for visitors. The members have access to the rest of the center."

"Rooms?" Hilary parroted. "What happens in these rooms?"

The man's smile widened. "Whatever your imagination allows."

Katie felt her throat tighten and she gave a little hoarse cough. "We're just doing some research."

"Personal research," Hilary added.

"Ah." The man's eyes lit with understanding. "You're just curious, but not committed."

Katie gave a swift elbow to Hilary's stomach, knowing she was going to make some committed-in-an-institution comment. "Exactly."

"I was going to ask if you were a top or a bottom."

"Excuse me?" Katie looked down at her outfit as the man studied her. What was wrong with her PVC vest, black miniskirt and knee-high leather boots? Sure, her magazines hadn't recommended this particular combination—she couldn't find any helpful advice on what to wear at a bondage scene—but she thought she looked edgy enough. She was even inspired to wear a velvet choker as her only accessory.

"A top is the dominant one, and those shoes you are wearing are a submissive's dream."

"Maybe that's why Ryder hates them," she muttered to Hilary.

"But the choker," the man said, "is a sign that you are already claimed by a dominant."

Katie's hand went straight to her throat. "That is what it means?" A thought occurred to her. "What if it's a regular piece of jewelry?"

The man considered the question. "Any piece of jewelry could be considered a symbol. Many think a wedding ring is a public claim."

Katie grinned. That must be why Ryder had given her those earrings instead of a Christmas ornament.

A woman wearing a simple black dress approached the man. She bowed low, her eyes downcast. "Excuse me, sir. May I have a word?"

The man excused himself and the woman trailed behind him. "His submissive?" Hilary asked.

Katie smiled wryly. "Obviously you don't work in an office. That was his assistant."

"Well, I don't know about you, but I think we've learned a lot. Walk three steps behind your boss and don't wear a choker with dominatrix boots. What more is there to discover?"

"Hilary, we haven't looked in the other rooms."

She looked at the double doors from the corner of her eye. "I think I would like to keep it that way."

"I thought you wanted an anthropological experience. You of all people should have an adventurous spirit and an open mind."

"Yeah, but I don't want to require a mind eraser after this night." Hilary took a deep breath. "Okay, we'll go look, but only for ten minutes."

"A half hour," Katie bargained.

"Twenty minutes and then we go back to our hotel room and do something more our speed, like eat everything in the minibar and watch *Golden Girls*."

"Fine. You drive a hard bargain," Katie said as she headed for the double doors. The closer she got, the more it sounded like a party was going on behind the doors. "And the next twenty minutes are going to fly right by. You'll see."

She opened one of the doors and dragged Hilary inside. The room was shadowy and packed with people. She saw the gleam of chains and inhaled the rich scent of leather. She twisted her head and gawked at the riding crop in an elderly woman's hand. Katie grabbed for Hilary's arm and held her close as they navigated the dark room with shuffling steps.

"Oops!" Katie tripped and would have done a face plant if Hilary hadn't been holding her up. Katie looked down and saw a young athletic man kneeling on the floor in front of his master. "Sorry!"

Katie was beginning to believe that Ryder had a valid point. She was not ready for this place. She didn't think she would last the whole twenty minutes. "So . . . what do you think?"

"I think the bar is over in that corner," Hilary yelled over the noise.

Katie gave her friend a strange look. "We just walked by a grand-mother in a leather bustier, a half-naked guy kneeling on the floor waiting for his next command, and all you can see is the bar?"

Hilary shrugged. "It's a gift."

"And a helpful one," Katie decided. "Lead me there."

They took a couple of steps, when Hilary skidded to a halt. "Huh, well, that's interesting."

Katie couldn't imagine what would have captured Hilary's attention in this room. "What is?"

She craned her neck to get a better view. "I think I just saw Darwin."

"Darwin?" Katie's voice squeaked. *"Darwin Jones?"* She instinc-tively ducked.

"How many Darwins do you know?"

"One more than I should. What is he doing here?"

"Well, it's logical that he should be here since he's the one who gave me directions to this place."

"What?" Katie jerked Hilary down to squat next to her. "I thought Jake gave it to you."

"He wouldn't. So I asked around and Darwin was the only one who would fess up to knowing this place."

Katie rubbed her aching head. "I don't believe this."

"Uh, let's just get to the bar and plan our next move," Hilary said as she pulled Katie up. "People are staring at us."

"Staring at us? We're the most normal people here."

"Now where is your open mind?" Hilary teased as she herded Katie through the crowd to the bar. "They say BDSM is an art, but I'm thinking it's more like a different world."

"I won't argue with you on that one," Katie said as she rested her arms on the bar.

"Think about it," Hilary said. "Their clothes represent something about them, and they have their own vocabulary. They have a set of rules and expected behaviors."

Katie nodded as she flagged down a bartender.

"The question is: Do you want to be part of this world?"

Katie had been wondering that the moment they arrived. "There is no easy answer to that question," Katie finally said. She wanted to be with Ryder, but she wasn't interested in anything she saw here.

She liked the idea of being with Ryder because he was rougher around the edges than any man she knew, but she hadn't experienced enough of his dangerous side yet. And while she was fine with the blindfold, she had taken it off when she was fed up with it. Maybe she was as bratty as Ryder accused her of being, because she wasn't into depriving herself.

Then again, she loved it when Ryder was protective and possessive. Also, her secret fantasy was to tie him up and have her wicked way with him, so she must have some kink in her. And she wouldn't be opposed to the idea of reversing positions as long as Ryder was overwhelmed with desire for her.

But would she have to give up her sexual fantasies to hang on to Ryder? Was she in love with a man who was sexually incompatible with her?

But maybe she was looking at it wrong. Would being with Ryder open up a new and exciting world? Would it tap into fantasies she was too unsure of to uncover?

"Oh, no." Hilary set down her drink with a thud. "Darwin is wearing the same pants that I am."

Katie froze, knowing from past experience it was best not to make any sudden moves. "He spotted us?"

"No, he's making the rounds. Tell me the truth, do I look better in these pants than Darwin does?" Hilary did a fashion model turn.

"Yes, of course."

Hilary gave a sigh of exasperation. "You didn't even look at him to make the comparison."

"Where is he?" Katie looked in the direction Hilary had indicated earlier. Did she really want to see Darwin in PVC?

"He's right over there." Hilary squinted. "Huh. Well, he *was* right over there."

"You lost track of him?"

"Don't worry," Hilary said in a placating manner. "Just look for a guy in a studded dog collar."

Katie's eyes widened as she mouthed the words. *Dog collar?* She hoped Darwin was far away from the exit because she'd just decided her twenty minutes were up.

She felt a large masculine hand clamp around her wrist. Double damn. Darwin had found her. She felt dread twisting her stomach. She needed to talk fast before the guy maneuvered her into one of the members-only rooms.

"Well, fancy seeing you here," she said with a forced smile and looked up. "Ryder?!"

Ryder was clearly furious. A muscle twitched in his rigid jaw as his dark eyes glittered with savage anger. She glanced at Hilary, who had decided that now was the best time to chug down her drink.

Katie looked back at Ryder and only then noticed her brother standing behind him. She couldn't tell what Jake was thinking because he was too busy panting after a woman in leather hot pants. Jake never worried about his little sister. Maybe he thought she was too much of a good girl, or maybe he knew that Ryder would handle it. The only advice she got solely from Jake was to leave Ryder alone. Her brother obviously thought she hadn't changed much from the annoying brat she used to be.

She noticed that neither Ryder nor Jake had dressed for the

club. Ryder wore a long-sleeve blue T-shirt, jeans and running shoes. There was nothing that hinted at his sexual taste, but then Ryder didn't need to emphasize his dominant traits. One look at him and anyone would know that he was a leader and would take charge of any situation.

"What are you doing here?" she asked Ryder.

"That's what I should ask you." His grip tightened. It wasn't painful, but she was very aware of how much he was trying to control his temper. "I told you to stay away from this place. Jake and I are here," he said, his words crisp with anger, "because we heard you decided to join the club."

Hilary snorted with laughter. "Join the club? Not quite. Who told you we were here?"

"You asked all of Crystal Bend for directions," Jake said. "And then we saw Melissa, who was worried about you guys."

"Well, as you can see, we're safe and sound. And we rented a hotel room across the street." That piece of information mysteriously increased Ryder's anger. "So you don't have to worry about us driving all the way back home."

"It's time to leave," Ryder announced.

"I just got here." She wasn't totally sure why she was refusing Ryder's escort. A couple of minutes ago she had thought the same thing, but she didn't want to leave just because Ryder told her to. "I haven't had a chance to mingle or take a sip of my drink."

Ryder gave her a warning look and she knew she was pushing her luck. "I'm going to say it one more time," Ryder whispered in her ear. "We are leaving."

Katie pulled away. "I'll see you when I get back in town." She lifted her glass to her lips, but she didn't catch a drop as Ryder bent down and slung her over his shoulder, fireman-style.

"Ryder!" she shrieked as she dropped her glass.

Ryder acted like he didn't hear her or feel the thump of her fist on his back. "Jake, you get Hilary out of here. Rent another hotel room and we'll meet up in the morning."

"I can take Katie," Jake said, and something in his voice alerted Katie. Did he not trust her with Ryder?

"Wait a second," Hilary interrupted. "No one is taking anyone anywhere. You can't just haul Katie out of here. What are you planning to do?"

"I'm going to lock her up and throw away the key."

"Sir?" Two men in dark suits with earpieces suddenly flanked them. "Put the woman down."

"Don't worry." Ryder patted the curve of Katie's ass. "She is mine."

CHAPTER NINE

She is mine. Katie couldn't stop the exhilaration flooding through her. She hoped she wasn't smiling as Ryder carried her out of the club. He'd actually said those three little words. *She. Is. Mine.* She had always wanted to hear him say that.

She heard the heavy door slam and the cold, wet night air hit her skin. Katie shivered and lifted herself up over Ryder's shoulders. She saw they were outside and that the downtown street was quiet. As far as she could tell, no one was around, but that could change any minute. And, knowing her luck, it would be someone she knew. She pushed the heels of her hands against Ryder's back. "You can put me down now."

"Forget it." He strode across the sidewalk like a man on a mission.

"Fine," she answered pertly. "If you want me to flash all of Se-attle, that's your choice. . . ."

Ryder immediately stopped and slid her down the length of his body. He was all hard muscle. When her boots hit the sidewalk, Ryder didn't let go. He held her upper arm in an unbreakable grip as they crossed the street to the small hotel. Katie had to skip and hop to keep up with him.

"Give me your hotel key," he said as they reached the revolving door.

Did he really think she was going to make it easy for him? That she didn't have a say in anything? If she had been at the café in Crystal Bend, she wouldn't have let him yank her out of there and drag her across the street. "What makes you think I have it?"

"Because you always have to be in control." He stopped in front of the hotel and held out his hand, knowing she had a key.

The sad thing was, she hadn't realized how much she needed to be in control until he took it away from her. But she was getting better about it.

If she wanted to, she could refuse to give him the key. She had the power to walk away from him right now. But she didn't want to leave. Ryder had come after her tonight and she wanted to see this through. Katie reached into the pocket of her black miniskirt and pulled out the plastic key card.

As Ryder snatched it silently, Katie knew that she wouldn't have been able to simply walk away. If she had tried to leave him in the street, he would have done something very uncivilized. She was just fooling herself, thinking she had power over this situation.

Ryder guided her into the hotel and tersely asked for her room number. She hesitated and he stopped in the middle of the old-world lobby. The atmosphere was hushed and elegant, and she was feeling anything but that. Something raw and feral pressed against her chest, ready to break through. She quietly recited the numbers, trying to maintain her composure. Ryder grabbed her upper arm again and escorted her to the room, his sense of direction eerie.

But then again, he may have been here before. Countless times, even, Katie realized as they took a short ride in the claustrophobic elevator.

The elevator doors opened and Ryder hustled her down the hall. He located the small room and closed the door with a sense of finality. He didn't turn around, his head low, as if he was gathering strength. A trickle of apprehension slid down her spine. She backed away, the back of her knee catching the edge of the bed.

Ryder turned and leaned against the door. He looked at her in silence, but she could tell he had quite a lot to say. She didn't think she had ever seen him this angry. She suspected he wanted to punch a hole in the wall, but the tremor in his hand and the muscle twitching in his clenched jaw were the only visible signs of his emotions.

"We agreed that you would not go to the club," Ryder said, his voice dangerously low.

Katie would have preferred yelling to this carefully controlled voice. She licked her lips. "We said that you wouldn't initiate me at the club."

"You knew I didn't want you at the club."

She couldn't talk around that statement. He'd made his feelings about the bondage club very clear. "You knew I expected more last night."

"Is that what this is about?" He stepped away from the door and she took another step back. "You want to punish me for last night?"

"No," she said, her voice high and squeaky. "I came here to see what bondage was all about."

He shook his head. "You came here knowing I would follow."

"No!" But as she said it, she wasn't so sure. Was this all to provoke a response from Ryder? She knew he would have kept his distance from her after last night, and this was a surefire way to have him come to her.

"You weren't secretive, asking everyone for directions," Ryder pointed out.

"Hilary asked around, not me," she defended.

"And you conveniently left Melissa in Crystal Bend to tell me your plans."

She scoffed at that accusation. She was not that conniving. "She didn't want to go."

"*She* was smart."

Katie knew it was time to stand her ground. "Why is it okay for you to go to this club, but I can't go anywhere near it?" She put her hands on her hips and glared at him. "I can't believe you would be so hypocritical."

"I don't care what you believe." And he really didn't. She could tell her words didn't make him pause. "That is the way it's going to be."

His arrogance was too much. "Just keep telling yourself that when you pack up and leave."

"You can throw all the accusations you want at me," Ryder said as he took another step toward her. "It's not going to change my mind, and it's not going to change the fact that you broke your promise."

"I did not." She took another prudent step back.

"You broke the rules." He reached for his belt.

Katie's eyes bugged out as she watched him unbuckle the strap of leather around his waist. "What are you going to do?" She could barely get the words out.

"You knew there would be consequences," he said as he jerked the belt from his jeans and held the ends in his hand.

Perhaps she hadn't been specific enough. "What are you planning to do with . . . that?" She pointed at the belt.

He paused and Katie saw the devilish glint in his eye. "This?" Ryder thwacked it hard against his palm.

She took another hasty step back. "If you touch me with that belt, I will scream this place down and I will never, ever forgive you."

His eyebrow went up. "Katie, what is going through that little head of yours?"

Okay, so he wasn't planning to spank her with that. Her relieved sigh was weak as her heart stopped pumping frantically. Now she was embarrassed and really mad at herself—as well as worried that she might just have given him an idea. She tossed her hair back and thrust her chin out defiantly. "Maybe I'm kinkier than you think."

His mouth twitched with a smile. "You are as vanilla as it gets."

Katie frowned, but she didn't take her eyes off the belt. She wasn't sure what being vanilla meant, but it didn't sound very complimentary. It made her sound bland and boring.

Ryder dropped the belt onto the carpet, but Katie could tell that she was still in trouble. He was bent on showing her the consequences of her actions, and she couldn't predict what he was planning. She wasn't scared, but the not knowing was killing her.

"Well, thank you, Ryder, for showing me the error of my ways," she said as she inched away, wondering how far she was from the bathroom. She didn't think she could hide in there all night, but if he really was as mad as he seemed, she might need to try. No, she reminded herself—when would she ever get Ryder alone in a hotel room again? She needed to make the most of this opportunity.

"You're not getting off that easy," he said, grabbing the collar of his shirt and pulling it off.

"And I promise that I will never return to the club." She held her hands out as if giving a pledge. "Cross my heart and hope to die."

"You've shown me how much your word means."

She didn't like that accusation at all. "Can you guess why I went to the club? It was to figure out what I needed to do so you wouldn't walk away from me the next time I'm naked, vulnerable, and desperate for you."

Ryder paused. "I did that for your own good."

"You did that because you don't trust yourself with me."

"That, too," he admitted as he threw his shirt on the ground. "You have my full attention now. I'm not planning to go anywhere."

She stared at his muscular chest, the excitement pressing inside her. This was the moment she'd been waiting for all year. But she wasn't going to be a sure thing or an easy lay for Ryder Scott. She'd learned her lesson from last time—if she gave him too much power, would he abandon her when she was naked and panting for more? She edged closer to the bathroom. "So, what is my punishment going to be? An early bedtime?"

He raised an eyebrow. "You're very bratty for someone who is already in trouble."

"I can be, because you're not going to punish me," she taunted.

Suddenly, he pounced. Katie's surprised yelp fizzled in her throat as he cornered her. He flattened his hands on the wall, trapping her. As he leaned in, she felt his body heat. "Wanna bet," he whispered.

Maybe she had a bit of kink in her because the only thoughts in her head were: *Don't hold back! Punish me good!*

"Get rid of your choker."

His command surprised Katie and her hand went to her throat. "Why? I kind of like it."

"I didn't give it to you, and I don't touch another dominant's submissive."

Good point. Katie untied it from her throat and tossed it over Ryder's shoulder. "Happy?"

He didn't answer as his gaze slid down past her shoulders. "Take off your vest."

He wanted her to strip in front of him. She suddenly felt shy and she hated it. This moment felt different from when he had taken off her dress yesterday. Their emotions were both running so high now. "If you want it off, you take it off."

He looked into her eyes. "Take off your vest."

It was a battle of wills. He didn't use threats, but she knew he would walk away if she didn't follow his rules. She wanted to appear powerful and confident, but she wanted to play this game even more.

She watched his expression as she unsnapped the PVC vest. It was more out of shyness than design that she slowly peeled the polyvinyl off her chest. She liked how his eyes blazed when he discovered she was wearing nothing underneath. Her skin tingled, her nipples tightening as she waited for his touch.

"Now your skirt," he said hoarsely.

She nervously licked her lips as she squeezed her thighs together. The shyness she felt was very inconvenient. "Why don't you put your hands to good use?"

"Katie"—his mouth was right against her ear—"take off your skirt or I will tear it from your body."

Naughty excitement licked through her veins. "You wouldn't," she said huskily, knowing full well that he would.

She saw the wicked flash in his eyes and felt his hand bunch up her skirt. But she still gasped when he gave it a violent tug and she heard the fabric tear. Katie couldn't help but look down and watch the skirt fall to the floor.

She stayed very still, her nipples tightening, as Ryder stared at her bare body. Her toes curled in the leather stiletto boots. "Take off my boots," she whispered.

"No," he said as he glanced down at them. "They stay on."

Ryder wanted her to wear them to bed? Her hips twitched as

the sexual excitement curled and tightened deep in her pelvis. "I thought you hated them."

"I do," he said, "but you need to learn that you don't give the commands."

"Are you saying I have no power?" She leaned into him, rubbing her hard nipples against his chest. Katie was secretly thrilled that he didn't move away. "I'm told there is a power exchange between a dominant and his submissive."

"So?" he asked gruffly.

"I have as much power over you as you have over me." She tilted her head and licked the love bite on his neck that she had given him days ago, reminding him of her claim. "I'm going to get exactly what I want tonight. So are you."

"That should be interesting since you still haven't earned the right to touch me."

That rule really bugged her. "I'm touching you right now."

He gave a nod. "But not with your hands."

"Do you plan to keep track of my hands all night long?" she asked, and then a possibility occurred to her. "Or are you going to tie me up?"

"You still aren't ready for bondage," he said, still not moving away from her as she trailed a string of kisses on his throat. "You never will be."

"Don't be too sure about that." She boldly placed her hands on his shoulders. "I have you now. You'll surrender by morning."

Just as she'd expected, Ryder gripped her wrists and pinned them against the wall above her head. "You'll be the one under me begging for more."

Oh, she hoped so. "Promises, promises."

Ryder kissed her hard as he ground his hips against hers. When he yanked his mouth away, they both were gasping for air.

"Is this how you punish your submissives?" Katie asked as she batted her eyelashes. "I bet they never learn their lesson."

Ryder grazed his lips along the pulse point above her collarbone. He caught the flesh between his teeth and sucked. Katie moaned but didn't try to get away. She wanted him to brand her, and she loved that she felt the pull all the way to her core.

When he let go, she still felt the throb at her throat. "Does this mean I'm yours?" she asked.

"It means I'm your master."

She'd never agreed to that, and no branding of her skin would symbolize it. "And you bear my mark," she said with a smile, "so that must mean . . ."

He captured her chin with his thumb and forefinger and directed her gaze to meet his. "No, you surprised me with the love bite, but that doesn't mean you can master me."

She narrowed her eyes. "Keep telling yourself that and one day you might actually believe it."

He tightened his grip on her chin. "You are begging to be punished, aren't you?"

She smiled. "Well, I'm hoping for more than a love bite."

Ryder's eyes darkened with desire. "Tell me what you want," he said in a rough whisper.

This was no time for shyness, she told herself. She needed to tell him exactly what she wanted and not hold back. "I want you underneath me, naked, hot and sweaty," she said as she brazenly looked into his eyes. "I want you deep inside me, filling and stretching me as I ride you hard."

He swallowed audibly.

She had him now. The eagerness in his eyes gave her the confidence to continue. "Take me to bed, Ryder," she whispered as she wiggled her body against him. "I want to mount you."

Ryder closed his eyes.

"And then I want to sink onto you." She rubbed her thighs together as her silky, slippery core clenched with anticipation. "Slowly and deeply before I ride you fast and hard."

"Didn't you forget something?" He slowly opened his eyes. "You haven't earned the right to touch me."

"Don't worry, Ryder," she said as the confidence overflowed from her. "I can do you with no hands."

Ryder abruptly gathered her in his strong arms and moved swiftly to the bed. Katie couldn't stop the triumphant laugh tumbling past her lips.

The bed was cool and soft against her back, but as she reached for Ryder, he flipped her onto her stomach. The move disoriented her. Katie's eyes widened as she saw the busy pattern of the quilt.

"Get on your hands and knees," Ryder said from behind her.

Okay, that sounded a little too submissive for her. "I will once you get underneath me."

"Katie," he said as he lifted her by her hips, making her settle on her knees, "do you think I'm going to reward you for breaking your promise?"

Damn, had she fallen into a trap? Now she was in a perfect position to get spanked. She was very aware of how vulnerable she was, and her skin tingled with a mix of dread and excitement. She flinched when she felt his hand follow the curve of her ass.

What was she worried about? This was *Ryder*. He wouldn't hurt her. But she still had to ask, because she hadn't been able to predict his every move. "What are you going to do?"

"I'm going to mount *you*," he said in a low, husky voice as he rubbed his finger along her wet slit. He reached under her with his other hand and squeezed her breast roughly. Katie arched and dipped her spine as she enjoyed the sensations he created inside her.

"And then I'm going to sink into *you*, slowly and deeply, before I ride *you* fast and hard."

Katie's fingers curled into the quilt, her hands shaking with anticipation. This wasn't how she'd dreamed their first time in bed would be. This was much, much better.

"Stay still," he ordered as he withdrew his hands. Katie was tempted to look over her shoulder to see what he was doing, but she decided it was time to follow his instructions. She would surrender if it meant Ryder would claim her in the most basic, primitive way.

She heard him take off his jeans, followed by a rip of foil. When she heard him roll on a condom, she dug her fingers into the quilt, wishing she could have done the task for him. She wanted any excuse to wrap her hand over his big cock.

Katie felt the sag of the mattress. He was kneeling behind her, his chest hovering over her spine, and she felt the heat of him and inhaled his aroused, masculine scent. Ryder reached underneath her and played with her breasts. His aggressive touch made her moan and rear back.

He reached down and cupped her sex. Katie panted eagerly as he teased her clit. He knew exactly how to touch her, aware of every move and sound she made. When she thought she would come, he immediately backed away.

She murmured her disappointment as he guided her reluctant body back to her hands and knees. He was firm about her keeping the position, even as her arms and legs trembled. So this was the punishment? Would he get her so close to a climax and back off?

Katie stiffened when she felt the rounded tip of his cock pressing against her. She dipped her spine as he rubbed his cock along the length of her wet slit, again and again. Katie bucked against him, desperate for more.

Just when she thought she would go crazy, Ryder gripped her hips and slowly sank his cock into her hot, slick core. She gave a long, guttural groan as he filled her to the hilt.

Katie's flesh clung to him and Ryder shuddered when she squeezed her pelvic muscles. Her arms and legs were shaking. Her boots felt so heavy and sweat beaded on her skin. She'd never felt so good. So wild and alive.

Ryder reached out and smoothed her hair from her face. He gathered her long black hair and twisted it around his hand. She wished she could watch his face. He had said nothing and she really needed to see his expression.

With one hand clenched on her hip and another wrapped so tightly in her hair that her scalp tingled, he began to ride her. He pumped his cock in shallow thrusts, teasing her.

"More," she whispered.

"More, what?" he asked as he plunged his cock deep into her.

She gasped as black dots danced before her eyes while white-hot heat lit up and sparked inside her. *More, what?* How could she answer that? More cock? More, please? More, Master?

Master? Was that what he wanted her to say? Forget it. She clawed at the quilt and dug her knees into the mattress. She wouldn't call him that. She could last this out.

His pace was designed to drive her wild. A couple of short thrusts and then a deep plunge to remind her of what she wanted more than her next breath. She understood why he chose to place her in this position. He had all the control. She couldn't see him, couldn't touch him, and couldn't set the pace. She was at his mercy.

Was it wrong to enjoy it so much?

"Please, Ryder." The words escaped her mouth before she knew it.

"Please, what?" he asked. She noticed his voice was shaky, too. He had set this pace to make her submit, but he might be the first to surrender.

She closed her eyes, relishing the ache building in her body, ready to splinter inside her. "I need you."

He slowed down.

"All of you." She licked her lips. "Everything you have."

Ryder's hand tightened painfully on her hair before he released it. He clamped both hands on her hips and surged forward. Katie almost lost her balance as he drove into her. Oh . . . my . . . God . . . Ryder demonstrated his full power and strength as he set a fast, ferocious speed. There was no rhythm, no design. He showed her exactly how much he wanted to be deep inside her, to claim her. His control slipped and suddenly he was on top of her, tilting her hips, and he drove into her. His hoarse, animal cry echoed in her ears.

She couldn't fight it anymore. She didn't want to. Katie surrendered to Ryder, body, heart and soul. The ache inside her splintered and whirled. The pleasure mingled with pain and she heard her scream from a distance.

Ryder sagged against her. He was heavy, and his body almost too hot to touch, but she didn't protest. As she gulped for air and her heart pounded hard in her ears, Katie knew she had him right where she wanted.

This was a beautiful start to a wild love affair.

Ryder watched Katie fall asleep in his arms. He couldn't take his eyes off her as she snuggled into him. He was surprised at the show of trust. He didn't deserve it. And if he wasn't careful, he would find himself doing the same to Katie and curling up against her, feeling safe and warm in her embrace.

The moment he'd tossed Katie over his shoulder in the club, he'd known they would wind up in bed together. He wanted it to happen, and he wouldn't let Jake interfere, even though that would have been the safest course of action.

Ryder knew he had acted like a caveman, carrying Katie away. He had been uncivilized and he hadn't cared. He had embraced it wholeheartedly. He never let himself get completely out of control, but there were moments when he skated right at the edge between control and recklessness.

Katie had provoked him and pushed him to the limit. Their battle of wills was more erotic than anything he had seen in the club. Katie had teased his senses and tempted him until he couldn't see straight. She saw that he was a demanding lover who was more rough than romantic. But she was with him every step of the way, her enthusiastic response hitting him like an aphrodisiac.

Still, he should have been gentler. He wasn't wrong about her. She was vanilla and he'd probably shocked her to the core. She was an eager lover and he found intense pleasure initiating her. He wanted to show her everything he knew and test her boundaries.

Ryder stiffened. What was he thinking? This was a one-time thing. If he let it continue she would see right through him and find out how unlovable he really was. He glanced down at Katie and saw that she was sleeping as if she hadn't had a decent sleep for the past few nights. Ryder gently pulled away from her. She frowned and murmured something, but didn't wake when he tucked a blanket around her nakedness.

Ryder sat up and slowly turned away from her. He was surprised that he hadn't been knocked down with regret and shame for his failure to uphold just one simple rule: Don't get into bed with Katie Kramer.

He was sure regret and shame would find him soon enough, but right now he wanted Katie one more time. He wasn't restless or feeling empty. If anything, he wanted this sense of deep satisfaction to linger. Once more with Katie and then he'd put a stop to it.

Ryder winced at his promise. He should have known that one night with Katie was all that it would take to become addicted to her. He needed to stop this now.

Then again, *Katie* had wanted an affair. Ryder rubbed his hands over his face, knowing he was grabbing for the very idea he had hated a mere few days ago. But Katie wanted something hot and wild that lasted a few days, not some happily-ever-after fairy tale.

Which was a good thing, because he couldn't give her that. A couple of weeks, maybe even a few months, and Katie would discover like everyone else that her prince was nothing more than a toad.

He didn't want that to happen, and that meant he had to give her up now. Cold turkey. Once they returned to Crystal Bend, he had to leave her alone and not look back. It was the only way he would get through the next couple of days.

CHAPTER TEN

❦

December 28

So much for being a beautiful start to a wild love affair, Katie thought glumly as she drove home from Seattle the next morning. She glanced in the rearview mirror and saw Ryder's truck a couple of car lengths behind her. Even on the I-90, he was doing his best to keep his distance.

Last night had seemed to be perfect. She vaguely remembered Ryder tucking her in. She had been exhausted and a little fuzzy as he placed the sheets and quilt on her naked body, but it was a sweet gesture. Katie honestly believed it was yet another facet of his protective side.

It was only in the morning that she'd realized Ryder hadn't slept in the same bed. And this morning he'd managed to keep a few feet, or a piece of furniture, between them in the small room at all times. Ryder wasn't rude or cruel, but he was distant.

But it didn't interfere with his need to protect and provide for her. Katie noticed that Ryder made sure she ate breakfast. He also checked her car before they headed out of the city, and made sure she had everything she needed. But he barely spoke to her and the strained silence between them was unbearable.

What she needed was a hug. Maybe some reassurance that the previous night had been a major event in his life, too. But she saw how Ryder tensed when she looked in his direction, or took a step back when she approached. If she was more confident, or felt more powerful, she wouldn't have let it get in her way.

So much for waking up with him by her side. Or snuggling in his arms. Katie sighed and pulled her gaze away from the rearview mirror. Why did she think last night would have brought them closer? Had she learned nothing? If anything, she was back to square one. Maybe even further than that.

"Are you always this quiet the morning after?" Hilary asked from the passenger side. She gobbled down a cinnamon chip scone and knocked it back with a hot chocolate and extra whipped cream.

"No, I usually sing 'Like a Virgin' at the top of my lungs," Katie deadpanned and immediately regretted it as the song started to loop in her head. "Do you always get a sugar fix on your morning after?"

"I do when I don't get any," Hilary muttered before wolfing down the rest of the scone.

"Say what?" Katie's car swerved and she immediately righted it, hoping Ryder didn't notice, but that man missed nothing.

"You heard me." Hilary took a fortifying sip of her hot chocolate. "I thought I was going to get lucky last night. Jake takes me out of the club and rents a hotel room for us. And guess what?"

Katie hunched her shoulders. Did she really want to know about her brother's exploits or, uh, underperformance? "I'm almost afraid to ask."

"Nothing!" Hilary splayed her hands in the air. "That's what happened. Absolutely freaking nothing."

Katie frowned. Was she missing something? "My brother didn't lay a hand on you?" she verified.

Hilary looked out the passenger window. "He slept on the floor. I don't think he knew I was in the room," she said softly.

Ouch. That had to hurt. "I am so sorry."

Her friend shrugged. "When a woman spends the night with a womanizer and he doesn't make a move on her, then she has hit an all-time low."

"Womanizer?" Great, now Britney Spears's song was going through her head. It was going to be that kind of morning.

"What else would you call Jake?" Hilary asked. "The guy only dates sex-crazed bimbos."

No, he had some variety like . . . well . . . Katie clucked her tongue. "You're right. He's a womanizer."

"Let's just keep my night a secret, okay?" Hilary pleaded with Katie. "I don't think I could handle anyone knowing that I failed to seduce Jake."

Katie pressed her hand against her heart and vowed, "I'll take your secret to the grave."

"Thank you." Hilary straightened her shoulders and pulled down the sun visor to check her appearance. "I look like a raccoon. You should have told me it would take a chisel to get all this makeup off."

"I thought a genius like you knew it was going to take more than soap and water."

"I use my brainpower to fight the forces of evil." Hilary rubbed the black mascara circles from under her eyes. "I can't spare it on things like makeup and dating."

"Maybe that can be your New Year's resolution," Katie said slyly.

"No way," Hilary said and snapped the visor closed. "I refuse to take part in that antiquated custom. Next you'll stuff black-eyed peas and cabbage down my throat."

"Hey, those are for good luck on New Year's Day."

"Don't get me started on the whole concept of getting lucky. But wait a minute!" She turned and faced Katie. "You keep changing the subject on me. Tell me about your night."

Katie groaned. She didn't feel up to discussing it, but she was trapped in the car with Hilary.

"Come on. How was it?" Hilary leaned over her seat and looked down at the gas and brake pedals. "Oh, I guess it wasn't that great. I'm so sorry."

Katie cast a curious look at her friend. "Why do you say that?"

"Katie, you're wearing ballet slippers." Hilary patted Katie's arm with sympathy. "You needed a cinnamon scone more than I did. Why didn't you tell me?"

"I have no idea what you're talking about."

"When I see you wearing ballet slippers, it is the equivalent of me pouring sugar packs down my throat. Stop at the next Starbucks and I'll find you something sugary."

Katie wiggled her foot and gave a quick glance at her black ballet slippers. "Are you saying my shoes reflect my mood?"

"No, just the height of your heels. I've noticed the phenomenon this year. When you're ready to take on the world, you wear your highest heels. When you're feeling unsure, you wear flats."

"I do not! I'm wearing these shoes because they are easier to drive in."

"Uh-huh. If you say so." Hilary brushed the crumbs off her cardigan. "So, how was last night?"

"It was great." Katie felt a blush coming into her cheeks. "At least, I thought it was. But there was no bondage involved, and now Ryder can't look me in the eye." She took another look in the rearview mirror. Ryder's truck seemed to be even farther away.

"That doesn't mean anything bad," Hilary said. "He might be overcome by the life-changing moment."

"I seriously doubt that."

"Okay, let's focus on the positive." Hilary started listing the items, ticking them off on her fingers. "You had sex. You had good sex."

"Amazing, life-changing, but bondage-free sex," Katie corrected her friend.

"Just rub it in, why don't you?" Hilary said with a smile. "And you had sex with Ryder Scott. Even more important, you fulfilled your New Year's resolution. The one you've made for the past two years!"

"No, I didn't." Katie hadn't gone through all this for one night. "One night of sex does not make an affair."

Hilary dismissed the definition with a wave of her hand. "Don't quibble over the details."

"I don't quibble. I don't even know what that means. But I do know that one night of sex means it's a one-night stand."

"Well, how long is an affair?" Hilary asked. "Two nights?"

That still sounded too short and insignificant. "No, that's a wild weekend."

"What about three nights?"

"That's a fling."

Hilary gave her a suspicious look from the corner of her eye. "You are making this up as you go along, aren't you?"

"Yes," Katie admitted. "I want an affair, and to me that means something meaningful and . . . and important to both people."

Hilary pursed her lips as she tried to understand Katie's definition. "So the relationship is consequential if it lasts longer than three nights?"

"I guess." She was thinking more in terms of weeks. Months. And yes, even years.

"Then you have a problem because you don't have that much time left."

Katie sighed. "I know."

Hilary sat up straight. "Unless you make the most of your afternoons."

"You mean *this* afternoon?" Approaching Ryder that soon would be like walking into a minefield.

"Sure, why not? He's had enough time to recover."

Katie wasn't really thinking about his sexual recovery time. "Ryder doesn't want to be around me right now."

"Who cares? You wait too long and he'll come up with a whole list of reasons why he can't have sex with you. Not to mention the fact that he'll be halfway to Dubai."

"You're right." Katie was reluctant to admit it. "Any idea how I can drag him into my bed this afternoon? And incorporate bondage while I'm at it?"

"He's a man. You don't need to be too creative when it comes to sex," Hilary said. "All you have to do is show up, eager and willing, and he'll think you were gift-wrapped especially for him."

"Gift wrap! That's it. That's what I'll do." Katie turned to her friend. "Hilary, you really are a genius."

"I'll take your word for it."

Katie stared up at Ryder's front door. Why didn't he hide a spare key outside like normal people? And did he really have to live on the second floor of an apartment building?

Katie wrapped her long overcoat tighter around her body as the wind started to kick up. She slung her shoulder bag around to her back and tried to accurately gauge the distance of the stairwell to Ryder's balcony.

She could make it. She grimaced and decided to check again. Her chances would have been better if she had been wearing jeans and rock-climbing shoes. Something with more traction than her ballet slippers.

She glared at the black flats. She didn't care what Hilary believed. The level of her self-confidence was *not* measured by the height of her heels. She happened to be very confident in the plan she had hastily put together once she got back to town. She knew she had to bombard Ryder today before he built up any resistance.

She just wished the plan wasn't necessary.

Katie grabbed the short safety wall next to the stairs and kept her eyes on the railing of Ryder's balcony. The wet, slippery railing was still covered with clumps of snow.

She wasn't going to think about that. Katie glanced down. It wasn't *too* far to the ground. She could do it. She sat on the safety wall, slinging her bare legs over the side. She leaned forward and grabbed on to Ryder's balcony for dear life.

Katie pressed her feet hard against the safety wall, her fingertips turning white as she clung to the balcony. Her coat was flapping in the wind.

Okay . . . now what?

She really should have thought this through, she thought as she hung there like a suspension bridge. All she knew was that she had to get into Ryder's apartment while he was out. She had no idea where he had gone or for how long. She just had to be in place when he got back.

She took a deep breath, clung to the edge of Ryder's balcony and pushed off the safety wall with her feet. Swinging her legs, she banged into the wood structure. Katie winced and refused to let go of the balcony. Her body banged against the structure again.

Katie wasn't sure what she had hoped to accomplish, but dangling from Ryder's balcony was not it.

A cold wind tugged at Katie's long coat. This was probably not the best time to have gone commando.

Certain that someone would walk by and look up—because that was just how her luck was going—she grunted and groaned as she hoisted herself up and over the balcony's wall. Katie's feet slid over the ledge and hit the balcony floor with a thud. She lay there, gulping for air, her arms shaking from the exertion. She really needed to stay away from the Christmas candy and get back into the gym.

"Yoo-hoo!"

She heard an older woman's voice from a distance. Oh, crap. Katie's pulse started to gallop. Did she have a witness? Was someone calling the cops on her?

That wouldn't be good. While she was dressed for an easy strip search, she wasn't wearing enough for a night in a holding cell. Katie knew she needed to talk fast to get out of trouble.

She sat up and peered over the wall. Ryder's neighbor waved at her from the balcony on the other side of the stairwell. Katie gave a tentative wave. "Uh, happy holidays, Mrs. Graham."

"Katie Kramer, what are you doing?" the older woman called out. "You could have fallen and broken your neck."

"I . . . uh . . . am here to help Ryder pack." She slowly stood up and brushed the dirt off her coat.

"Sure." Mrs. Graham dragged the word into several syllables. "That's what the other girls said. Only they used the front door."

Katie's stomach gave a twist and she glanced inside Ryder's apartment through the sliding glass door. "Other girls?"

"You know them. Sasha and Tatum come by the most."

"They've been here?" Her stomach gave another sickening twist. She should have expected that her competition would be one step ahead of her.

Mrs. Graham rested her elbows on her balcony wall. "Not for long. Ryder shooed them away. Don't worry, the coast is clear."

Katie blushed. "I'm only here to . . ."

"Uh-huh." The woman rolled her eyes. "I know why you're here. No one climbs a balcony to help pack up some moving boxes."

"Okay, you caught me." Katie injected an exaggerated sarcastic tone. "I'm planning a sneak attack to seduce Ryder."

Mrs. Graham slapped her palm on the railing. "Good for you."

Katie's blush sizzled through her cheeks. "I was kidding." Why was it that exaggerated sarcasm only worked on TV shows?

"No, you weren't. You've been after Ryder for ages. It's about time you've done something."

"Oh, my God." Katie thrust her fingers in her hair. "Mom was right. The whole town knows!"

"But aren't you one to wait until the last minute?" Mrs. Graham suddenly turned to look inside her apartment. "Oh, my phone is ringing."

"Mrs. Graham," Katie urgently called out to the older woman and clasped her hands together in a form of prayer, "can we just keep this between ourselves?"

The older woman gave a snort. "I'll do my best."

Katie's shoulders sagged in defeat. That meant Mrs. Graham would tell whoever was on the phone. Katie hoped it was a telemarketer living in India. "Thanks!"

"Good luck!" The woman waved at her and ran for her phone.

"I'm going to need it," Katie muttered to herself and waited until Mrs. Graham disappeared. She turned and faced the sliding door.

Wait a second. What if *this* door was locked as well? And why was Ryder locking doors anyway? This was Crystal Bend, for crying out loud. What were the chances of someone jumping onto his balcony and entering his apartment? Well—Katie rolled her eyes—apart from her, of course.

Katie closed her eyes and made a quick wish. She grabbed the handle and almost wept with relief as the door slid open. She quickly stepped inside and closed the door behind her.

She halted as she saw the changes in Ryder's apartment. She hadn't been around for a while, but it looked totally different. The walls were bare and boxes were stacked up everywhere. Packing supplies littered the couch cushions.

Katie slowly made her way to the kitchen. It was crammed with boxes. He really was moving. She opened the cabinets and found most of them empty. Panic began to bubble inside her. Katie placed her hand on her stomach to calm it down, but it was useless.

She wasn't sure why she was so surprised. Ryder had said he was moving, and that guy always followed up on his word. But she hadn't seen any evidence of the impending move until now.

Worse, she didn't think she could stop him from leaving. Hell, she couldn't keep him in her bed. She wished she was enough of a reason to make him stay.

Katie wasn't sure how long she had been standing in Ryder's kitchen before she spotted Ryder's pickup truck entering the parking lot. She ducked, hoping he didn't see her in the window. For her plan to work she needed the element of surprise.

She hurried to his bedroom and swung the door shut behind her. There were boxes in the corner, but his bed was still in one piece. That was a good thing, especially since she was counting on using the headboard.

She grabbed her purse and pulled out the bright red Velcro handcuffs she had bought this morning after returning from Seattle. Katie hadn't had a chance to try them out, but she was sure they would be fine. After all, how dangerous could Velcro be?

Katie scurried onto the bed and threaded the handcuffs through a rail in Ryder's headboard. Once she had the handcuffs perfectly aligned, she reached for her purse and pulled out a shiny red bow. Taking off the sticker to reveal the gummy side, she affixed the bow on the handcuffs.

Katie paused to study her handiwork. Perfect. She flinched and looked over her shoulder when she heard the front door. She was really cutting it close. Katie shucked off her ballet shoes and kicked them onto the floor. They landed softly as she removed her winter coat and tossed it after the shoes.

She looked down at the white nightie she wore. The spaghetti straps were as fragile as they appeared, and the hem reached her thighs. It was the prettiest piece of lingerie she owned. She liked the romantic embellishments of seed pearls, sequins and lace. But it was only at this moment that she realized it looked a lot like a wedding dress.

That was going to be a turnoff for Ryder, but there was nothing she could do about it now. Unless she decided to get rid of it, too. Katie hesitated, her fingers clenching on the spaghetti straps. No, she couldn't do it. She was already putting herself in a vulnerable position and she needed something, even a flimsy piece of lingerie, as a shield.

Katie fluffed out her long black hair and positioned herself in the center of the bed just as she heard Ryder turn on his stereo in the other room. The hard, pulsing rock music wasn't her first choice of a romantic accompaniment, but it could be worse. At least it wasn't one of the songs that had been playing in her head all morning. She wrapped one handcuff around her wrist and then struggled to close the other cuff.

The moment she accomplished that, she sagged against the mattress and exhaled. Wow, she had made it with seconds to spare. She looked expectantly at the door and waited.

Nothing.

No problem. That would give her time to adjust her position. Katie posed with one knee bent, allowing a tantalizing glimpse of her hip. Hmm, probably not sexy enough. Maybe she needed to emphasize that she was gift-wrapped for Ryder's pleasure. She wiggled down the bed a little until her arms were fully extended. Perfect.

She stared at the door and waited. And waited some more.

He was coming to the bedroom soon, wasn't he? Otherwise she might lose all circulation in her hands and arms.

Katie heard footsteps and held her breath. This was it. He was going to open that door and discover her. And then he was going to pounce. Katie arched her spine, thrusting out her chest. She saw the doorknob turning and she forgot about breathing.

Suddenly the door opened and she saw Ryder. He wore a gray Crystal Bend Community College sweatshirt, snug jeans, and a stunned expression.

Ryder came to a dead stop at the threshold. His jaw dropped but no sound came from his mouth. He slowly blinked and opened his eyes wide.

She gave him her best come-hither smile.

As if he was on automatic pilot, Ryder took a step back into the hallway and closed the door.

CHAPTER ELEVEN

Ryder was hallucinating. That was the only possible explanation for why he'd thought he'd seen Katie tied to his bed. Wearing next to nothing. Except a big, red bow.

No, he hadn't imagined it. Damn, it was like his greatest fantasy had come to life. He was already tense and ready to pounce and he'd only had time to catch a glimpse before shutting the door.

Focus. He had to focus, and not on how great Katie looked spread out on his bed, waiting for his touch. Ryder rubbed his forehead, the sweat already beading on his skin. He was sure Katie had planned this to the very smallest detail. Too bad she hadn't considered the possibility that someone else would be here, too. Someone like her big brother, Jake.

This was not good. He whirled around and faced Jake, wondering if he'd seen anything. His friend didn't look stunned or horrified. He looked . . . confused.

"What's the problem?" Jake asked. "You don't want to dismantle the bed?"

The bed. Ryder's stomach did a somersault. Oh, hell no. There would be no dismantling of the bed.

Ryder prayed that Katie wouldn't call out to him. He had to warn her somehow. "You know what, Jake?" he said loudly, despite the fact that Jake was standing at his elbow. "Let's postpone the packing."

"I'm right here, dude. You don't need to yell over the music," Jake said as he took a step forward. "And I'm here to help you pack, so let's do it."

Ryder blocked the door as his brain threatened to shut down in something close to panic. If Jake found his little sister here, in his bed—not to mention tied up with a bright red bow—all hell was going to break loose.

And Ryder was not going to let that happen. And not because he didn't want to ruin his friendship with Jake. Nothing so noble. He wanted Jake out of here so he could enjoy every delicious second Katie was about to offer him. He was going to go to Hell for it, but at this moment, he didn't care.

"I'm hungry and there's nothing here," Ryder improvised. "We can go to the café and grab something."

"No way," Jake said. "You have to stop procrastinating. You aren't going to finish in time if you keep going to parties and pulling Katie out of trouble."

Ryder glanced at the door, wondering what Katie thought about that. He hoped that she had at least heard Jake's voice and was smart enough to keep her mouth shut.

Jake made a move for the door and Ryder threw his arms out, preventing Jake from reaching the handle. He knew he was acting suspiciously, but if he had to, he would wrestle his friend to the ground to keep him from opening that door.

"I . . . forgot to tell you," Ryder said, his words coming out in one big rush. "Sasha came by earlier. She's looking for you. And she said she'll swing by later."

Jake's groan was so loud that Katie had to know he was here. "Can't that woman take a hint? She's suffocating me. Okay, this is what we'll do. I'll hide in your bedroom when she drops by."

"No!" Ryder exclaimed, pressing his back against the door. His eyes widened when he heard a frantic rustling sound coming from the bedroom. He immediately conjured up the image of Katie writhing on the bed, struggling against the bindings.

Oh, God. He couldn't think about that right now. He was not going to imagine Katie swaying from side to side, rocking the bed. He wasn't going to think about climbing onto the bed and holding Katie still as he covered her body with his.

"No, that won't work," he insisted hoarsely. "She'll see your truck parked out front."

"You're right," Jake admitted with frustration. "That woman drives me crazy." He turned and walked toward the front door.

Ryder followed Jake, barely listening to his elaborate plan to outwit Sasha. Ryder hoped that Jake wouldn't find out that Sasha wasn't looking for him at all.

The moment Jake was out the door, Ryder closed the door quickly and locked it. His heart was pounding harder than the music as he ran back to the bedroom.

Katie heard footsteps coming closer and she froze. They were swiftly eating ground and she had no chance to take cover as the door swung open. She sighed with relief when she saw Ryder alone at the threshold, hands on hips, and a look of utter incredulity on his face.

"Oh, thank God," she said with great feeling. "For a second, I thought you were Jake."

Ryder took a deep breath and rubbed his forehead as if he was getting a migraine. "He just left. What are you *doing* here?"

She blew her hair from her eyes. "I wanted to surprise you."

"Oh, I'm surprised."

He didn't say anything else. He remained standing on the other side of the room, staring at her.

She hadn't expected that. She imagined that after one glimpse of her chained to his bed, Ryder would tear off his clothes and launch himself at her like a heat-seeking missile. He didn't seem too eager to join her in bed, and she wondered what she had done wrong last night. She did her best not to show her disappointment, confusion and hurt.

"I thought we could pick up where we left off last night," she said with a bright smile.

Ryder was already shaking his head. "Last night was a mistake."

Katie rolled her eyes. "I knew you were going to say that." He had probably prepared a speech and practiced it all morning.

Ryder thrust a tense hand into his hair and looked away. "I was too—"

"Ryder, if I had a problem with last night," she said firmly, determined to block any excuses, "I wouldn't have encouraged it and screamed for more. I would have stopped you."

"You don't understand," he said as he approached the bed. "Last night I don't think you could have stopped me. That's why I had to stop myself. I couldn't sleep next to you without going crazy."

Katie smiled wide. This was music to her ears. Ryder desired her so much that he had lost control. "That's great!"

"No, it isn't." He sat on the end corner of the bed. "I've managed to resist you all this time and it's become harder. I'm days away from removing myself from temptation"—he gestured at the moving boxes—"and I did the one thing I swore I wouldn't do."

Katie stared at Ryder as the words played over in her mind. "You *are* leaving because of me." Wow, her mother was right. Two times in a row. This was freaky, and possibly unprecedented.

"And I'm not going to make the mistake again," he vowed.

She hated to hear him say that their night together was a mistake. What they did, what they shared, was beautiful. There had to be something she was missing. Katie gathered her courage and asked the one thing she really wasn't sure she wanted to hear the honest answer to. "Why are you staying away from me?"

"Isn't it obvious?" He clasped his hand on her ankle, as if he couldn't resist touching her, that he needed the contact. "Look at how I took you last night."

That was why he was keeping his distance? Because he hadn't claimed her in a missionary position? He must think she was a fragile woman with a delicate disposition. Hadn't she done everything she could to correct that assumption? "I liked it."

"You don't have to say that to make me feel better." He looked down and patted her ankle. "You deserve a guy who can treat you like a lady. Someone who is tender and romantic."

Katie made a face. "Where did you get that idea? I've known guys like that and they bore me," she confessed. "I know what kind of man I want and it's you."

Her claim didn't please Ryder. "You're saying that because you don't know any better." He absently stroked her ankle, sending waves of pleasure up her leg.

"I'm not looking for someone who tries to charm me into bed, or who wines and dines me hoping to sixty-nine me," she said bluntly. She needed to get through this man's stubbornness and time was running out.

The look he gave her indicated he didn't believe a word she said. "You are telling me that you don't want the roses and champagne route?"

"The guys who offer me that always turn out to be shallow and they run at the first sign of trouble. I want a guy who will make the same sacrifices that I would to protect what we have together. A man who wants and needs me as much as I want and need him. I want someone who understands me, who has been with me through the ups and downs. And I want to offer the same for that guy. *You* are that guy. We are perfect for each other."

Ryder wasn't convinced. "So last night was your romantic fantasy?"

She paused. Okay, that question might trip her up. Last night hadn't been her romantic fantasy. Katie had dreamed that their first time would include flowers, champagne and words of love. Last night she had been surprised, but only in the beginning. "Last night was exactly what I needed and wanted."

"You didn't answer my question."

"I have a lot of fantasies," she admitted. "Some of them are romantic and some of them are dirty. All of them include you."

His gaze collided with hers for a moment before he dragged his attention away. "Is being tied to my bed one of your fantasies?" he asked as he continued to rub his callused hand around her ankle.

"Actually, I thought this would be one of yours." Although she did enjoy the feel of his hand holding down her ankle like a cuff.

Ryder pulled his hand away from her. "Katie, you shouldn't be here."

She wanted to kick him. Scream. When was he going to get it

through his head that he didn't need to protect her from himself?

"I can't think of anywhere else I want to be," she said honestly.

"Obviously. I can't believe you tied yourself to my bed." A thought suddenly occurred to him. He looked at the window and then at the bedroom door. "How did you get in here?"

She gave a nervous chuckle. If Ryder found out, he would go crazy, and she would rather spend her time driving him insane in bed. "You don't want to know," she said in a confidential whisper and gave a small shake to her head.

"You should leave," he said as he got up from the bed.

"I want to be here with you," she insisted.

"You don't know what you're in for." He thrust his hand into his hair again. "I'm not the knight in shining armor that you think I am. I'm not chivalrous or thoughtful. I'm not even sweet or kind."

"Believe it or not, neither am I."

He laughed softly at that.

"What?" She demanded an answer. "It's true."

Ryder leaned down, his face over hers. His eyes darkened as he studied her face. "You are so sweet I can taste it." To her surprise, he kissed her lips tenderly.

She poured everything she felt into that kiss. Katie knew that she was opening herself up for a cutting rejection. Tied to his bed and confessing how much she needed him laid everything out in the open.

The only thing she couldn't do was tell him how much she loved him. Because if he rejected her now, she wasn't sure what she would do. She couldn't handle the possibility that he might completely crush her dreams.

Ryder pulled away and she tried to follow, but the damn cuffs halted her. He stroked her cheek before allowing his hand to trail down her neck. His eyes narrowed as his fingertips brushed along the love bite.

"It doesn't hurt," she reminded him.

He didn't listen. He pressed his mouth against the love bite and gave it a kiss. She liked the gentleness, but it worried her. Did he think she couldn't take all of him, the roughness *and* the tenderness? The frustration as well as the patience? She wanted the whole man, the good along with the bad. And Katie wanted Ryder to accept the same traits in her.

Katie didn't want Ryder to be all sweet and soft with her. Not now, and not when he thought she couldn't handle anything else. Katie was desperate for his mouth, but she couldn't reach him. Exasperated, she jerked at her cuffs and heard a small tear of Velcro.

He froze at the sound. Ryder looked up at her and then at the handcuffs. "Do you want me to free you?"

She wondered if there was a deeper meaning to that question, but she couldn't figure it out. She had to answer the question carefully. "I want to be tied down only if you're going to take advantage of it."

There was a wicked glint in his eyes before he cupped her face with his hands. His kiss was slow but relentless. By the time he lowered his hands to caress her throat and chest, she was out of breath.

Katie squirmed and she sighed as Ryder straddled her hips and possessively grabbed her breasts. She arched, thrusting to offer him more. The sequins and seed pearls pressed into her flesh, but she didn't complain. If anything, the pressure added to her excitement.

"You shouldn't have worn this nightgown," he told her.

She pouted. Yes, it looked too bridal, but it wasn't slutty or overly suggestive. It made her feel beautiful, especially the way Ryder was looking at her. "You don't like it?"

"It's very pretty," he said as he slid between her legs, "but it's going to get ruined around a rough guy like me."

She smiled. "I think the designer would be offended if you *didn't* tear it off my body."

He glanced at the red handcuffs anchored on his headboard. "Are you sure you want to be cuffed?"

"They're Velcro," she revealed to him. "I'm fine. Why do you keep asking?"

"I don't want you to get hurt," he admitted in a low, raspy voice as he removed his hands from her heavy, swollen breasts. "And I don't want to scare you."

She bit her lip, catching the "awww" that was sure to displease him. "You couldn't."

He didn't reply to that. Instead he bent down while bunching her nightie up to her hips. Her breath caught in her throat as Ryder laid kisses against her inner thighs. She offered no resistance when he parted her legs wider. He left a trail of kisses along her legs, getting closer and closer to her wet slit.

Katie could barely breathe, her sexual hunger pressing down on her. Her heart began to pound as Ryder hooked her knees over his shoulders. He immediately claimed her sex with his hot mouth. His boldness shocked her.

Katie's hips lifted off the mattress as he circled his tongue and flicked it against her swollen clit. She rocked her hips up and down as he teased her unmercifully. She wanted to grab him by the hair and bury his face deep between her thighs. She needed to guide him and have him thrust his tongue deep inside her until she climaxed. But she couldn't do any of that with her wrists still bound above her head.

Ryder pushed her nightie to her stomach and she wished he would just rip it off. He slid his hands under the satiny fabric to play with her breasts. She twisted and arched her spine as he stroked her. Each time he pinched her nipple she felt the jagged pinch in her clit. She rolled her hips to alleviate the building sweet pressure, but there was no escape.

Ryder hummed with pleasure as he lapped her sex. She couldn't help but blush at his pure satisfaction. Katie had never had a lover who enjoyed sex with all of his senses. She instinctively knew he wasn't doing this just for her pleasure; he was enjoying it as much as she was.

When Ryder sucked on her clit, it was an abrupt change from the gentle lapping. Katie's eyes rolled back and her moan echoed in the bedroom. Goose bumps blanketed her skin as her breaths came out in shallow pants.

"You like that?" Ryder teased her, his voice vibrating against her flesh.

"Yes," she answered in a faint whisper. She licked her lips as she tried to catch her breath. Ryder went down on her again, suckling her clit with such force that the pleasure lingered on the edge of torment. Ryder showed no leniency, until she thrashed from side to side.

Sweat gathered on her skin and her nightie clung damply against her curves. Heat spread from her core down her legs and up her chest before radiating out.

Ryder stopped sucking her clit and licked her moist entrance. Katie closed her eyes as her head spun from the rich, vibrant sensations. She rocked her hips, trying to get closer as Ryder teased her with the tip of his tongue.

"Please, Ryder," she said, but she wasn't sure why she said it. "I need . . . I—"

He thrust his tongue into her core. Buried it deep. Oh, yeah. That was *exactly* what she needed. Katie started to shake, the sensations so intense, she couldn't contain them.

Ryder slid his hand from her breasts and trailed them down her quivering stomach. She flinched when he boldly placed his thumb against her clit. He tapped the swollen bud as he pumped his tongue in and out of her sex.

She felt the barriers inside her falling down like dominoes. Any control she thought she had was long gone. She was defenseless and at his mercy. Katie could ask him to release the bindings, but she didn't want to. The sense of being out of control was scary, but it offered a sense of freedom. She wanted him to take her, grab her, claim her any way he could.

Ryder pulled his mouth away from her wet core. She felt the loss sharply. Katie frowned, and murmured her protest as she wondered what he would do next. She had been so close to coming, her arms and legs shaking as the power inside her grew.

Ryder removed his hand from her clit and started to rub her slit. She wiggled against his hand, wanting more than that. She really hoped he wasn't planning to start over again from the beginning. She couldn't take it. She needed all of him right now.

He tapped her clit with his tongue. The little flicks of his tongue were fast and furious. She felt the waves of pleasure lapping at her, but it wasn't enough. She needed him inside her. She needed his cock so much she was willing to submit and follow every ridiculous instruction he gave. She was so far gone, she would call him Master if it meant deep, thrusting penetration.

As Ryder lashed his tongue against her clit and pumped his finger in her sex, he cupped his other hand under her ass and slid another finger along the cleft of her buttocks. He tapped his finger against her rosebud. The onslaught was too much. She twisted and rocked her hips, but she couldn't escape.

Just when she thought she couldn't take much more, she came violently. She lurched forward, the handcuffs tightening against her wrists as she arched wildly from the bed. The climax tore through her, stealing her strength, squeezing her last breath, until she collapsed on the mattress, bewildered and exhausted.

She was dimly aware of Ryder crawling above her, his body barely touching hers. She stared at him, in a daze, as he reached for her cuffs. Katie heard the rasp of the Velcro and her arms dropped on the mattress above her head. They felt heavy and not quite a part of her.

Ryder reached for one of her arms and roughly massaged her from her elbow to her fingers. She groaned and winced. The pinpricks of sensations stung as she regained circulation.

"You shouldn't have been in these cuffs this long," Ryder lectured her gruffly as he reached for the other arm.

"Next time don't argue with me for so long," she said lazily and her head lolled to one side.

"I mean it, Katie. You are too new to bondage to stay in these cuffs for long periods of time."

"I'm lucky to have such an expert taking care of me," she said with a cheeky grin. Her smile disappeared when she saw the guilty look on Ryder's face. She knew from past experience that his expression meant trouble. "What's wrong?"

He absently rubbed her arms hard enough to make her wince. "We need to talk," he said, as if he had just made up his mind.

Katie's stomach gave a painful twist. She didn't think she could cope with any more of Ryder's surprises. But nothing could be worse than his announcement that he was leaving, right? "Well, don't keep me in suspense," she said, trying to offer a nonchalant smile.

"I don't know where you got this idea about me. Well, there were the old rumors, but it's not who I am today."

Katie gave an impatient sigh. "Ryder, just spill it."

He looked directly into her eyes. "I'm not deep into the bondage lifestyle."

She blinked and stared at him as his words packed a punch straight to her chest. *"Excuse me?"*

"I don't need to tie women up every time to enjoy sex. I don't know where you got the idea that I did." Ryder's mouth slanted into a devilish smile. "Not that I'm complaining."

CHAPTER TWELVE

"You are a rat bastard!" She grabbed the pillow from under her head. Her arms were still weak and stinging, but that didn't stop her from hitting Ryder squarely on his chest. "What do you mean, you aren't into bondage?"

"I have fun with it, and there was a time I was seriously into it, but it isn't something I *need* to do." He shrugged his large shoulders. "I like variety."

She couldn't believe it! Katie hit him again with the pillow and it glanced off his shoulder. "How did you know about the club?" She thwacked him again, this time on the side of his head. "And you had a blindfold!"

He grabbed the pillow and tossed it on the floor. He leaned in, his hips grinding into hers, until Katie was lying on her back and her hands were on either side of her face. "Bondage was something I experimented with years ago."

She didn't care how long it had been for him. That didn't change one important fact. "I let you blindfold me!" She couldn't believe she had been through all of that when it wasn't necessary. She was outraged. She was embarrassed.

"It's not something to be upset about. I—"

"Don't get upset?" Spoken like a guy. "I don't think you get it. I *tied* myself to your *bed*."

His dark eyes twinkled and she knew he was remembering the moment he walked in and saw her gift-wrapped just for him. "I got to admit, that was pretty hot."

She grabbed the collar of his sweatshirt, pulled him down until his crooked nose bumped against the tip of hers. Katie glared at him. "You wanted me to call you *Master*."

He ducked his head and a red flush streaked his cheekbones. "I know, I know. I went too far. I don't know what got into me. It was like the role took over." He glanced back at her. "But I knew you would never call me that."

She hadn't been so sure. There had been too many close calls when she would have said anything to find the ultimate satisfaction with Ryder. She hoped he would never find out the truth or his arrogance would have no bounds.

"I don't believe this." She let go of his sweatshirt and tried to push him away, but he was too strong and heavy. "All this time I was worried that I wanted a guy who was sexually incompatible."

"Believe me, that is no longer something to worry about," he said huskily as he sat up and caressed her arms, each stroke leisurely and possessive.

She swatted his hands away, not willing to forgive him quickly. "Why didn't you correct my assumption?"

He rubbed the back of his neck, clearly uncomfortable to admit the truth. "I thought it would ward you off. How was I supposed to know it would make you more interested?"

Now she was the one blushing. The kinky side of Ryder had fascinated her. She pointed at him, jabbing her finger into his chest with each word. "You owe me."

"Hey, it's not a complete lie." Ryder grabbed her hand and brought it up to his mouth. He brushed his lips along her knuckles before turning her hand over and placing a kiss at the center of her palm. "I like a little kink. Who doesn't?"

She curled her hand and tried to pull away from his grip. "You are not getting off that easy."

"I know," Ryder admitted with another charming smile. "But what made you think I was heavy into bondage? My past isn't that well known."

"It's known to your ex-girlfriends." They knew he had some experience, but they *also* must have known that he wasn't deep into the lifestyle. When Hilary had started asking around, she'd failed to take into account that Tatum, Sasha, Jessica and Emily were all friends with one another. Low-down and dirty friends.

Katie's eyes narrowed into angry slits. They must have purposely told Hilary stories to make Katie run in the other direction. They had played her well, but they made the tactical error of thinking she was too much of a good girl to go after someone as kinky as Ryder. "I'm going to kill them," she said in a vicious growl.

"Why?" Ryder asked as he captured her wrists and pinned them down on either side of her head. "You had fun."

Okay, yes, she had. She had enjoyed some experiences more than others. But even more than that, she discovered some things about herself, both good and bad. But that wasn't the point!

"I don't care," she insisted as she attempted to wiggle out of his grasp with no success. "I'm going to get even with you all. One by one. Starting with you!"

Amusement gleamed in his eyes and he indicated her predicament with the tilt of his head. "How do you plan to do that?" he purred, wrapping his large fingers around her wrists.

Good question. She probably looked ridiculous making these

bold claims while Ryder was straddling her and pinning her arms down, and after he had claimed her so intimately. "Just watch your back, Ryder. I'll make my move when you least expect it."

Her intimidating words had the opposite effect, as Ryder started to chuckle. Katie knew she was a fool in love, because as much as his reaction irritated her, her heart gave a funny little flip as she watched him laugh.

"I'll tell you what," Ryder said as he released her wrists. "I'll let you tie me up."

"Say what?" She sat up abruptly, her head clipping Ryder's chin.

"Just once," he said as he rubbed his hand over his jawline. "Then we'll call it even."

Katie maneuvered into a kneeling position. "That doesn't quite balance the scales," she complained. This guy had her jumping through hoops, wearing fetish clothes in *public*, and visiting bondage clubs. She deserved more than one time.

His smile disappeared. "I'm not making this offer lightly."

Katie knew that. Allowing her to take control and letting her have her revenge while he was tied up took courage. Especially for someone like Ryder, who was always in total command of his surroundings. She hoped he wouldn't regret it.

"Have you ever been tied up before?" she asked.

"No, you'll be the first." He curled his finger under her chin and lifted her face to look directly into her eyes. "But I trust you."

She knew it, but the words meant a lot to her. "Don't think that's going to make me go easy on you," she teased, trying to lighten the mood that had grown suddenly serious.

"So, how about it, Katie?" He waggled his eyebrows, making her laugh. "Are you going to tie me up?"

"Now?" Her X-rated fantasy bloomed in full Technicolor before her eyes. She could easily imagine him tied to the bed, spread-eagled and aroused, calling out her name as she rode him hard.

"Now," he confirmed, the wicked glint in his eyes making her shiver with anticipation.

She ran her tongue along the edge of her teeth. She could do this. She could be the confident, sensual, powerful woman of her dreams. This was going to be fun. "Take off your shirt."

His eyebrow went up. "Are you giving me orders?"

"Yes, I am. Do you have a problem with that? You had your chance to be dominant—now it's my turn."

"I wasn't pretending."

She didn't doubt it. Ryder had that kind of personality. He had a commanding presence and often managed to take over without anyone realizing it. But he was going to find out that she could also take control in the bedroom.

Katie reached for his sweatshirt and pulled it over Ryder's head with his assistance. Once he tossed the shirt over his shoulder, Katie ran her hands along the planes and indentations of his chest. She moved closer and laved her tongue against his flat brown nipples while exploring his washboard abs with her hands.

Katie bit down on his nipple and smiled when Ryder lurched. When she licked his nipple, Ryder grabbed the back of her head, threading his fingers through her long black hair. She had a feeling Ryder was not going to submit easily.

She released his nipple and looked up at his face. The desire glittering in his eyes heightened her excitement. She felt naughty and she wanted to test her limits and push her luck. "Ryder," she said sweetly, "you haven't earned the right to touch me."

His jaw dropped open before a reluctant smile tugged at his mouth. "So, you're going to play it *that* way."

"It's only fair," she told him as she reached down and rubbed his hard cock through his jeans. She cupped him and gave a hard squeeze. Ryder inhaled sharply, the air hissing through his clenched teeth. "Let go of my hair," she said.

There was a pause as he wrestled against his natural inclination. She could see the internal battle shining from his dark eyes. She gave her hand a little twist and Ryder flinched.

"Surrendering isn't easy," she said knowingly. "Now you know how I felt."

Ryder slowly untangled his hand from her hair, taking his sweet time about it. He let it be known that he was humoring her. He didn't see her as a force to be reckoned with. At least, not yet. Maybe she should bind his hands before continuing. Ryder was so much stronger and more experienced that he could take control from her if she wasn't careful.

"Lie down," she told him, knowing that she had to make her request firmly but sweetly. If she barked at him like a drill sergeant, he would quit on the spot. Katie placed her hands on his shoulders and guided him down. When he was sprawled onto the mattress she straddled his hips. Ryder placed his hands on her legs and caressed her thighs.

"Hands above your head," she ordered, hoping he would listen. Silently, he did as she asked, but his eyes still twinkled. Here she was trying to be tough and Ryder found it entertaining. How amusing would it be when he was tied to the bed, vulnerable and trusting her?

She leaned over him to cuff his wrists. Her breasts dangled enticingly over his mouth. She dipped her spine a little more than necessary to tease him. Ryder tilted his head and playfully closed his lips over her laced-covered curves.

Katie tried to focus on her task, making sure the cuffs were extra snug. It was difficult when Ryder was teasing her breasts with his mouth. When she completed the job, her nipples were tight and red, her nightie wet and transparent.

"Take off your gown," Ryder said in a husky voice.

"No." She shook her head slowly, even though the nightie no longer served as a shield. "You don't give the orders. Just for that I will *not* take off my clothes."

His eyes flashed with annoyance, but his jaw was set when he recognized those words. To her surprise, he didn't complain. He had known what he was getting into when he made this offer, but obviously he hadn't expected it would be this difficult.

Katie crawled down his body, placing random kisses on his body as she went. She allowed her long hair to drag along Ryder's chest and loved the feel of his muscles twitching beneath her.

She removed Ryder's belt before she slowly unzipped his jeans. She shoved the denim and underwear down his hips. Katie had planned to strip him bare, but at the last moment she decided to stop midway. With his clothes bunched at his knees, it restricted his movements. She wanted to heighten his sense of being trapped.

Kneeling at his side, Katie ignored Ryder's questioning look as she left his jeans dangling on his legs and focused her attention on his cock. She cupped his length with both hands and felt the tremor sweep through him.

Katie gripped him hard and pulled up, one hand after the other. She did it again and again, listening to Ryder's deep, uneven breaths. Just when he got used to the rhythm, Katie gave her tight fist a twist.

Ryder's hips vaulted from the mattress as his growl echoed in the bedroom. Was it wrong to enjoy having Ryder beneath her, unable to stop her from doing everything and anything she wanted? When lust and power mixed in her blood, it was a heady combination.

She knelt down and covered the tip of his cock with her wet

mouth. The growl transformed into a low moan. Ryder's lean hips rocked as she bumped his cock with her hands while swirling her tongue along the rounded trip.

Katie hummed with pleasure as she licked him. He tasted of hot, aroused male. She wanted more and drew him deep in her mouth. She continued to pump him with one hand as she fondled his balls with the other.

"Katie," Ryder said with a hint of warning in his voice, "if you keep doing that, this will end before it starts."

Katie reluctantly released him, his cock sliding from her mouth with a pop. It was thick and erect, curving toward his flat stomach. As much as she wanted to tease Ryder, she wanted this fantasy to last as long as possible.

She turned to face Ryder, noticing the rigid expression as he tried to hold on to his slipping control. She licked her lips and watched the ruddy color suffuse his face. "Tell me you have condoms," she said.

One of his eyebrows lifted. "After all the planning you did to get in here, you didn't remember condoms?"

"Ryder." He had better have condoms or they were going to be in for some very torturous moments.

Ryder grinned when he saw the flash of concern on her face. "In the drawer." He angled his head toward the bedside table.

Katie got off the bed and opened the drawer. "No toys?" she teased as she pulled a foil pouch from the box. "Not even a blindfold?"

"You have my blindfold," he reminded her.

"I wish I had brought it here," she said as she opened the foil and removed the condom.

He shook his head. "You would never have gotten it on me."

"Oh, I'm sure I could have convinced you," she said as she returned to the bed, giving a little naughty sway to her step.

"You couldn't even bribe me to do it."

Katie smiled as she straddled him again. She'd let him think that, but she knew differently. Ryder wouldn't have thought he'd let her tie him to his bed, and look at where he was now. She was beginning to understand just how much power and influence she had over Ryder.

But as she rolled the condom on his cock with such agonizing slowness that Ryder bucked and thrust his lean hips, Katie realized she shouldn't do anything to abuse her power. She wanted to test their boundaries, but she didn't want to cause a rift in their relationship. She wanted this kind of closeness, and she wanted moments like these when he would demonstrate his trust in her—even if she only had a couple more days to do it.

She held his cock in her hands and guided it to her slick, hot entrance. Katie watched Ryder's face as she gradually sank onto him. His hands were knotted into fists, his jaw clenched as desire blazed from his eyes.

Ryder bucked his hips to bury himself deep inside her, but this time Katie controlled the pace and she wasn't going to surrender the power. She gritted her teeth and pressed her lips together as she took all of him.

Sweat glistened on her skin and her body shivered from the intrusion. She gave a tentative rock of her hips and moaned as the pleasure whipped through her.

"More," Ryder whispered.

Katie knew she could tease him. Make him beg or even ask him to call her Mistress. She smiled at the idea, knowing it would not go over well. She knew what she wanted and that was to grant both their wishes.

Katie made small, gentle circles with her hips as she grabbed the hem of her short nightie. She looked directly into Ryder's eyes as she removed the gown inch by inch.

"Come on, Katie," Ryder said gruffly, as if restraining his primitive instincts was causing him pain. And maybe it was.

The nightie cleared her hips and she offered him a clear view of their intimate joining. Ryder reached for her and his arms snapped back. He muttered something raw and ferocious, prompting Katie to laugh.

"Not so easy, is it? Why don't you just lie there and enjoy?" she asked as she pushed her nightie over her waist and rocked her hips a little faster.

"Ride me harder," he said, his breath growing choppy.

"I will," she said as she revealed her breasts and pulled the nightie over her head. "Soon."

"Now." His tone was harsh.

She increased the pace a little, moaning as his cock rubbed a sensitive spot inside her. Again and again and again. She wasn't sure she was going to last much longer. Katie tossed her nightie to the floor and glided her hands over her body, secretly wishing it was Ryder touching her.

"Don't you wish you could touch me?" she teased Ryder as she squeezed her breasts.

His eyes darkened and he swallowed audibly. "You are a brat." He pulled at his cuffs and the headboard rattled against the wall.

She rolled her hips deeply and Ryder tensed. "You love my bratty ways," Katie declared, thrusting her breasts out and pinching the nipples.

"I think the power is getting to your head."

She rode him a little faster and slid her hands down her stomach to her hips. She brushed her hand over her clit and shuddered. "Ooh, that felt good."

"Katie, I'm going to count to three," he said in a low, dangerous growl, "and then I'm taking over."

"We'll see about that." She couldn't wait to see him try. She was sure the coup he would stage would be as successful as it was glorious. She leaned back, riding him hard as she started to rub her clit. Katie tilted her head back and moaned.

"One . . . ," Ryder said.

She grabbed her breast, pushing it up high so she could dart her tongue along the puckered nipple. She didn't look at Ryder but she heard his sharp intake of breath. She continued to rub her swollen clit with her other hand. She couldn't get enough.

"Two . . ."

Katie rolled her hips, riding him as fast as she could. She couldn't catch her breath. Every move sent a shower of sparks through her veins.

"Three!" Ryder announced and ripped his wrists from the Velcro cuffs. He sat up and grabbed Katie by the waist. Ryder ground her hips down on him and their cries mingled.

"Put your hands on my shoulders," he told her.

"I'm the one giving the orders here," she replied, tossing her long black hair away from her face.

"In case you hadn't noticed, you've been overthrown." He reached for her hands and guided them onto his shoulders. "Hold on tight."

She did as he requested. Her fingers dug into his strong shoulders as she rode him hard and fast. Ryder held on to her hips, driving his cock deeper.

Katie felt the sweet ache tightening inside her pelvis. It coiled tighter and tighter, gathering power at lightning speed. She tried to hold it off. She knew she was being greedy, but she wanted this to last.

Katie looked into Ryder's eyes, determined to hold on to this moment when they were joined as equals. She lowered her mouth against his, their lips clinging as she climaxed. The coil of need unleashed something wild inside her. She arched back and rode Ryder so fast that everything else was a blur. The sensations lashed at her and she cried out. It felt like she was splintering into shards and falling.

Katie grappled for Ryder as he tossed her onto her back. Her head dipped past the mattress as Ryder knelt between her legs. He buried his cock deep inside her, each harsh thrust wringing the climax from her body.

Ryder burrowed his face in the curve of her throat as he drove into her one last time. His hoarse shout was muffled, but Katie knew it was a cry of victory. Of relief and deep satisfaction. It was exactly how she felt.

When she could catch her breath, Katie reached down and tousled his hair. "You cheated," she felt obliged to point out.

"I gave you fair warning," he replied without an ounce of apology. "I counted to three."

She smiled down at him and was rewarded with a devilish grin in return. Katie wanted to stay like this, lying together skin against skin. She wanted to curl against Ryder and have his arms around her.

She wasn't sure what her own eyes revealed, but she saw the guarded expression creep back into Ryder's features. He cleared his throat and looked out the window.

She knew he was about to come up with a lame excuse and find a reason to get out of bed and get her out of his home. Her heart couldn't handle that. She needed to beat him to the punch.

"Well, this has been fun," Katie said in the breeziest tone she could manage, "but I'll have to go soon."

Something dark glittered in his eyes. She couldn't define it, but it made her very wary. "Is this some sort of hit-and-run?" he asked as he rolled off her and got out of bed quickly.

"I wasn't planning to spend the night," she lied. "Unless you need help packing."

That seemed to anger him even more. "No, thanks. Jake has offered to help."

"You sure you don't need an extra pair of hands?"

"I'm sure. We should get you home before he comes back." He strode out of the bedroom like a conquering warrior. A gloriously buck-naked one.

Well, she beat him to the punch, Katie thought as she watched him close the bedroom door, leaving her alone. She should be proud. So why did she feel like she had ruined a beautiful moment?

Ryder stood under the showerhead, the cold water like stinging needles against his head and shoulders. He stared at the white tiles of the shower stall as the hot anger swirled inside him. He hoped Katie was already dressed and leaving because he didn't trust this mood he was in. He would probably say something he would regret.

She didn't want to spend the night with him. Ryder couldn't understand it. Katie had gone through a great deal to sneak into his apartment and tie herself to his bed. He thought she was going to be there for good, but she wasn't looking for anything more than a couple of hours of sex. His cock was practically still inside her and she was ready to leave.

That hurt, and the reason scared him. He wanted more than sex with Katie. He enjoyed the intimacy they shared. Didn't she realize that when he let her tie him to the bed? He didn't do that for just any woman.

It hadn't been easy for him, but he had loved watching Katie take control. She was bold and naughty, and he didn't last long before he had to get his hands on her. Afterward, he wanted to hold her close and stay in bed with her all day. For a moment that need spooked him. He was getting too close, too fast. His desire for Katie overruled his caution. But before he could gather her in his arms, she was ready to hop out of bed.

It didn't matter that he had left her in the Seattle hotel. That was different. When he had sex with Katie that night he had broken the one rule he had sworn he would always uphold. He needed to distance himself. But Katie was ready to leave now because she'd gotten what she came for.

If she wanted a guy simply for sex, she could have had her pick of men in Crystal Bend. She managed to do just fine all year long. Why him? And why now?

Well, he knew the answer to that. Ryder turned off the water and stepped out of the shower. He was leaving and she hadn't been able to check him off her "Men to Do" list. If Katie thought she could get away with that, then he had better set her straight.

He reached for a towel, wrapped it around his waist and strode out of the bathroom. "Katie?" he called out as he entered the bedroom. He came to an abrupt stop when he saw the empty bed.

She had already left. Just like he thought—had hoped—she would. So why did that make him feel worse?

CHAPTER THIRTEEN

❧

December 29

The Crystal Bend Café was busy, as it was every morning. The scent of sizzling bacon, maple syrup and fresh pastries wafted from the old brick building and into the streets. It was one of the few places in town to hang out, and the café brewed a coffee that would instantly jolt you awake. Katie passed on the coffee—her nerves were already jittery.

Katie saw her friend Melissa at the cash register and waved her down. Her friend's cheeks were rosy from the cold morning, and her blond ponytail was bouncing from side to side as she made her way to the table.

"Good morning," Melissa said in a chirpy voice as she removed her red puffy vest, revealing her yellow warm-up jacket. "Isn't it beautiful outside? The sun is shining and the air is cool and crisp, perfect for jogging."

"I can't stand morning people," Hilary muttered, her red hair flopping in her face like a curtain. She burrowed deeper into her oversized gray cardigan, as if she couldn't face the day just yet. "No one in their right mind should be this happy before noon."

Melissa just smiled, which prompted a cranky growl from Hilary. She plopped down in the booth opposite Hilary and Katie. "I'm glad to see you survived the bondage club and are both back in one piece."

"You should have gone with us," Hilary said, pouring a packet of sugar into her coffee. "We were the belles of the ball."

Katie wanted to roll her eyes as she listened to Hilary's revised history. Belles of the ball? Couldn't her friend have tried to get a little closer to the truth? Like that they were so invisible nothing had happened?

"I bet you were," Melissa said as she scanned the menu. "I wish this place would offer something low-carb."

Hilary growled in the back of her throat.

"Getting a sore throat?" she asked Hilary.

"January first is two days away," Hilary informed her. "Pig out now and detox in the New Year."

"I treat my body like a temple," Melissa informed her with a haughty tilt to her chin, "not like I'm on a bender in Vegas."

Hilary arched her eyebrows. "What exactly are you trying to say? That I treat my body like a casino?"

"I wouldn't dream of saying such a thing." Melissa closed the laminated menu with a slap, as if indicating she was changing the subject. "So, how was your Seattle trip? I was worried about you guys, and when Jake and Ryder came by asking questions, I thought it was best to tell them."

"Don't worry." Katie patted Melissa's hand. "They weren't happy to find us there, but everything turned out fine."

Melissa put her elbows on the table, then looked around the crowded café before asking in a low tone, "Did you *finally* complete your New Year's resolution? And, Hilary, what about you and Jake?

Rumor around town is that you guys didn't get home until the next morning."

Katie was struck by something in Melissa's questions. She tilted her head and considered the eagerness in her friend's face. "Melissa, did you send them our way because you were worried about us, or to help us with our goals?"

"I don't know." Melissa thought about it for a moment. "Both, I guess. I figured you wouldn't mind your knights in shining armor riding out to save you."

"Did you hear any other rumors?" Hilary asked, pouring yet another sugar packet into her coffee. Katie sensed the tension in her friend. She hoped Jake hadn't revealed anything about their night in Seattle.

"I heard this strange one about Katie that didn't make much sense. Something about her dangling off a ledge half-naked to get Ryder," Melissa said and shrugged.

Katie felt the sizzling blush flooding her cheeks but chose not to say anything. She was sure she had Mrs. Graham to thank for that rumor.

"I assumed it was some kind of metaphor. Although"—Melissa wagged her eyebrows at Katie—"last night I heard something about you visiting the sex shop and coming out with a very little bag. Anything you'd like to share?"

"You know what they say." Katie leaned closer to Melissa. "Good things come in small packages."

"So you *were* there." Melissa's eyes brightened with interest. "And what's this about you dangling naked on a ledge?"

"That's not true," Katie said, waving her hand carelessly. "I was wearing lingerie."

A shadow fell on her. "Helloooo, Katie."

Katie winced as she heard Darwin Jones's voice. It was the third time in a week he had surprised her. Something was definitely off with her Darwin radar. She must be so focused on Ryder that she was blind to everything else that went on around her.

"Good for you on taking my advice," Darwin said, leaning his hip against her booth and giving her a close-up of his belt buckle. Today he wore the one that spelled out "Stud" in gold and rhinestones.

"I . . . did?" Darwin gave her advice? What was he talking about?

"You went to the sex shop," he reminded her in a booming voice. Katie sensed people turning their heads, but she wasn't going to look around to confirm it. "But why didn't you call me? I would have been glad to show you around."

"That's okay," Katie said politely. "I managed all on my own. It was so nice seeing you, but—"

"And you were supposed to call me the other night," Darwin complained, not taking the hint that she wanted to talk to her friends alone. "What happened?"

Katie narrowed her eyes as she tried to follow what he had just said. She really had no idea what he was talking about. "I was? I don't remember that."

"When I gave Hilary the directions to the bondage club," Darwin explained, gesturing toward her redheaded friend. "I gave her my cell phone number so we could hook up. That was the price for my information."

Katie gave Hilary a threatening look. She had made a deal with Darwin to hang out with him? Was she nuts? "Is that right?"

Hilary shifted uncomfortably in her seat. "Must have slipped my mind," she muttered against her coffee cup and took a big swallow.

"I could have gotten you the VIP treatment," Darwin confided, slicking back his already slicked-back hair, "but I didn't see you until Ryder carried you out."

"He carried you out?" Melissa repeated, her eyes widening. "Were you drunk?"

"I would have stopped him," Darwin said, puffing out his chest, his tight TV test pattern sweater stretching to the limit, "but when he claimed you as his own, I couldn't interfere. You know the rules."

"Here comes Ryder now," Hilary said, perking up. "He doesn't look happy that you're talking to his woman."

Katie saw Darwin turn several shades of green as Ryder strode from the cash register to where she was sitting. Her heart did a funny little flip as she watched his approach. Wearing a black hoodie, jeans and hiking boots, he wasn't dressed to impress, but it didn't matter. Ryder Scott was a force of nature in this tiny café, and his dark masculine beauty took her breath away.

Ryder towered over their table and gave a nod of acknowledgment to her and her friends before focusing all of his attention on the hapless Darwin. The men were the same height, but Darwin seemed so insignificant next to Ryder. Darwin was heavier, but Ryder moved with such a lethal grace it was obvious that he could take Darwin down in a split second.

"Jones." Ryder's low, husky greeting hinted at the anger roiling underneath the surface.

Darwin gave a wheezing cough. "Ryder. I was telling Katie—"

"I heard what you were saying to Katie." Ryder didn't move closer, but there was something in his voice that made Darwin lean back. "And you must have been mistaken."

"M-m-mistaken?"

"Ryder, you don't have to concern yourself with this." Katie tried to inject herself in the conversation before Darwin lost all bladder control.

Ryder didn't listen to her. He kept his laser focus on Darwin, who was beginning to perspire. "I don't like it when people gossip about Katie."

"It's not gossip," Darwin babbled nervously. "I saw her."

Ryder leaned forward and lowered his voice. "Be very careful about what you decide to say next."

Darwin paled and Katie decided she'd had enough. As much as she appreciated Ryder's protection, he didn't need to traumatize guys like Darwin. She slid out of the booth and stood between the two men.

She flattened her hand on Ryder's chest. "Ryder, leave Darwin alone. He meant no harm."

Ryder glanced down at her. His expression hadn't changed. She knew why Darwin was sweating bullets, but she wasn't afraid. "Sit down, Katie."

"No."

Displeasure flickered in his eyes. "Katie"—he wrapped his hand around her wrist and pulled down her hand—"I need to talk to you. Privately."

She gave a sigh of impatience and looked over her shoulder. "I'll be right back," she promised her friends.

Ryder ran his hands through his hair as he escorted Katie away from the table.

Just when Darwin slumped against the booth and sighed, Ryder backtracked and stared down at the other man. "I got my eye on you now, Jones." Then Ryder kept walking, not waiting around for Darwin's reaction. He knew his words would have a strong effect.

"You don't have to intimidate Darwin like that," Katie whispered fiercely as Ryder guided her past the other tables. "He's annoying, but he doesn't mean any harm."

"You shouldn't lead him on like that," Ryder said in a harsh and low voice, his self-control slipping. He stopped into the alcove with the pay phone next to the restrooms. Katie needed to understand why she drove him crazy. "Do you need to have every man in Crystal Bend panting after you?"

"Lead him on?" Katie's jaw dropped. "I do not! I'm trying to be nice because I don't want to hurt his feelings."

"Stop encouraging him," Ryder ordered. It amazed him that Katie didn't understand her sex appeal with other men. "Don't talk to Jones, don't look in his direction, and stop smiling at him."

"Oh, you are being ridiculous." She put her hands on her hips and glared at him. "I am not going to be rude to Darwin because you're jealous."

Ryder's eyes widened. "Jealous of *Darwin*?" His voice rose in disbelief. "Now who is being ridiculous?"

It sounded ridiculous. Outrageous. And yet, he knew there was some truth to it. Katie had chosen to be with him right now and he didn't want any guy—even Darwin—intruding on his time with her. He was a possessive man and he didn't share. At all.

"Darwin is *not* harmless. I heard everything he said the moment I walked in here," Ryder continued. The guy was lucky he'd held back, because otherwise Darwin would be kissing the sidewalk right now. "Everyone heard him. I did what I had to do in order to protect your reputation."

Katie rolled her eyes. "You're trying to protect my reputation? In case you haven't noticed, I didn't have much of one until this year."

Oh, he'd noticed all right. He'd noticed the guys she dated and hated every minute of it. But she was his now and that meant he protected everything about her, including her reputation.

She gave him a sharp, sudden look. "Unless it's your reputation that's really worrying you."

He scoffed at the suggestion. "I don't care about that." He never had. Katie should know that.

"But you don't want people to know about us, do you? Am I your dirty little secret?" she asked, crossing her arms, as if the possibility hurt. "You can give it to me straight, Ryder. I can handle it."

Ryder rubbed his hands over his face, digging the heels of his palms against his eyes. How had he gotten into this conversation? One minute he was warning her about the dangers of Darwin and the next he was defending himself. "You could never be anyone's dirty little secret."

"Thanks, I think."

Ryder lowered his hands. "I don't care what people say about me, but I do care what they say about you." Didn't she understand that he wanted to protect her from prying eyes?

His motives weren't completely noble. He didn't want her to have a single moment of regret over what they experienced together. Some people in town would gladly pick at what he shared with Katie. He would keep the ugliness at bay for as long as he could, giving their relationship some time to bind and strengthen, so that when he left, Katie would remember him with love and affection.

"I can take care of myself," Katie insisted. "My methods are different, but they are just as effective."

"I'm trying to protect what we have," Ryder said, splaying his hands in the air to emphasize his point. "You don't approve of my methods? Too bad. I will do what I think is necessary.

"I will not have your reputation dirtied because my name is associated with yours," he continued. Ryder pointed toward the tables in the café. "Right now, no one other than Darwin is going to give you trouble because I'm around. Once I leave, it's going to be a different story."

Katie pressed her lips together and looked away. He couldn't tell what she was thinking, but it looked like she was trying not to cry. Okay, what had he done now? "Katie? Are you listening to me?"

She turned to face him. "Yes, I am." Her eyes dulled and the expression on her face was blank. Katie's words were clipped as she kept her gaze straight ahead at his chest. "I promise I won't do anything to encourage the rumors. Is that all?"

He watched her carefully, trying to figure out why she was guarding her emotions from him. Katie was someone who argued passionately and challenged him every step of the way. He had never felt like she was mentally pushing him aside until now. He suddenly felt cold.

"And stay away from Darwin," he ordered, waiting for a flicker of spirit in her eyes. None came.

"I will do my best," she promised with a tight smile. "But we just gave everyone in the café something to talk about. How about if you leave first and I'll follow in a couple of minutes?" She headed toward the restroom. "Who are you with?"

"I owe Jake breakfast, but he's late as usual," Ryder answered, watching her carefully. She was cool, distant and agreeable. That wasn't good.

"I'll eat fast and get out of here," she offered.

"Forget it," Ryder said with an impatient growl and walked away from her. "I'll do takeout. Jake won't mind." How was it that she had agreed to do what he asked, but he still felt like he'd lost a major battle?

Katie watched him leave. She exhaled shakily and entered the women's restroom. As she washed her hands, taking time to recover, she looked at her reflection in the mirror. She was surprised to see how composed she appeared. No watery eyes, pale complexion or red cheeks advertising how stressed she felt.

And she was stressed, Katie admitted as she turned off the faucet and grabbed a paper towel. This should have been a wonderful time for her because the man she loved was in her life and in her bed. She should be happy. Walking tall. Freaking glowing. But he was still determined to leave.

And that didn't make any sense. She wadded up the towel and viciously threw it in the wastebasket. He'd already given in to temptation, so why was he still planning to move? Wasn't that like closing the barn door after the horses escaped? There had to be something else going on. How was she going to figure it out before he left in two days?

No wonder she was stressed! She tightened her long ponytail until her scalp tingled with pain. Straightening her pink leopard-print hoodie over her sparkly black yoga pants, Katie glanced down at her pink athletic shoes and groaned. Maybe Hilary had a valid point about the height of her heels reflecting her mood.

She flung open the bathroom door. Calm down, she reminded herself. Chin up and shoulders back. She knew people would look at her the moment she went back out on the floor. She was going to show the whole of Crystal Bend that she was unaffected by their attention.

Just as she passed the alcove, Katie collided with another person.

Great entrance. What's your encore going to be? She felt big hands grab her arms to keep her from falling down.

"Darwin!" She noticed he wasn't as pale or sweaty anymore. The guy managed to bounce back fast. "I'm sorry. I wasn't looking where I was going. Are you all right?"

Darwin scoffed at her question and moved, guiding them back into the alcove. "I'm fine. I wanted to check on you and let you know that I have your back."

"You have my back?" She pressed her lips together and gave a solemn nod. "Thank you, but it's not necessary." She tried to step away but Darwin didn't let go.

"And anytime you want to go to the bondage club, just call me." He leered. "You can be my special guest."

Okay, *now* it was time to follow Ryder's advice. She placed her hand on his chest, and pulled it away when she decided it would be too encouraging. "No, thank you. I saw enough of the club to know that lifestyle is not for me."

"It's okay," Darwin said, glancing up at the ceiling. "Ryder won't be around to complain."

"What are you looking at?" Katie looked up and saw that all this time Darwin had been positioning her under something leafy and green hanging from the ceiling by a floppy red bow. Mistletoe. "Oh, you have got to be kidding me. Do you have a death wish?"

Darwin didn't answer as he smothered her mouth with a wet, sloppy kiss. Katie wondered why she was never wearing those killer boots when she needed to kick someone hard. She pushed Darwin away and he went flying.

That surprised her, and just as she was questioning her own strength, she saw Ryder holding Darwin by the back of his test pattern sweater. Darwin's feet weren't kicking in the air, but his toes were barely touching the floor.

She saw fury tightening Ryder's harsh features. She held out her hands in a placating manner. "Ryder, it's okay. I have this under control."

"Oh, yeah. I can see that. Jones had you backed up in a corner and was making unwanted advances."

"No!" Darwin's voice squeaked. "It doesn't count if there's mistletoe involved."

Ryder reached up and tore the sprig of mistletoe from the ceiling with barely restrained violence. "Do you know what you can do with this mistletoe?"

"Ryder!" Katie said urgently, yanking at his arm. "You don't want to cause a scene."

"You're right. Let's take this outside, Jones."

Fear twisted Darwin's face as Ryder dragged him through the café and out the door. Katie followed their trail, aware of heads turning and the murmurs of shock. After all the intimidation Ryder used on her dates in high school, Katie should have had enough experience to defuse the situation. But something was very different this time. Ryder truly saw Darwin as a trespasser.

She walked outside and yanked at Ryder's arm before he laid a hand on Darwin. "Ryder, please stop."

He didn't lower his fist, but he didn't shrug her off. "I told you not to encourage him."

"He isn't going to talk to me ever again. Isn't that right, Darwin?" She caught Darwin's gaze and nodded with exaggeration, prompting him to answer correctly.

"Right," Darwin said, hunching his shoulders. "I didn't know Katie was yours. She never said."

Oh, right. Like this was all her fault for not wearing a T-shirt that said "the personal property of Ryder Scott." She swallowed back a retort, knowing the situation would be resolved faster if neither man lost face in this showdown.

"There, you see, Ryder?" She pulled at his arm. "No harm, no foul. Now put Darwin down."

Ryder let Darwin go abruptly. The man took a giant step back and straightened his sweater. "I-I—"

"Why are you still here?" Ryder asked him coldly.

Darwin gulped, turned and ran.

"He runs away fast," Katie remarked with surprise. The guy was already on the next block.

"He's had a lot of practice," Ryder replied, looking at her instead of the retreating Darwin. "You didn't correct him."

Katie rolled her head with exasperation. "I didn't expect him to make a move after you scared him. I thought he had more brains than pride."

"He said you were mine, and you didn't argue." He placed a finger under her chin and lifted her head. She couldn't avoid his gaze.

"I am yours," she replied. Her heart skipped a beat and then went into overdrive.

"Is that right?" His eyes narrowed on her lips.

"Don't make me have to prove it," she teased him, but he didn't smile. He pressed his thumb against her lips and slid it hard across the length of her mouth. He wiped away her smeared lipstick and, she suspected, Darwin's claim.

Ryder held her chin tight, as if she might try to get away. When was he going to learn that she wasn't going anywhere? Ryder claimed her mouth with a possessive kiss. She put her hands on his shoulders, wanting to lean into him, melt into his heat, when they were interrupted.

"What the hell?"

Katie broke away from the kiss. She recognized the voice and it had the effect of a bucket of cold water. Still, she had to turn to confirm that her mind wasn't playing tricks.

Jake stood next to them on the sidewalk outside the café. He was staring, stunned, his face flushed. And she had never seen him so angry.

CHAPTER FOURTEEN

Katie stared at her brother, the cold breeze whipping her hair in her eyes. Her stomach twisted into knots so tight she felt nauseated.

Driven by instinct, Katie moved between Ryder and Jake. She didn't consider it a courageous move. She knew her brother and Ryder wouldn't hurt her. But they might hurt each other. The tension emanating from Ryder was nothing like the dark emotions rolling in waves from her brother. She had to keep this from coming to blows and prevent any angry words that could never be taken back.

She would do whatever it took to protect Ryder. He might think that was unnecessary, but she knew he was suffering. Jake was his best friend and Ryder couldn't bear the thought of hurting him. She wished she could have done something to keep him from this confrontation, but she wasn't going to waste time agonizing over something she couldn't change. Katie faced Jake defiantly, her arms outstretched in a protective gesture. She sensed the men's surprise at her stance.

"Jake," she began, holding his gaze and refusing to back down from the anger she saw, "I can explain."

"I can figure this one out on my own," Jake said, his voice carrying a bite. Jake braced his legs and stuffed his hands in the pockets of his thick red hoodie. "How long has this been going on?"

It was a simple question, but Katie wasn't sure how to answer it. She wasn't going to admit anything until she knew what Ryder's story would be. So far he had offered her no clue. He was silent, not saying a word in his defense. Why had he withdrawn into himself? She had never seen Ryder unsure of how to act before.

"I don't know what you're talking about," she said and blew the hair from her face. When in doubt, play dumb. It had worked for Katie at the office countless times, but it wasn't so successful in this situation. Her answer only seemed to anger Jake even more. He slowly took his hands out of his pockets and Katie wondered if he was about to make a move.

She sensed the tension escalating in Ryder. She didn't have to look at him to know he was ready to pounce. Katie figured she only had a few more moments to settle things before Ryder took over and ended it his way.

"Since Seattle?" Jake asked. "When you guys shared a hotel room? I should have known!"

Katie didn't answer. She wasn't going to discuss what had happened in that hotel room with her brother. That was a private, intimate moment between Ryder and her. Katie saw a movement from the corner of her eye. She looked and saw curious faces pressed against the café window. So much for not causing a scene.

"*Before* Seattle?" Jake asked in a raised voice.

She winced and bit her lower lip. The cold was seeping into her bones. Oh, how was she going to answer this and not land herself in deeper trouble?

"Wait a second." Comprehension hit Jake and his hands curled into fists at his side. He looked at Katie with horror. "That night when Ryder asked me to drop by the house. You were—" He gestured at her, his hands flying in every direction. "You were— *Eww!*"

"Hey!" She pointed at her brother. "Now, that is just uncalled for."

Suddenly Katie felt Ryder's hands circling her waist. She flinched and tried to pluck his fingers off her. Had Ryder gone crazy? Didn't he realize that this was the *worst* time to indulge in public displays of affection?

But Ryder wasn't getting her message as his hold tightened. He lifted her up effortlessly. Katie squawked with surprise, her fingers digging into his as he physically removed her from the line of fire.

"What are you doing?" she called out, her legs swinging wildly in the air. "Put me down!"

Ryder set her gently on the ground and stood in front of her. She moved to the left and Ryder blocked her, without even looking in her direction. His attention was directed straight at Jake. She sighed and moved to the right, but Ryder anticipated that, too.

"Say what you want to me," he told Jake, his voice raspy and low, "but you will not talk like that to Katie."

"Aww!"

Melissa's voice jolted Katie. She looked in the direction of the café's front door and saw her friends blocking the entrance, watching from a safe distance. Melissa's hands were clasped to her chest, her eyes wide, mouth slack, totally enamored with Ryder's protective display. Hilary stood on the top step, dipping her toast in a little plastic jam container.

Katie placed her hand on Ryder's shoulder blade. "I have this under control," she said softly. "Maybe you should leave."

"I don't think so," Ryder replied, not taking his eyes off Jake.

"I'm not leaving and you definitely don't have this under control. It was against my instincts to let you do the talking, but I thought this was between brother and sister. I should have known better."

"Maybe you should leave." Jake glared at his friend. "I was talking to Katie before you interrupted."

Oh, here we go. This had to be Ryder's biggest nightmare coming to life. He hadn't acted on his desire for her because she was Jake's little sister. Ryder and Jake had been the best of friends for as long as anyone could remember. But she couldn't be sure that their friendship wouldn't crack under the strain of this test. Katie didn't want to be responsible for driving a wedge between them.

"Katie, come here." Jake snapped his fingers and pointed at the spot next to him. "I want to talk to you alone."

Katie bristled but didn't move. She did not appreciate that tone at all. Especially in front of Ryder and her friends. Not to mention half the town.

"She's not going anywhere," Ryder said. He didn't hold on to her, and he didn't make any move to keep her behind him. Maybe he knew he didn't have to.

The tug-of-war had already started. Lines were drawn. She felt like a bone being fought for between two dogs. And as much as she appreciated family ties, her loyalty was with Ryder.

"Jake," she said from over Ryder's shoulder, "whatever you have to say to me, you can say in front of Ryder."

"Oh, to hell with this." Jake reached around Ryder and grabbed Katie's arm.

Katie didn't even have time to protest when she saw Ryder's grip on Jake's wrist. She had to get Jake away from Ryder. "Ryder, please," she said softly, hating how her voice quavered. "Let me talk to Jake for a minute."

Ryder seemed to be frozen on the spot. She could see the tremor in his arm. She knew he was fighting back his instinct again because of her. He wasn't happy with her request, but he wouldn't deny her anything. Ryder suddenly let go of Jake and looked at Katie. His expression was ice cold. "You have two minutes and then I'm coming after you."

Katie heard Melissa's sigh of approval and ignored it. Her friend didn't realize that it wasn't so much of a promise as it was a warning. She gave a short, choppy nod to Ryder and allowed her brother to yank her arm as they headed to the corner and turned. "You've made your point," she hissed at Jake. "You can let me go now."

He didn't listen. "Parking lot. Now."

"I have had enough of your attitude." She jerked her arm from her brother's grasp. "You are blowing this all out of proportion."

He stopped where his bright red truck was parked behind the café. "How is that?"

She flattened her hands on her chest. "I may be your little sister, but I'm a twenty-five-year-old woman. Your concern is a little late and completely misplaced."

"You have known Ryder forever. You know all about him." He tossed his hands in the air. "What the hell were you thinking?"

Katie straightened to her full height. She was still shorter than Jake, but she knew she had right on her side. "Believe it or not, what I do or don't do with Ryder is no concern of yours."

"He is my best friend!" Jake gestured in the direction where they had left Ryder. "I watch his back, even if it means keeping him away from you."

"What? What are you saying?" She was getting this all wrong. Jake wasn't worried about *her* well-being. He was worried about *Ryder's*. Katie stared at him, dumbfounded.

Jake held up both hands, pinching his thumb and forefingers. "Let me explain it to you in teeny-tiny sentences and itty-bitty words."

"Watch your mouth, Jake," she warned her brother, glaring at him through narrowed eyes. "It's been a while, but I can still wrestle you to the ground."

Jake wasn't listening. "You wanted to date different guys this year, that's fine, even though you dated my *boss*. After all, who am I to get in the way? But you have no right to play games with Ryder."

She put her hands on her hips. "Was there a 'hands-off Ryder' policy I wasn't aware of?"

"Yes!" He stomped his foot, the last of the slushy snow spraying from the impact. "It's understood! Ryder has a soft spot when it comes to you. And what do you do? You use it to your advantage!"

"What do you mean by a soft spot?"

"What do you think?" he asked, his voice raising an octave. "He's got this totally wrong idea about you. That you're sweet and adorable." Jake rolled his eyes.

"I can be if I put my mind to it." But she knew what Jake was saying. She wasn't sweet. She had told Ryder that, but he didn't believe her.

"I don't know why," Jake said, "but you represent something very special and elusive to Ryder. And what do you do? You are using him for sex."

Katie found that a very uncharitable opinion. "That's very rich, coming from you."

"At least I'm honest about it. The women I date know that I'm only interested in one thing."

Katie wanted Ryder in her bed, but she was looking for more than that. She wanted an intimate, loving relationship. Why was that so hard to see? "You don't know how I feel about Ryder."

"Yeah, I do. You've been throwing yourself at him since high school. It was funny at first, not to mention embarrassing. Then it got annoying. I never thought it would cause serious trouble."

"You mean you didn't think I'd be successful," Katie tossed out. She started to walk away. She was so fed up with her brother.

"You still don't get it. Ryder is a very vulnerable guy."

She stopped in her tracks and looked over her shoulder. Jake looked like he had just betrayed his brother for saying that. He was lucky Ryder hadn't heard him.

"*Ryder?*" Katie asked. "No one messes with him. He's strong and—"

"And hurt," Jake finished for her. "You know his history. You know that his mom's never been there for him and he's had to fend for himself since he was a teenager. That messes with a guy's head."

"I'm not going to hurt him." She couldn't believe she had to explain that to Jake.

"No, you're in it for some fun and action." Jake looked at her with disgust. "So help me, you better be careful with him. Treat him wrong and I will never forgive you."

Katie watched, stunned, as her brother climbed into his truck and slammed the door. "Where are you going?" she asked as he turned the ignition.

"I'll be damned if I'll sit back and watch you wrap Ryder around your little finger." He gunned the engine and drove off, wheels squealing.

She didn't move as she watched him leave. He swerved out of the parking lot and the back of his truck fishtailed. Stomping on the gas, he turned out of sight. Katie rubbed her forehead, the ache blooming at her temples.

Well, she hadn't expected this. Katie lowered her hands and took a deep breath. She knew that Jake would not calmly accept Ryder and her as a couple. She'd predicted that he would shout and fuss and make his opinion known. But she didn't think, not in a million years, that he would accuse *her* of taking advantage of Ryder.

She crossed her arms tightly and stared at the graffiti on the back wall of the café without really seeing the colors and shapes. She had to calm herself down before she saw anyone, especially Ryder, but then he could probably take one look at her and know exactly what was going through her mind.

As much as she admired Jake for looking out for Ryder, his interpretation of her actions hurt. She wasn't after Ryder just for the sex. It had developed into so much more than that. And anyway, what kind of person did her brother take her for? She might not be the sexiest woman in the area, but she didn't need to go through all this for a good lay.

But what really stunned her was that Jake was more worried about Ryder's feelings than he was about hers. Ryder was insistent on leaving town in two days and not looking back. She was going to be left here, abandoned and heartbroken. Was her brother too blind to see something so obvious?

She saw Melissa's head pop around the corner of the café. Katie jumped, slapping her hand over her pounding heart.

"Are you okay?" Melissa asked.

Katie hurried over to her friend. "How long have you been standing there?" She didn't want anyone to hear Jake's words about her, but it was more important to her that no one knew what Jake said about Ryder.

"I saw Jake leave like a bat out of hell and thought I should check on you." She wrapped her arm around Katie's shoulders. "And I really couldn't take much more of Ryder's pacing. It's like watching a caged tiger."

"I bet." She walked down the short sidewalk with her friend. "Sorry I caused such a scene."

"Oh, stop worrying. It isn't your fault. And so what if you are now the talk of the town? It'll die down in a couple of days."

Katie winced when she heard that. She could imagine the café buzzing. The people were probably still staring out the window as if they were watching a sporting event. "Ryder was doing his best to keep that from happening."

"Then Ryder shouldn't have kissed you passionately in front of the breakfast crowd on Main Street."

"Good point," Katie said with a smile. Ryder hadn't cared where they were when he kissed her. She wondered if that was a sign of her getting under his skin and making him lose control.

She turned the corner with Melissa. Just as her friend had described, Ryder was pacing the sidewalk. She noticed that his agitation didn't mar his athletic grace. He turned and came to a halt when he saw her.

"Hey, Katie," Hilary said as she walked down the café's front steps. "What did Jake do?"

"He just yelled a lot. Nothing I'm not used to." She waved off the concern, but she felt knots building in her stomach as she looked at Ryder. Ryder's reaction was worrying her a lot more than Jake's.

Ryder's body tensed at the sight of Katie. He studied her face for a clue about how she was feeling. He *knew* he shouldn't have let things get this far—he couldn't bear to see her looking so hurt when it was all his fault. "What did Jake say?"

"Oh, the usual." Katie gave a shrug. "You're his best friend . . .

yadda, yadda, yadda. I'm not so sweet. Blah, blah, blah. I'm not good enough for you. . . ."

Ryder flinched and took a step back. Jake had said that? That was harsh. He had thought Jake was mad at *him*, but he was mad at Katie! That was uncalled for and Ryder couldn't let it go unchecked. Maybe he should appreciate Jake protecting him, but he didn't. Not when Jake thought Katie was the opponent. Ryder wanted Jake to always put Katie first. Always. No matter what. The moment he saw Katie home, he was going to hunt Jake down and make sure that happened from this moment on. Jake had to start looking out for her after Ryder left town, otherwise she'd be all alone.

"He. Did. Not," Melissa said. "What kind of brother would—"

Jake would, Ryder thought as disappointment crashed through him. He saw the flash of pain in Katie's eyes and it nearly undid him.

"Come on, Melissa." He vaguely heard Hilary urging Katie's other friend toward the café. "Let's finish breakfast and give these guys some space so they can get their story straight."

Get their story straight? Ryder frowned at Melissa's choice of words. He didn't need any story. There was no need to lie about him and Katie. As much as he wanted to protect her, the truth was out and he wasn't going to hide it. All he had to do was explain to Jake that blood was thicker than water.

Melissa's eyes narrowed with confusion. She looked at Katie, then Ryder, then back at Hilary. "What are you talking about? What stories?"

So Katie didn't kiss and tell. Interesting. He would have pegged her as the type who was generous with the details. Was their time together too special to her to share? Maybe that was wishful thinking on his part, but he liked his spin on it.

"Never mind and just come on." She pushed Melissa toward the café entrance.

Ryder kept his eye on Katie, who looked increasingly uncomfortable with him. She was studying him beneath her lashes, clearly trying to gauge his mood.

Katie crossed one arm over her chest and held her other arm at her side. It was an awkward position that mirrored her discomfort. "I didn't realize that I was so selfish pursuing you," she said in a soft voice that only he could hear.

Ryder blinked with surprise. Katie was never selfish! "You weren't." What the hell else had Jake said to his sister?

Katie looked down at the sidewalk. "All this time I've been trying to prove that I'm the best woman—the only woman—for you," she said with a wry twist of her lips.

"You never had to prove it," he said. He already knew, whether he liked it or not. At times he felt like she was the worst, definitely the most dangerous woman for him. But that had never stopped him from wanting her.

"Oh. My. God." Melissa's blaring voice carried down the sidewalk. Katie's mouth twitched with clear annoyance. Ryder glanced at Melissa and found her staring back as if Katie had sprouted another head. What was going on now?

Melissa pointed at Katie, ignoring how Hilary was trying to get her inside. "I just figured it out! You guys slept together! Why didn't you tell me? To punish me because I couldn't keep the whole bondage club thing a secret?"

Ryder closed his eyes as he heard the buzz in the café. First Darwin and now Melissa. By the time he left Crystal Bend, Katie was going to have the worst reputation in town. He opened his eyes in time to see every head turning to look out the café window.

"Gee, Melissa," Hilary said. "Could you speak a little louder? I don't think the people in Idaho caught all that."

Melissa clapped her hand over her mouth as she blushed. "I'm sorry." She dropped her hand, ran back toward them and threw her arms around Katie's neck. "But this is great. This is—"

Ryder couldn't care less about how Melissa felt. His and Katie's relationship was none of Melissa's business. He was busy trying to convince Katie that she hadn't ruined his life. This was the trouble with small towns. Everybody interfered, interrupted and influenced every conversation.

Katie pushed Melissa away and waved both her hands, as if trying to get her friend to stop talking. Ryder frowned at Katie's gesture. It was usually a sign of someone trying to stop information spilling out. What was she trying to keep quiet?

"Okay, Melissa," Katie said as something that sounded like panic raised her voice. "We got it. You're happy for us. Why don't you go inside now?"

Ryder slowly looked from Katie to Melissa and Hilary. He felt the undercurrents between the friends and he didn't like it. Melissa's joy was out of place. What did they know that he didn't? What were they keeping from him?

"What's going on?" he asked Katie. He saw the flash of guilt before her cheeks flushed red.

"But this is reason to celebrate!" Melissa gave a congratulatory slap to Katie's back. "You actually completed your New Year's resolution!"

Ryder stilled. New Year's resolution? What was Melissa talking about? New Year's wasn't for another couple of days. Unless . . .

His world slowly stopped moving. Having sex with him was Katie's New Year's resolution? *That* was what all this was about?

"What did she say?" he asked hoarsely, his gaze fixed on Katie's face.

Katie stared helplessly at him, and he knew he hadn't gotten it wrong. He'd risked every important relationship he had, broke his code of honor and gave Katie the wild affair she asked for.

All for a stupid New Year's resolution.

"You were cutting it close," Melissa continued, oblivious to the growing tension. "Only two days left, but you did it! High five, girlfriend!"

Ryder stared at Katie. He couldn't believe he'd fallen for all her tricks. Maybe Jake was right about her. She wasn't so sweet. In fact, she knew just how to hurt him.

CHAPTER FIFTEEN

Katie was horrified. Melissa often got in trouble for saying the wrong thing at the wrong time, but Katie never thought she'd act *this* dumb. Why couldn't she keep her big mouth shut? Now everything was ruined!

Melissa kept her hands up for a few seconds until she realized no one was in a celebratory mood. She curled her fingers in her palm and hesitantly lowered her hand. "Did I just say something I shouldn't have?" she asked in a small voice.

Hilary snorted. "Understatement of the year."

Ryder's gaze never left Katie's face. It felt like he was searching for something underneath the surface. "New Year's resolution?" he repeated dully.

Katie nervously licked her lips. How could she possibly repair the damage? "You are more to me than—"

He lifted his hand to stop the excuse bubbling past her lips. "It's a yes-or-no question, Katie. Was I your New Year's resolution?"

She couldn't get out of this. She had to tell him the truth, and she didn't even have the courage to look him in the eye. Katie glanced away and focused her attention where his truck was parked a few spaces behind him. "Yes."

Ryder didn't move a muscle. The quiet seemed to screech down her spine like nails on a blackboard. Katie looked up at him from below her eyelashes and then wished she hadn't. He held himself erect and proud, as if he would crumple if he moved. The pain shone in his dark eyes and was etched in his face. He suddenly looked older.

"My resolution was about more than sex. I wasn't aiming for a one-night stand or a fling," she hastily explained.

"Really?" he drawled. "Your actions for the past week have said otherwise."

She frowned, trying to remember. "When?"

"When you tied yourself to my bed," he reminded her. "You announced you hadn't planned to spend the night."

Melissa jerked her head, her face turning bright red. It was only then that Katie remembered Melissa was still standing right there. She felt Melissa's shocked look before Melissa scurried backward to give them some privacy.

"That—that—" Katie exhaled with frustration and tried again. "You can't use that against me. I only said that because it seemed you were going to kick me out of bed. I was protecting myself."

"It wasn't obvious to me." Ryder dipped his head and rubbed his hands over his face. "Why would you make me your New Year's resolution?"

"You make it sound like it's a bad thing."

He lifted his head and gave her a look of disbelief. "That's because it is! How would you have felt if I'd made a resolution to get you into my bed?"

She put her hands on her hips and thrust out her chin. "Honored?"

"Think again." Ryder shook his head. "This is like making a bet or putting me on a to-do list. You weren't being honest. You used me so you could cross the event off and move to the next item."

"Oh, please." He had no idea what she'd been through just to make the resolution, to even write it down. It was scary to decide to go after your greatest fantasy, knowing that you could go all out for it and never have it granted. "You act like it was so easy and unemotional. You have no idea how much courage it took just to flirt with you."

His face tightened and his jaw was rigid. "I'm sorry it was such a hardship," he said in a hoarse whisper.

Katie gasped when she realized what Ryder was thinking. Didn't he know that she desired him so much it scared her? "You are twisting my words. I made you a New Year's resolution because I have—" She pulled back just in the nick of time. "I have wanted you for years and I was too shy to act on it."

"You didn't have any problems this week."

"That's because having a New Year's resolution pushed me out of my comfort zone," she said. "But I still wasn't making any headway. When I found out you were leaving for good, then I knew I had to do something drastic or I would regret it forever."

He kept shaking his head. He couldn't even look at her. "A New Year's resolution," he muttered. "A freaking New Year's resolution. And all this time I thought you were so sweet."

Just because she was shy and invisible, people automatically thought she was sweet. And now it sounded like that was the kind of fantasy girl Ryder actually wanted. "I can be sweet," she said. It just didn't come naturally.

"You told me you weren't, and I didn't believe you." He looked up in the sky and shook his head. "What a fool I was!"

"Ryder, I am so sorry." She grabbed for his arm, wanting him to stop and listen, really listen to her. "I didn't mean to hurt your feelings."

He slowly looked down at her hand on his arm. Most people would have been smart enough to snatch it away, but she needed to hold on to him before he slipped through her fingers forever.

He gave her a sidelong glance. "How did you think I would feel?"

"I don't know." She hadn't really considered it, but in all honesty, she hadn't thought he would ever find out. "I thought you might have found it funny or cute. You might even have been flattered."

"Cute?" His tone sharpened, and his eyes were dark and stormy. "I risked my friendship with Jake to be with you."

Katie paled. She was slowly realizing just how foolish she'd been.

Ryder flicked her hand off his arm. "I tested my relationship with your parents. The very people who took me in and asked for nothing in return. And you thought I would have found your motivations *funny*?"

Kate flinched. When he put it like that, she seemed like the bitchiest, most selfish woman he could ever come across. "I would never have asked you to make that kind of choice," she said, shame-faced.

He towered over her. "I never thought to ask *why* there was an urgency for you to be in my bed. I thought it was because you couldn't wait to be with me."

"That was true, but you were also leaving town," she insisted. "What else was I supposed to do?" She tilted her head to meet his eyes. "This New Year's resolution was not as coldhearted as you think."

"What was the resolution?" he asked, his eyes glittering savagely, his voice quieter than she'd ever heard it. "Tell me, Katie. Word for word."

"Ummm . . ." She hesitated to tell him, not sure how he would interpret it. She'd really walked into this one. "Well, if you hear it out of context it—".

"Word for word."

Katie's shoulders sagged in defeat. "To have a wild love affair with Ryder Scott."

His whole body flinched. He was fighting to keep his emotions in. The struggle was so fierce that he went pale.

Katie knew she should have lied, but she wasn't good at thinking on her feet. She could easily figure out that he had a huge problem with the word "affair." Had he heard the word "love" before it?

All this time she had used that terminology because she was afraid to reach for the impossible. She didn't want to ask for something more substantial and permanent because she was afraid she wouldn't get it. She had played it safe and now that decision was going to haunt her.

Ryder abruptly turned his back to her and silently walked to his truck.

"Ryder? Where are you going?" She followed him. "You can't just walk off in the middle of an argument."

"Watch me."

"I made a resolution to get closer to you," she insisted. "There is no reason to punish me for it."

"You made a resolution to have sex with me," he corrected her as he got into his truck. "Mission accomplished. Cross it off your list and focus on the next item, because we have nothing more to say."

"I have plenty to say." She marched over to the driver's side of his truck. "You are the one who had sex with me knowing you were going to leave a few days later."

He didn't look at her as he turned the ignition. "You knew it, too."

"So how are your actions different from mine?" She tried to open the truck door, but he had already locked it.

"Because I didn't set out to seduce you," he said, looking down at her. His eyes were dead, his voice low but neutral. "I didn't decide to turn your life upside down just to scratch an itch. And I wasn't the one who thought our 'wild love affair' meant there would be no consequences."

She closed her eyes in defense. There was that "no consequences" offer being thrown in her face, too. She had really blown it with him.

"Because I took you to bed knowing the risks," Ryder continued, "knowing the consequences, and I *still* chose you above all else. I only wish you had chosen me, not because it was a game, but because you couldn't imagine being without me."

"I did feel that way! I still do!"

"I don't believe you." He put the car in drive and slowly inched out of the parking space. Katie walked to keep up with his truck.

"What about the risk I took?" she called out as he maneuvered the truck into the driving lane. She had to walk fast to keep level with the driver's side. "I turned my life upside down. I put all my trust in you. I didn't do anything lightly."

He pushed on the brakes and looked at her. "You went to bed with me because you craved the sexual danger. You wanted to know what it felt like to have sex with the town's bad boy. I hope it was worth it for you."

She thrust her hands in her hair. "Ryder, haven't you heard anything I've said? What is it going to take for you to believe me?"

"Nothing. There are no words to convince me. There is nothing you can do. It's too late." He took his foot off the brake and drove off before she could catch up with him. Katie stood in the middle of Main Street and watched his truck disappear.

"I am so sorry, Katie," Melissa wailed for the millionth time in the back of Hilary's purple hatchback. "I didn't mean to ruin your life."

"Melissa, if you don't shut up," Hilary warned as she sharply turned the steering wheel, "I am going to throw you out of the car. And I'm not going to slow down while I'm doing it!"

"I thought he knew," Melissa said as she automatically clung to her seat belt as the car tilted with the deep turn. "I really did. I don't know why. We've talked so freely about it, so I assumed . . ." She let her voice trail off, deeply upset.

"Stop worrying about it. It was an honest mistake," Katie said as she looked out the passenger-side window. At first she had been so tempted to place all the blame on Melissa, but Katie knew it would be wrong. She was solely responsible for this disaster, and her friend had just said the wrong thing at the wrong time.

"Oh, there!" Katie sat up straight when she thought she saw Ryder's truck. Then she realized it was the wrong model. "Sorry, no. It's not his truck."

"I had no idea there were this many trucks in Crystal Bend," Hilary said as they sped down yet another residential street.

"Where could he be?" Katie asked as she kept looking out the window. "We have been everywhere."

"We probably keep missing him," Hilary said. "Maybe we crossed paths on one of the side streets. Do you want to go back to the point of origin and start over?"

"No." Katie propped her aching head on the window, which

jostled and shook from Hilary's erratic driving. "We've been at this for hours."

"Maybe he already left Crystal Bend," Melissa said.

Hilary slammed on the brakes in the middle of the deserted road. Katie lurched forward and slammed her hands on the dashboard. Her heart felt like it had fallen and shattered, but not from the movement of the vehicle. What if Ryder had already left town? It was possible. He could have arranged to get an earlier flight.

Katie and Hilary looked around in the back of the car and glared at Melissa.

"Out of the car," Hilary ordered Melissa. She pointed at the door. "Right now. Get out."

"I didn't mean that." Melissa held out both hands in surrender. "I really didn't. It just sort of slipped out."

"Fine. This is your last chance," Hilary said. "Keep it up and you are just sort of going to slip out of the car at high speed."

"I won't say another word," Melissa promised. She mimed the motion of zipping up her lips and throwing away the key. Melissa settled back in her seat, her lips firmly pressed together.

Katie looked at Hilary. "Do you think he left already?"

"God, I hope not." Hilary pressed on the gas and they lurched to the end of the road.

Katie quickly looked out the passenger window as the tears stung in the back of her eyes and clawed her raw throat. "I can't have him leave thinking the worst of me."

"We'll find him," Hilary assured her. She reached out and patted Katie's arm. Katie appreciated the gesture, but she really wished her friend would keep both hands on the wheel. "And when we do, you are going to tell him the truth."

"Hilary, I'm sure you saw and listened to the whole thing. I told him the truth and look where it got me."

"I'm talking about the whole truth," Hilary said, checking both sides of the road before she squealed across it. "That you love him."

"The forever and always kind," Melissa added.

Hilary shot a warning glance in the rearview mirror. "Ryder needs to hear it."

"Maybe, but the timing is all wrong," Katie explained. "He's not going to believe me."

"Then make him believe you." She slammed back in her seat as they went down a winding, steep hill. "You can be persuasive."

Katie looked out the window again, not really seeing the trees passing by in a blur. Panic and urgency squeezed her chest. She felt like she couldn't breathe. She could easily imagine trying to persuade Ryder, being on her hands and knees while declaring her undying love. And he wouldn't say a thing as he walked right over her and out the door.

"It's not that easy," Katie insisted quietly.

"Yes, it is," Hilary argued. "Just say those three little words: I. Love. You. And in that order."

Melissa leaned forward, her face between the front seats. "It's not that easy, because if Ryder still leaves town after she says those three little words, then she knows that her love didn't mean a lot to him."

"Is that true?" Hilary looked at Katie. "Is that what you think?"

"More or less." Katie shrugged, but she was stunned by Melissa's insight. That was exactly her greatest fear. That, when all was said and done, her love wasn't going to be that important to Ryder.

"Oh, God, woman!" Hilary said in a fit of frustration. "If that's what happens, then just suck it up."

Melissa patted Hilary on the shoulder. "And this is why we don't have you handle the pep talks."

"You are not telling him how much you love him just to keep him here," Hilary told Katie.

"That would be manipulative," Melissa said, leaning against Hilary's seat to look at Katie. "Which you are not."

"And," Hilary continued, "you are not saying it to see if he loves you in equal measure."

"Because that's competitive," Melissa said, "which you are also not."

Hilary pointed at Katie as she made a wild one-handed turn. "You are telling him something he needs to hear before he goes off in the world alone," she explained.

"Think of it as a . . ." Melissa rolled her wrist, trying to grab on to the word she was seeking. "Think of it as a gift."

"Exactly." Hilary punched on the horn. Katie wasn't sure if it was for punctuation or because the car in front of them was going too slow for her taste. "He needs to know that there is someone in the world who loves him. Who is thinking of him and wants the best for him."

"He needs to know that you're going to love him even when you're not going to be with him," Melissa said.

Katie leaned her head on the window and crossed her arms. "When you put it that way, it makes me feel horrible and selfish for keeping it all to myself."

"Which you are not," Melissa said, "because you're going to tell him the minute you see him."

"If we find him," Katie said. The possibility didn't look good for her. "How much do you want to bet he's already left town?"

"I don't know," Melissa said. "How much money do you want to put on it?"

Hilary hit the brakes again and swung her car next to the curb, her tires rubbing against the cement. She pointed at the door. "Out of the car now, Melissa."

"No, no." She pressed her hands together in the universal sign of begging forgiveness. "I'll be good. I promise."

"Maybe we should go back to the café and separate," Katie said. "Three cars in different directions have to be more efficient than all of us in one car. What do you think?"

Hilary leaned back in her seat. "I think you're saying that so you're not stuck in a car with Melissa."

"That's one reason." Hilary's driving was another reason.

"Hey!" Melissa exclaimed. "Don't pick on me. I'm here to help."

"But with all of us in one car, I'm afraid we're going to miss him," Katie admitted.

"Forget it," Hilary said. "I'm nixing the idea because you, Katie Kramer, are in no state to drive."

"But we've been at this for hours and Crystal Bend is not that big," Katie complained. She didn't want to give up, but she was running out of time and options.

"We need to think like Ryder," Melissa suggested. "It's just like in sports. We have to get into the opponent's—I mean Ryder's—head. Come on, you know him better than anyone else."

"I thought I did," Katie said.

"No negative thoughts, please. They aren't helpful. Now think," Melissa ordered as she stared off into the distance. "Where would Ryder go to hide out and lick his wounds?"

"We tried his apartment," Katie said. When they had found it empty, the icy dread started trickling down her spine. "And I don't think he's going to be back there for a while because he knows I can break in."

"And we can scratch off the pool hall, the ski slopes and his favorite lookout point." Melissa ticked the list off on her fingers.

"We tried Jake's place," Hilary said, "which was a waste of time. And what was Jake doing there with that slut? What happened to Sasha?"

"Hilary, let's focus on Katie's love life for a minute, since hers is real and yours is all in your head."

"Not funny," Hilary said. "But I'm focusing, I'm focusing . . . and I've got nothing."

"You guys, I give up," Katie said as she battled the regret and disappointment pressing against her chest. "Can you just take me home?"

"Now is not the time to give up!" Melissa insisted. "You need to push through the pain and—"

"Melissa, this is not a coaching opportunity," Hilary declared as she turned the car around to head back to Katie's home.

Hilary dashed through the maze of streets and Katie was relieved that her friends were finally staying silent. She didn't think she could hold herself together for much longer. She didn't care as Hilary made one sharp turn after the other.

The car bounced and swayed when it hit the alley behind Katie's house. The poor road condition didn't deter Hilary. She sped down the alley, hitting every pothole.

"Well, I'll be damned." Hilary slowed down her car and leaned over the steering wheel to peer through the streaked windshield. "What is Ryder doing *here*?"

Katie stared at Ryder's truck where it was parked in the carport.

"It doesn't make any sense," Melissa said, pressing her nose against the car window.

"Maybe he's cooled down and wants to talk to Katie in private," Hilary said.

Hilary's words sounded almost too good to be true. Katie had been sure she would never see Ryder again. Now he was here, waiting. She couldn't blow this opportunity.

"Go on, Katie," Melissa encouraged her, pushing at her shoulder. "Show him the love."

Katie slowly stepped out of the car, her eyes on Ryder's truck. Her legs were shaky and not cooperating. She turned back to her friends. "What if he doesn't believe me or . . . or what if it's not enough?" She gasped when she revealed her deepest fear.

Melissa and Hilary looked at each other and back at Katie. "Then he's an idiot," Hilary said. "And then you'll know and move on."

Melissa smacked Hilary hard on the shoulder. "You are the worst at pep talks. What are you trying to do? Scar her for life?"

"That's it." Hilary shoved the car into park. "Out of my car. And, Katie . . . ?"

Katie looked at the house and back at Hilary. "Yeah?"

"Whatever you do, this is not the time to hold back."

CHAPTER SIXTEEN

Ryder stood by the Christmas tree in the Kramers' living room. He had turned on the lights, and immediately remembered how Katie had stood before the Christmas tree, blindfolded, almost naked and waiting for his touch.

He closed his eyes, trying to shove the image aside, but it was too late. The memory twisted at him, and not because she had been incredibly sexy, or that she had demonstrated a level of trust no one had given to him before. It was because he screwed up.

Rather than take what she was offering, he had walked out on her. He wasn't proud of that moment, even though he did it for Katie's good. He thought he had been strong, making that decision and walking away, but it had been a cowardly move.

Ryder didn't want to make that same mistake again. He was going to wait for Katie to come home and talk to her. He needed to see her one last time before he left.

He'd been sorely tempted to just throw his suitcases in the truck and leave town. But he couldn't do that to Katie, even though she'd hurt him badly. They needed to at least have one last discussion. He needed to know why she had made the stupid resolution, and why she had chosen him. He didn't think he was going to like the answer.

Ryder bunched his hands into fists as he fought the urge to leave. He needed to calm down or he was going to make a mess of things again. In an attempt to steady his nerves, Ryder reached out and touched one of the Christmas tree ornaments he'd given Katie years ago. It was faded and chipped, but well loved. Kind of like him. He was rough around the edges but Katie showered him with affection.

But Katie was generous with herself and her affection to a lot of people. Ryder had forgotten that. Over the years he thought he was important to Katie, but that New Year's resolution knocked him back into reality. She saw him just like every other woman in Crystal Bend did: someone to guide her through the wild side of sex.

A part of him wished he had never known Katie's true motivations. He would have liked to think that a good girl would break all the rules because she loved and desired him so much she didn't care what others thought. But it was probably for the best that he found out the truth. He would have always wondered if he had walked away from the best woman in his life.

He heard the back door open. Ryder tensed and for a moment he wanted to make a run for it. He didn't want to face the drama, or worse, the disappointment in Katie's eyes. But she deserved better, and that was the only thing that kept him still.

"Ryder?" Katie called out and waited for a response that didn't come. She thought she knew Ryder, that she was an expert on him, but today she couldn't even guess his mood or his next move. She was shocked to see his truck outside when she had convinced herself he must be halfway to Dubai by now.

She hurried through the kitchen and dining room and came to a halt when she saw Ryder standing by the tree, holding on to one of the ornaments he had given her. A mix of relief and anticipation swirled in Katie's chest as he turned to face her.

She wanted to run to him and throw herself in his arms, asking for forgiveness before declaring her love. And if she had been the confident, sensual and powerful woman of her dreams, she'd have done it without a second thought.

But she wasn't anywhere close to being that kind of woman. The sexy clothes weren't going to help her find the confidence to speak from the heart. Her crazy antics wouldn't get her any closer to Ryder.

She felt shaky, her mouth dry, her heart going a mile a minute. As she walked into the room, she knew she had reached the moment of truth. She could only hope that she was woman enough to see it through.

"There you are," she said softly as her blood pumped wildly in her veins. "I've been looking everywhere for you. I didn't expect to find you here."

"Why's that?" he asked as he stroked the ornament with his fingertips.

"Because I live here. And you're mad at me!" She thought it was obvious. Katie took another step into the room. "I want to explain about the New Year's resolution. Just hear me out."

He let go of the ornament and crossed his arms. The closed expression on his face wasn't encouraging, but she wasn't going to back down. She needed Ryder to know how important he was to her.

"I made you my New Year's resolution this year and the year before that." She paused before adding sheepishly, "And the year before that."

His expression didn't change.

"In case you haven't figured out what the rest of the town knows, I have always liked you. A lot," she confessed and felt a wave of shyness. Katie looked down at her feet. "It started out as a crush. Maybe an infatuation."

"I know."

Okay, his indifferent tone wasn't making it any easier. She licked her dry lips and forced herself to continue. "But I never went after you because I kept waiting for you to come to your senses. I wanted you to come after me." She glanced up at him, wondering what he thought.

"Are you finished?"

She frowned and gritted her teeth. Couldn't he tell how difficult this was for her? "No, I'm not finished." She took another step closer to him. "When you made it clear that you weren't going to touch me, I knew I had to take matters into my own hands. I knew you wanted me and I was determined that we would have a chance together."

He looked at the tree as if the ornaments were more interesting than what she had to say. "You went through all this for an affair?"

"I was kind of aiming low on my resolution," she said, catching her bottom lip with her teeth.

A dark stillness seemed to invade Ryder. He swung his head and pinned her to the spot with his gaze. The hurt shimmered in his eyes. "Is that right?"

She belatedly realized how he had interpreted that confession. "Not with *you*. I wasn't aiming low by going after you. Oh, my God. How can you think that?"

"Because you are such an innocent good girl and most of the women I know see me as just a walk on the wild side before they find someone better. Why would you want me for anything more than an affair?"

"I was aiming low in my resolution to *only* have an affair with you. I want a lot more. Too much, maybe." She felt the tears sting in her eyes. "Because the truth is that I love you."

"What?" He took a lightning-quick step away from her.

She had hoped for a better reaction. She wasn't expecting an "I love you, too." That was reaching for the stars, but Ryder's response was not doing a lot for her confidence. "Come on, Ryder. How can you not see this? I have always loved you."

He held up both hands, as if to stop her from saying it. "No, you don't."

Now she was getting angry. Katie crossed her arms and glared at him. "Who are you to say that?"

"You think you love me because we slept together and—"

"You may think that I'm innocent and naïve"—which was something she planned to disabuse him of at her earliest convenience—"but I know the difference between sexual satisfaction and love."

"You can't be in love," he said angrily. He started to pace, rubbing his hand hard along the back of his neck.

"Why can't I?" She didn't understand why her words caused him such agitation. "Because you don't love me back?"

"I didn't say that."

That answer gave her a flash of hope. But he didn't say he loved her, either. "Because it's inconvenient for you?"

"No!" He kept pacing.

"Then why?" she asked as she watched him pace back and forth. "Why can't I love you?"

He stopped in the middle of the room. "Because I'm not lovable!"

She stared at him. Of all the things she had expected him to say, that was *not* it. He hunched his shoulders and looked down. She had never seen Ryder look so vulnerable. Lost and alone.

"That's not true." Her voice was almost a whisper. She wanted to reach out and hold him, but he would not accept that. He would think it was out of sympathy or pity. "You know it's not true. I love you."

"Stop saying that!" Ryder closed his eyes and held up his hands, which trembled as he held back the turbulent, painful emotions. "Stop saying that. You think you love me, but just wait. It won't take long for me to ruin that. In a couple of months you'll wonder what the hell you were thinking."

"I'm not the only one who loves you. Jake would take a bullet for you. When we were fighting this morning, Jake was angry at *me* for going after you, remember? He was protecting you."

Ryder looked away. "That was wrong of him. He's your brother and he should look after you."

"He's your best friend and he's loyal to you. And don't forget my parents," she added. "They adore you. I swear, you can do no wrong in their eyes."

"Which would change the instant they found out about us." He shook his head as he considered what he thought he'd lost. "It's a good thing I'm leaving before I see their disappointment."

"They're not happy that you're leaving," she insisted. "And my mom thinks it's about time I go after you."

"She does?" Ryder looked stunned. He opened his mouth as if to say something, then closed it again. Finally he asked, "And your dad?"

"He knows how I feel about you, and I think he approves," she said truthfully. "Otherwise he would have said something."

Ryder leaned against the fireplace. "I don't get it."

Katie felt like she finally did. He thought the love the Kramer family showed him was conditional. After being abandoned by his only parent, maybe Ryder thought he would get it right the second time around. He did his best to never make a wrong move with the Kramers. He displayed a fierce loyalty, protected his adopted family with a vengeance, and was there whenever they needed him.

It must have been torture once he started to desire her, Katie realized. And then worse when she reinvented herself and threw herself at him time and time again. She didn't want to think about how much he had struggled as she kept testing his restraint.

Ryder must have been torn between the affection her family had already demonstrated and the possibility of something more with her. He really took a risk in choosing her with no guarantee that it would work out. Katie was humbled by the knowledge.

"I didn't fall in love with you because of what you do for me and my family," Katie wanted him to know. "Love is not something that is earned. I fell for the man you've become."

"I didn't earn it?" he asked and she saw the fear in his eyes. She hadn't meant to tap into one of his deepest fears. He had no control over the love he received. If it was given to him without him doing anything, it could just as easily be taken away.

She slowly walked to Ryder, not wanting to crowd him. She stopped right in front of him and she took it as a good sign that he didn't step away. "Just accept that I love you."

"You're taking a big chance on me."

"You're worth it." She stood on her toes and brushed her mouth against his. She felt the tension coming off him, shimmering in the air.

He reached up and stroked her hair. She felt his hand trembling and continued to kiss him gently. He was nervous. He wasn't sure if he could trust her love.

And maybe he had good reason. She had gone after him because of a New Year's resolution. The main goal was sex, not love. Now she was going to have to try to demonstrate her feelings without sex.

Oh, she didn't know if she could do that. Katie stepped away from Ryder, and it took a huge effort. She hadn't thought she was a very sexual person until she'd made love to Ryder. Once he gave her pleasure, the world had become sensual. She didn't know if she could put a hold on that.

She looked into his eyes, wrestling with her plan. He was going to leave town in two days. She still wanted to fulfill as many fantasies as she could with Ryder before the New Year.

But he already thought that she was confusing love with sex. She knew the difference. He would be shocked to know that she did not have to be in love to have good sex. In fact, she had had sex for the hell of it and enjoyed it. But he didn't need to know that.

All he needed to know was that she loved him, and that she was of sound mind when she said it. That meant no sex. Even if it killed her.

"Why are you looking at me like that?" Ryder asked.

"I'm . . . I'm trying to work up the nerve to ask you to stay here just for today. I know you have a lot of things to do, but I also know you came here to find some peace and quiet."

"I always felt safe here, you know?" Ryder looked around the room. "Like I belonged."

"You do. So stay here," she said, hating how choppy her words were. Could he tell that she was trying to hold back? "Just for today. I won't crowd you. Promise."

"Okay."

"Good." And that meant no touching, kissing, drooling or staring at Ryder. She could do this.

"As long as I can stay the night," he said with a gleam in his eye.

"Even better." He wanted to spend the night. Here. With her. When she had just promised herself no touching, kissing, drooling or staring. How was she going to survive that?

Okay, new rule. She would be the good girl Ryder thought she was. She wouldn't *initiate* the touching and kissing. That would be better. And she'd let Ryder make the first move and every one after that.

It was going to be a really long night.

CHAPTER SEVENTEEN

December 30

He was officially domesticated, Ryder thought with a content smile. If Jake saw him now, he would claim that Ryder was completely wrapped around Katie's finger. Ryder wouldn't argue, although he would like to think that Katie was bound to him just as tightly.

Ryder looked down at Katie, who was snuggled against him on the couch. She looked so small and delicate tucked against his side. She wore a baggy sweatshirt and pants, but he couldn't think of a time she looked more feminine. Her scent teased him and he was drawn by her softness. He couldn't stop touching her. Katie's long black hair was draped over his arm and he was tempted to wrap the length of hair around his hand until he could palm the back of her head. Then he could kiss her just the way he wanted, for as long as he felt like.

He could do that right now. Katie wouldn't refuse him anything, and that knowledge heightened his senses, his need for her building. It was going to take hours to sate this kind of hunger.

He was surprised that Katie wasn't impatient to get him back in bed. Her body hummed with need, he could tell, and she was generous with her long kisses and sensual caresses, but she was holding back. In fact, she had been so sweet and attentive. Accommodating. Quiet and shy.

Something was up.

He wasn't going to say anything just yet. Why mess up a good thing? But Katie's biddable behavior niggled at him. Was she trying to show him what he'd be missing once he left? Most likely. But he was already taking some good memories with him, and most of them starred Katie. Some of those moments would have been insignificant to her, and others she would want him to forget, but he treasured the imperfect times just as much as a day like today.

These were the final moments he had with Katie. He thought he would experience a sense of frantic urgency. If anything, he thought Katie would try to cram a lifetime into a few hours until it felt like they'd run a marathon. Instead, the lazy winter day stretched into a warm, sensual night and drifted into another snowy day. As he held her close he thought about everything he would be leaving behind when he moved away. His friends, the sense of community in Crystal Bend—despite the small-town gossip that drove him crazy—even the weather. He wouldn't be able to enjoy lazy winter days like this when he moved to Dubai.

Ryder sighed and pulled her closer. He liked the sense of being cocooned in the house, away from the rest of the world. It gave them a chance to be a couple, no matter how little time they had. As he looked down at Katie he remembered the good times they'd shared in the past. Like when she had quietly let him in the back door at the Kramers' house when he had an angry ex-girlfriend chasing him down, or the numerous occasions when she'd pulled him out of bar fights if situations got out of hand. Katie was the only one who listened with understanding when he poured out his true feelings about his absent mother, and she could always offer a witty insight that made him smile at his own situation.

And now, Katie was making every one of his wishes come true, but secretly he hoped her docile behavior didn't last much longer. He missed the challenging, teasing temptress. The one who could handle him at his worst. At least he knew she couldn't be this submissive for so many consecutive hours. If she didn't unleash the bratty, naughty, unpredictable side of herself soon, he would have to do something drastic. A curl of wicked anticipation flickered deep in his gut.

Either way, it was a win-win situation for him.

Good-girl sex wasn't bad, Katie decided. There were some benefits, like letting Ryder do *all* the work, from the seduction to holding her when she fell asleep in his arms. He really pulled out all the stops, and it overwhelmed her. She enjoyed every moment.

However, she had to be on her very best behavior all day and all night. It was hard for her to remember that when the love of her life was kissing her so passionately that her toes curled. And being ladylike in bed meant no grabbing, biting or taking. That had been tough.

If Ryder had noticed her reserve, he hadn't mentioned it. He had made love to her so thoroughly that he probably attributed her quiet behavior to sleepiness.

She wasn't going to regret her decision to be the sweet, innocent good girl Ryder thought she was. It wasn't her fantasy, but maybe it was his. Ryder certainly made the most of their night together and she had no complaints. After all, one of her wishes had come true: he had spent the night in her bed.

And for once the planets were aligning in her favor. It was as if the gods approved of her decision and were rewarding her with an extra day. When she and Ryder woke up they discovered that it had snowed and iced during the night. Ryder couldn't leave until the snowplows came by and they hadn't shown up yet.

Sometimes it paid to be a good girl. She rested her head against Ryder's shoulder and curled up against him as they sat on the couch next to the fire. They enjoyed a lazy day alone.

She would have preferred to have spent the entire day naked in bed and blocking out the world with a couple layers of quilts, but good girls were too virtuous to have marathon sex. Damn those good girls. Instead of tying him up and enacting her wildest fantasies, she planned to do innocent things to pass the time, like cook breakfast with Ryder, and maybe watch TV or play cards.

Ryder held her in his arms and stroked her hair. Katie pressed her lips together and closed her eyes, trying not to follow her naughty instincts. She needed to think of something that wasn't sexy. Nothing came to mind at the moment. All she could think about was how good it felt to be this close to Ryder, and how much better it would feel if they were skin to skin.

How had Ryder maintained his distance from her all this time? Was he superhuman? She was already a trembling mass of need. Ryder gently massaged the base of her skull, working out the tension with his fingertips. She wanted to purr and stretch like a cat, and that was just from a simple touch.

Now she was getting a better sense of the torture she'd put Ryder through. Maybe the gods weren't smiling down on her. Maybe this was her penitence. She could ace this test. If Ryder had been able to do this for years, she could do this for a day or two. Definitely no more than two.

Ryder tilted her head and kissed her gently on the lips. Okay, good. Light kiss. She could handle it. She wouldn't claw at him, or try to strip him bare at the touch of his mouth.

He kissed her again. His touch was gentle but exploratory. Her lips clung to his as he nibbled at her mouth. His fingertips glided from the top vertebrae and slowly down to the small of her back, and then slid back up again.

He was trying to kill her. That had to be it. Destroy her restraint inch by delicious inch.

Katie knew she should have worn more layers, or at least a bra under her sweatshirt. A bra would have been good. Or maybe jeans instead of sweatpants. She needed more armor and something that couldn't slide off her body in a moment of weakness.

Ryder moaned with pleasure as she parted her lips and drew his tongue into her mouth. She hadn't meant to do that. He just sort of slipped in. She needed to be more vigilant.

It was really important to show Ryder that she wanted more than sex, but her resolve was weakening at his every touch. The boundaries she had set had moved so far that now she had only one rule: Don't be aggressive. She kept her hands to herself and she didn't instigate any touch, no matter how much she wanted to.

Ryder's hand slipped under her sweatshirt. The feel of his rough, callused palm on her soft bare skin made her shiver. Katie was getting to the danger point. If she didn't move away right this very minute, Ryder was going to find out just how much she wanted him for sex.

But Katie didn't move. It felt so good to be cradled in Ryder's arms. She was addicted to his long, wet kisses. She needed him to touch her, cup her breast and rub his thumb hard against her nipple.

Katie moaned and arched into his hand, wanting him to squeeze her breast. She grabbed the back of his head, bunching his hair in her fists and grinding him closer.

No, no, no. She couldn't do this. She had to show Ryder how much he meant to her besides sex. Katie reluctantly let go of his hair and pushed herself away. She was breathing heavily as she jumped off the couch.

"Where are you going?" Ryder's voice was rough with desire.

"I need to check if the streets are clear." She went straight to the window and stared outside. It was beginning to turn dark and there was still a blanket of snow in the street.

"That's what you were thinking when you kissed me? Snow-plows?" Ryder was sprawled on the couch and Katie looked away. His chest rose and fell and she could see his aroused cock pressing against his jeans. She needed to stay away or she would jump him.

"What's going on, Katie?" Ryder asked quietly. "You asked me to stay and then you act shy around me."

"I'm not shy with you. I've been trying to show you that I'm not just interested in sex."

Ryder smiled wickedly. "That's what you've been doing?" He threw back his head and laughed out loud.

Ryder had been wondering what was going through her mind. At first he thought she was shy about declaring her feelings, and then he'd considered the possibility that she now regretted it. But that wasn't like Katie.

It wasn't until late in the night that he suspected she was already distancing herself from him. It bothered him, but what else could he expect? How could she give herself so freely and completely, knowing that he would leave her soon?

But he had never thought Katie was trying to prove that she was interested in more than his body. Good to know, but she didn't have to go to so many extremes. He couldn't stop laughing. Only Katie would do something like this.

Katie glared at him, obviously not in a laughing mood. "It's not funny. You said that I was confusing sex with love."

"I was wrong," he admitted quickly, doing his best to keep a straight face. He was willing to take the blame for putting that idea into her head. "You don't need to prove it to me."

She looked at him suspiciously. "You're just saying that so I will go back over there."

Katie knew him too well.

She frowned as his grin widened. "I'm serious."

He was worried about that. She seemed very determined to show that she didn't need to make love to him. He had to break down her resistance.

"So you won't touch me, and now I can't touch you." Ryder rose from the couch. "I'm sure we can work around this."

Katie crossed her arms. "I'm not trying to be difficult."

"I know," he said as he approached her. She was trying to show the depths of her feelings. He didn't mean to test her. "And it's very sweet of you."

"There you go again. I am not sweet," she insisted.

"I'm counting on that." Ryder picked up Katie and swept her into his arms, heading for the stairs before she could protest. He loved the small yelp she gave as she grabbed on to his shirt.

"This is not a game," Katie said as he took the first step. "I don't know why you see this as some sort of challenge."

"I'm not," he promised as he climbed up the stairs. "I shouldn't have said what I did. I'm sorry that you felt the need to hold back. And I know you're not going to give up without a fight, so I need to wear you down."

"By not touching me? Or me not touching you?" She scoffed at the thought. "I'd like to see you try."

"It's very simple," he said as he entered her bedroom, the lust pounding through him. "I want to watch you."

"Watch me do what?" Her eyes widened with comprehension. "Oh! You want to watch me touch myself?"

"Oh, yeah," he said, his voice raspy, as he laid her down on her bed. The wicked excitement pressed against his chest before curling into his belly. He wanted to watch Katie pleasure herself with abandon.

Ryder saw that the suggestion excited her. She pressed her mouth shut as she blushed. "I don't know if I should," she murmured, rubbing her thighs together.

"Please?" he asked, his mouth against her ear. "I fantasized about this. Wondering what you would look like, lying in your bed, thinking of me."

She gasped at his audacity. "And all you want to do is watch?"

Now that was a loaded question. He wanted more, lots more, but this was a good start. "I won't touch you," he promised with a smile. "You want to do this, don't you? I can tell."

She ducked her head. "What about you?"

"Don't worry about me." He wanted all the focus to be on Katie.

"You'll have to get undressed. I'm going to need some inspiration," she teased.

Ryder smiled as he pulled off his shirt. He was more than willing to fulfill that request. "You, too."

He watched Katie undress. He didn't think she intended it as a slow striptease. He could tell that she was a little nervous about masturbating in front of him. It was a deeply personal experience, and it required a level of intimacy.

Ryder was already naked while she stripped off her panties. His cock was erect and curving toward his flat stomach and it wouldn't take much for him to climax. He watched Katie lay back down on the bed and he knelt on the edge.

"Touch yourself," Ryder encouraged her in a husky voice. He wanted her to enjoy this moment, but was she ready to be this intimate?

Katie closed her eyes as she skimmed her hands along her breasts and down her stomach. Ryder clenched his hands into fists, wanting to touch her just like that.

As she glided her palms across her pelvic bone, Ryder noticed that she kept her eyes shut. He wasn't going to request that she open them, even though he wanted to see her eyes. Maybe she needed this one veil of privacy, and he was willing to respect that.

Katie parted her legs and cupped her sex. She let the heat coat her hand before she started to rub. Ryder's chest rose and fell, his breathing harsh and loud to his ears.

Katie boldly opened her eyes and their gazes connected. He couldn't look away even if he wanted to. Katie grabbed her breast and squeezed it as she watched Ryder's expression. His nostrils flared as the lust coiled tightly inside him.

"Touch yourself," she told him. "I want to watch you, too."

He felt a muscle twitch in his cheek but didn't say anything. If he touched himself, this was going to end faster than he planned. But he couldn't refuse. He wrapped his hand around his cock and started pumping in long pulls.

Katie seemed mesmerized by the sight. She rocked her hips as she played with her clit. Her finger flicked over the swollen nub in a light, fast touch while Ryder stroked his cock slow and hard. He bucked against his hand when he really wanted to thrust deep and hard into her. Katie wiggled her hips and parted her legs more, giving Ryder a glimpse of her hot and juicy pink core.

"I don't think you're going to last very long," Katie said.

It was true, but she wasn't going to last long, either. The lust glittered in her eyes and her skin was flushed. He could tell that the sound of his hand pumping his cock made her wet.

She let go of her nipple and brought her hand down to her slit. There was no hesitation or shyness at all. Katie wanted to show him how aroused she was. How much she wanted him. Her boldness made him hot.

"I think you're going to be screaming my name in the next couple of minutes," Ryder bragged, watching Katie dip her fingers into her wetness.

"What makes you so sure?" she asked as she parted her knees even farther and pumped her fingers inside herself quickly.

She was brazen and shameless, Ryder thought as he watched her every move. Katie loved showing off to him, and he couldn't get enough. If he wasn't careful, she was going to take total control.

Ryder leaned over to her bedside table. Katie looked like she was about to protest when he pulled the drawer open. He smiled when he saw what was hiding inside and removed the slim purple vibrator.

"How did you know about that?" she asked.

"I figured it out when you teased me about not having toys in my drawer." He switched on the vibrator and it quietly buzzed to life. He smiled as he considered all the naughty things he could do to Katie with this.

"You don't call this touching?" she asked and gasped as he reached down and rubbed the shaking toy against her inner thigh.

"I'm not touching you," he said as he moved the vibrator in small circles. He loved the way Katie moaned and the way her hands stilled as he teased her with the tapered end of the toy.

She gritted her teeth when he moved the vibrator closer to her slit. He saw the tremors sweeping through her. He could tell that she wanted to surrender.

With a long groan, she moved her hands away and watched Ryder rub the vibrator against the swollen folds of her sex.

She bucked toward him, desperate for more. Ryder wanted to toss the vibrator aside and touch her. He almost did when she bunched the bedsheets in her hands and rocked her hips. Ryder settled the toy against her clit and watched her as the vibrations sent her over the edge. Katie arched back, squeezing her eyes shut, as sweat bathed her skin.

"Can I touch you now?" Ryder asked with a knowing laugh.

"Not yet," she said.

Ryder's eyebrows rose as she challenged him. So she wasn't going to give in that easily. He switched the vibrator to the medium level. Katie shuddered as he drew the toy up and down her wet slit. The vibrations had an unpredictable pattern, but the designs Ryder drew along her flesh were even wilder.

Katie was trembling, but she didn't give in.

"Can I touch you now?" Ryder asked, enjoying every twitch and buck of her hips.

"No," she said. "Not now. Later tonight."

Ryder knew it was big talk, and he didn't bother to hide the arrogant smile playing on his mouth as he switched the level to high on the slim purple vibrator.

He saw Katie bracing herself for the onslaught. She locked her shoulders and hips in place and grabbed the sheets in her hands. Her feet were firmly planted on the mattress. She kept her gaze steady on him.

Ryder slid the tapered head of the vibrator into her core. The vibe was so fast, so intense, he was impressed that she didn't come right away. He didn't think she would last more than a minute.

"Now you can touch me," she told Ryder, her voice husky.

"Not yet," he mimicked before plunging the vibrator deep into her.

Katie groaned. Her muscles spasmed as they clutched onto the slim toy. Ryder pulled it almost all the way out, leaving her gasping.

"Not now," Ryder said and then thrust the vibrator deeper. Katie's hips lurched off the bed. He couldn't get enough of this. She was about to ride out the waves when he slowly withdrew the toy.

Katie made a desperate grab for the vibrator, knocking away Ryder's hands. He let her take it, smiling as she held on to the toy with both hands and pumped it inside her. She held his gaze as she rode it, showing him exactly how she liked it.

He didn't think he could take much more. He wasn't satisfied with just watching. He wanted to touch her, take her to the edge and back, again and again.

Her strokes faltered when the white-hot climax streaked through her. Suddenly Ryder's hands covered hers as he continued the pace she wanted. She watched him through half-opened eyes.

"But, Katie," Ryder said as he plunged the toy deeply into her core, "I promise I'm going to touch you later tonight. As much as I want."

With satisfaction, he noted that she didn't argue. He gave the vibrator a naughty twist that triggered a low, guttural moan from her. "And from now on, you will touch me as much and as often as you like."

Katie closed her eyes and sighed as he slowly withdrew the vibrator from her. "Sure. Now you tell me."

CHAPTER EIGHTEEN

December 31

Ryder placed the coffee mug on the bedside table and slowly turned to Katie. He braced himself, but just the sight of her sleeping was a punch to his gut. She was so beautiful, so sweet and loving, that he wanted to lie down next to her and curl his body against hers.

Katie lay naked under the blankets, her arms stretched out to where he had slept. The thought that she was reaching for him made his heart ache. He couldn't let that instinctive movement get to him.

Ryder allowed his gaze to drift to Katie's black hair tousled and spread across the pillow. He wanted to sink his hands into the long tangles, but he had to refrain from touching her. The longer he lingered, the more difficult it would be to leave.

He had to be strong. Ryder had reluctantly left Katie's embrace hours ago and forced himself out of bed. He was dressed and ready to go. If he was smart, he would write a note and leave before she woke.

Who was he kidding? It wasn't the smartest route; it was the easiest, and also the most cowardly. He couldn't do that to Katie. Even if she caused a scene, or created a drama that only Katie could do, it would be better than sneaking out. If he left while she slept, he would regret it.

Five more minutes, he decided. He would wake Katie up and leave within five minutes. It didn't seem like a lot, but his determination was already slipping.

He lay down next to Katie, knowing it was risky, that he might not get back up for hours. *If I don't curl up next to her, I'm okay.* He wanted to believe it, holding his body rigid, just in case he wrapped his arm around her.

He watched her sleep, inhaling and savoring her scent. Ryder felt the sting of tears in his eyes as his throat constricted. He squeezed his eyes shut, determined to push back the emotions rolling through him.

He knew he was already over his allotted five minutes, but he wanted to take just a few more with his emotions under control. But it was now or never. If he was a stronger man, he would explore what he had with Katie. Exhaust every possibility, ride it out until there was nothing left.

Katie might have the courage to do that, but he didn't. Katie had already stripped him of his armor and captured his heart. He had to retreat now, before this affair destroyed him.

Katie stirred when she felt the light, insistent touch on her bare arm. She grumbled and frowned, burrowing her head in the pillow. She wasn't ready to wake up, not when she was having the most delicious dream about Ryder.

"Katie, rise and shine," Ryder whispered close to her ear and gave her a soft kiss on her cheek.

"It's too early to get up," she mumbled. She had no idea of the time, or whether it was morning or night. She was worn out.

No one warned her how tiring it was chasing after a man. Probably because the exhausting part happened once he was captured. She didn't think she'd had much rest, trying to cram as many fantasies as she could into two days.

Katie smiled as she remembered how she'd spent the night. She felt the blush streaking up her neck and into her cheeks as a collage of memories flickered through her mind. Arching her back, Katie winced as her muscles protested. She ached and she was slowly becoming aware of the sting of whisker burn in a few places on her body. There was no telling what other marks and bruises decorated her skin.

She stretched leisurely, welcoming the twinges. Her fingers collided against something warm and solid. *Ryder.* Katie's eyelashes fluttered as she forced her eyes open. The first thing she saw was Ryder's smile. She sighed, the joy and contentment inside her overflowing. She reached for him and discovered that he was fully clothed.

"Why are you dressed?" Her voice was rough with sleep. "It's only going to slow me down."

The sparkle in his eyes dimmed. "I have to go."

Her fingers wrapped around the drawstring of his black hoodie. "Go where?"

Ryder's smile straightened into a firm line. He didn't say anything for several moments. "It's December thirty-first, Katie. This is my last day in Crystal Bend. I'm flying to Dubai early tomorrow morning."

The warmth that had invaded her body suddenly turned cold. Her body stiffened as it warded off the jarring effects of his words, and the serenity she had felt vanished as if it had never existed. "Your last day?" she repeated dully.

"Katie, you knew I was leaving."

She noticed the gentle and careful way he spoke to her. As if he could tell his reminder would cause a hairline fracture in her fragile composure. Did he know it wouldn't take much for her restraint to disintegrate and reveal the swirling, messy emotions inside her?

Katie swallowed the lump in her throat and scrupulously removed her hand from his drawstring. She wouldn't cry. She refused to. It wouldn't be right. She had always known Ryder's plan and she conveniently forgot about it yesterday, foolishly pretending things were different.

No, that wasn't true, Katie thought as she gradually sat up. She thought that since she hadn't held anything back, she had assured Ryder of her love. After last night, after enjoying an intimacy that took her breath away, Katie thought his plans were obsolete and he wouldn't want to leave.

That was stupid of her. Katie squeezed her eyes closed, horrified and angry with her mistake. Stupid, stupid, stupid.

She was aware of Ryder's gaze on her. He was probably waiting for the waterworks. That wasn't going to happen. She had promised herself that she wouldn't create drama if he chose to leave. If she expected him to accept that she loved him, then she would graciously accept that it wasn't going to stop him from leaving Crystal Bend.

She couldn't think of it that way. If she did, she would be a basket case before breakfast. She had to view it the way her friends explained it. She was gifting him with her love and expecting nothing in return. She was going to handle his desertion—no, his *departure*—with sophistication and style.

She would be on her best behavior until he passed the city limits. Then she would have the mother of all breakdowns.

"Katie?" Ryder's voice was laced with concern.

She jerked at the sound of his voice. Katie tried to cover up her reaction by rubbing her eyes, as if she was wiping the sleep away. "Sorry, I'm not really with it first thing in the morning. What time is it?"

"It just turned nine," he said and sat up next to her. Ryder didn't touch her, but she felt surrounded by him. "I brought you some coffee. It's here on the table."

"Thank you." The thoughtful gesture inexplicably irritated her, and she wasn't sure why. Probably because it was his final act of taking care of her. It was so simple and insignificant, but Katie couldn't look at the table. She didn't trust herself to look in his direction.

"I still have to finish packing and meet with my landlord," Ryder said. "I don't know how long it's going to take."

They wouldn't get to spend this final day together. That's what he was trying to tell her. Maybe it was for the best, but she didn't think so.

Katie knew she was being greedy. She'd gotten more than she'd ever hoped for, but it wasn't enough. Was it wrong to want every single minute with him before he left?

"It sounds like you're going to have a busy day," she said in a determinedly breezy tone. She forced herself to move and swung her feet to the floor. Katie felt uncoordinated and graceless as she got out of bed, but she kept going.

Reaching for her long terry-cloth robe, she hesitated. If she wanted to remind Ryder of what he would be missing, she should wear something silky and sexy. No, that wouldn't be enough. She should stay naked.

Forget it. Bad idea. Katie grabbed the robe and gratefully wrapped it around her cold, trembling body. She was already feeling defenseless and stripped of the last of her confidence.

Katie didn't look at him as she wrapped the robe around her and pulled the sash tightly. She stuffed her shaking hands into the oversized pockets before she finally turned around to face him. He continued to watch her with solemn, dark eyes.

"Let me make you some breakfast before you go," she offered with a bright smile firmly in place. That sounded like something a sophisticated lover would do. And it would delay him from leaving.

"There is no need."

"I insist." She headed for the door, wishing her legs would cooperate and not make her feel so ungainly and awkward. If it was this much trouble to walk, then making a meal was going to be disastrous. "I forgot." She stopped abruptly and snapped her fingers. "I don't have anything to cook for breakfast. No matter. We'll go out."

Ryder got off the bed and approached her. "Katie, you don't have to."

"I want to." She took an instinctive step back, not wanting him to touch her. "Please?"

"Sure," he said with a sigh. "Anything you want. My treat."

"Great." She struggled to keep her smile in place. It was easier if she didn't look directly at him. "Although I don't think I'm up for going to the café."

"I'll wait for you downstairs."

She nodded jerkily. Katie remained still and didn't watch him leave. When she heard Ryder close the bedroom door behind him, she let out a shaky breath.

He was leaving town and not coming back. Katie blinked rapidly. She wasn't going to last the morning, or even the next five seconds, without crying. Hopefully he wouldn't hear her sobbing in the shower.

Katie thought she deserved a crying jag. She had given her all, and it wasn't enough. She fought for her man and she lost.

A tear stung her eye before falling over her lashes and sliding down her face. She wiped it away fiercely. She couldn't cry yet, because once she started, she wouldn't stop. It was time to surrender to the inevitable. She would rather not do it with a bright red nose and swollen eyes. She needed to be gracious in defeat.

Or, in the words of Hilary, it was time to suck it up.

"So," Katie said cheerfully as she sat in Ryder's truck while he drove to town, "you are going to miss these winters when you're in Dubai."

"I'll survive," Ryder replied, his eyes on the road.

"You could always come back here on your vacation. Just to remember what snow looks like." Great. She only had an hour, two tops, with Ryder and she was discussing the weather. It couldn't get much worse.

"I'll think about it."

"You do that," she muttered. Ryder didn't sound enthusiastic about her plan. She understood that he wanted to start a new life with a clean slate, but that didn't mean he had to stay away forever.

Ryder glanced over in her direction. "I'm going to keep in touch," he promised.

Katie leaned her head back on her seat and looked out the passenger window. "No, you're not."

"What?"

"I'm sorry," she said with a sigh. "I didn't mean to put a damper on our last morning together, but it's true. You're not planning to keep in touch. You are making a clean break."

Ryder shook his head. "I would never abandon you."

She took an unsteady breath. She sure felt like she was being abandoned. Dropped and kicked to the curb. Maybe she wouldn't feel this way if he would just tell her why he had to leave so suddenly.

Maybe he was leaving today because he hadn't had a better offer. "You know, since we're kind of together . . ."

"Katie, no." He was shaking his head like he already knew what she was going to say.

"You could stay at the house," she offered. Katie sat a little straighter in her chair. She liked this idea. "I have the whole place to myself and it gets a little lonely."

"It wouldn't work."

"It worked just fine," Katie protested. "Better than fine. It was fantastic, if I say so myself."

"That was for a couple of days." Ryder stopped the truck at a stoplight, giving him a chance to look directly at her. "If I stayed for longer, soon you wouldn't be able to stand the sight of me."

"Oh, please." She made a face. "That's impossible."

"Not as impossible as you'd think," Ryder muttered under his breath and returned his attention to the street.

"Is that why you're leaving?" she asked, searching his face for any hint of what was running through his head. "You think it's only a matter of time before I fall out of love with you? Do you think I'm that fickle?"

"No!"

Huh. Katie looked out the window. She had been so sure for a moment there. But if that was the reason why he was leaving, she didn't know how to ease his fears. How could she prove that she wasn't going to fall out of love? There was just no way to give that kind of proof.

She saw the familiar yellow of the Merrill house coming up the street. It had been a few days since she'd last seen it, but she didn't think the old farmhouse would give her the peace she desperately needed. Katie frowned when she saw an addition to the for-sale sign posted at the edge of the neglected lawn.

"Stop the car!" Katie yelled as she took off her seat belt.

Ryder pumped the brakes and his truck slid to a stop just as Katie flung open the door. "What the hell is wrong with you?" he called out as she jumped down from the truck.

She wasn't listening. Katie marched right through the shoveled snow piled against the curb and stood in front of the sign. For years it had stood there like a limp white flag of surrender, and no one paid any attention to it. It had melded into the background until now.

"No . . . ," she whispered weakly as she stared at the red banner that streaked across the white sign. *Sold*.

Katie took a choppy breath, the cold air burning down her throat. Someone had taken her house. Not just taken it—*stolen* it from right under her nose.

"You're lucky there was no one behind us," Ryder said as he came up from behind. "What were you thinking?"

"Someone bought the house." The words weren't easy to say.

He looked at the sign as if he'd just noticed it. "Impossible."

She stared at the red banner. Sold. S-o-l-d. She'd read it right. It was no hallucination. Someone was buying her house, and taking away her dream in the process.

"Katie? Katie?" Ryder waved his hand in front of her face. "Are you listening?" He grasped her arm and guided her away from the sign. "Let me get you out of the cold."

Katie looked over her shoulder to catch one last glimpse of the farmhouse. "Someone bought my house."

"Someone saved you from a very big financial risk," Ryder said as he helped her over the pile of snow.

Katie yanked her arm away from Ryder and glared at him. "How can you say that? I loved that house. I wanted it."

"You can't always get what you want," he said softly, almost pensively.

There was no need to tell her that. She knew it firsthand. No matter how hard she tried, how much she changed her life, she was not the type of woman who got everything she wanted. She was the girl who just had to suck it up.

She reluctantly got into the truck. Ryder gave her a searching look before declaring, "I'm going to take you back home." Katie didn't respond as he closed the door. She leaned forward and pressed her forehead against the window. She still couldn't believe that the house had been sold right out from under her. Why hadn't the Realtor warned her?

She felt Ryder's hand on her arm. Katie dragged her gaze away from the house to see that he was now in the driver's seat. She met his concerned gaze. "Seat belt," he reminded her.

It took a couple of attempts, but she managed to take care of the small task as Ryder started the truck. She continued to stare out the window until the farmhouse was out of view.

"Have you heard a word I've said?" Ryder asked.

Katie looked at him. "What?" She recognized they were on her street again. The ride home had been a blur.

Ryder rolled his eyes. "I just spent the past ten minutes telling you why you couldn't buy the house. Why you *shouldn't*."

She was so tired of that word. *Shouldn't*. She shouldn't go after the Merrill house. She shouldn't go after Ryder. She shouldn't care. She shouldn't cry. Katie felt the sting in the back of her eyes and was afraid to blink in case the tears started rolling. She wasn't going to have their final moments end with her sobbing. Katie focused on her parents' house coming up. She could keep a brave face until she got inside.

"I—" She stopped as her voice hitched in her throat. To her horror the first tear started to spill before she could stop it.

Ryder parked in front of the house. "Katie?"

She skipped crying and went straight to bawling. Not little delicate tears and cries, but the heaving, gasping, scary sobs. She tore off her seat belt and reached for the latch, but Ryder moved faster. He had her in his arms before she could open the door.

"It's going to be okay," he murmured in her ear as he gently stroked her hair.

"No, it won't," she said, her voice muffled in his chest. She wanted two things out of life and she was getting neither.

"It's just a house."

Something froze inside her. Hardened and crystallized. She couldn't remember a time when she'd felt so cold. "Just a house?" She pushed away from him. "Did you say it was *just a house*? That house represented everything I wanted out of life."

Ryder stared at her. "*That* house?"

"*That* house was perfect." She sat back in her seat and pushed the hair from her face. "When I had a bad day at work or if you were dating some gorgeous woman, I would drop by that house and imagine what it could be."

"What?" He squinted at her, the confusion clouding his dark eyes. "What do I have to do with this?"

"Don't you get it?" She wiped the tears from her wet face. "Oh, you probably don't. And you probably don't want to know. It might scare you."

"Try me." He placed one arm on the back of the seat, the other arm on the window. His long, lean body was sprawled out and he seemed open to whatever came his way.

She paused. She wasn't up to telling him. Every time she opened up and shared a piece of her dream, he rejected it. All this time she hadn't wanted to scare him off because she might lose her opportunity. But what did she have to lose now? He never said he loved her, and after today, she would never see him again.

"Whenever I drove by that house, I could imagine what life could be like," she confessed, looking down at her hands. "It included you and me, creating a home together."

He sat up straight, his arms coming down.

She gave a humorless chuckle. "Scared you already? Well, brace yourself because that's just the tip of the iceberg. That house has enough rooms for children." Katie felt the sudden tension vibrate through him. "Yeah, that's right. I fantasized about having it all with you."

He ran his hand through his hair. "I thought . . . you only wanted a . . ."

"An affair?" she finished for him. "That was going to be the start. My New Year's resolution focused on us getting together. I really thought that would be our only hurdle."

She saw him pale and his jaw slacken. Ryder moved his mouth, but no words came out. When she saw the panic in his eyes, the last spark of hope fizzled.

"Yeah, that's what I thought you'd say," Katie said with a wry smile. She opened the truck door and slowly got out. "I'm usually very straightforward with you. I didn't tell you what I really wanted because I knew you wouldn't touch me."

"That's not true," he was compelled to say.

She leaned against the door. "You really would have entered a relationship with me knowing I wanted forever?" she asked, her eyebrow arching in disbelief.

Ryder's mouth opened and closed.

"I thought so." She slammed the door and walked to her parents' house. Katie heard the whine of the car window rolling down and knew Ryder wasn't going to let her have the last word.

"I'm not a family guy," he called out after her.

"Keep telling yourself that and you might start believing it," she called back over her shoulder.

"You of all people know I'm no good with families."

She whirled around. "You think that because you're basing everything on what your own family did," she corrected angrily. "And good riddance to them. But when you were with us, I saw how much you valued family."

"That's not the same," he argued.

"If we had made a family, you would have done anything to protect and provide for them. And so would I." She pressed her hand over her pounding heart. "I would have created the home you couldn't wait to get back to."

He continued to stare at her.

"I know that reaching that dream wouldn't be easy. There would be risks and mistakes and setbacks, but we could have made it work." She took a deep breath, feeling the tears stinging in her eyes again. "But not anymore."

"Because the Merrill house isn't available?" He pointed in the direction of her dream home.

She pointed at him. "Because you're leaving before anything can happen."

He hit his steering wheel with the palm of his hand. "That's not why I'm leaving."

"Yeah, you're leaving before you ruin how I feel about you," she said as she opened the front door. "You think I'm going to stop loving you, and you want to be long gone before that happens."

"You'll thank me later."

"Why?" she yelled back, her hands shaking as she gripped the door handle. "Why would I thank you for showing that whatever I do, it's not enough? That *I'm* not enough for you?"

"Katie!"

She stepped inside and slammed the door shut. She leaned against the solid wood, needing its support. She knew locking the door would be a waste of time. Ryder wasn't going to come after her. He was moving out and moving on.

When she heard the growl of Ryder's truck's engine as it sped down the street, Katie slid down the door and sat. Ryder was gone forever. Now she could cry.

Why? Ryder clenched his teeth as he drove off, the truck tires squealing in protest. He wanted to run after Katie and comfort her, and it took all of his willpower to leave her alone. After all, he was the source of her pain.

Creating a home together.

Katie's words wafted inside his head like a curl of smoke, provoking cozy images he couldn't allow. He really was no good with families. He wished he was, but didn't let that show, protecting that weak spot of his. It was hurtful enough that his own family didn't want him around.

But Katie wanted him, and was willing to take the biggest leap of faith by creating a family with him. Ryder winced and slowed his truck. Damn, why did Katie have to lay that on him now? Hours before he was leaving for good.

He did not need this. Ryder rubbed his aching head with a tense hand. He could drive away right now, throw his bags in the truck and leave without looking back.

I fantasized about having it all with you.

Ryder punched the steering wheel with frustration and continued driving. Yeah, he fantasized about that, too. In those unguarded moments, he imagined having Katie at his side, always there no matter what happened.

I wanted forever.

Ryder never allowed himself to dream about forever. His track record proved that no one could handle him for any length of time. Except for Katie, but she saw him differently. For years she had built him up in her mind as some sort of hero, and Ryder should have destroyed that image long ago. But he wanted to be the kind of guy Katie thought he was, and when he was with her, he felt like he could be. It was dangerous to think that.

Because eventually he would ruin everything, and her love for him would die. He couldn't live with that. Katie's love was the greatest gift he received, and he was afraid of losing it.

Ryder slowed down his truck when he saw the Merrill house coming up. He didn't know why he had decided to drive down this street. He parked at the curb and stared at the house, trying to see what Katie loved about it. The house was run-down and he could make a list of problems just from a glance. It could be a solid structure, if someone was willing to invest a lot of money, time and tender loving care.

Maybe Katie saw him the same way. He hadn't had a lot of success with families, with relationships, but she was willing to take the risk with him. Even more than that, Katie wanted to give him the one thing he didn't have the courage to go after.

He wished he could do the same for her. If there ever was a time to prove that he could be the guy Katie thought he was, this was it. It would mean throwing caution to the wind, and risking Katie's love, the most precious thing he had.

Ryder stared at the Merrill house, his heart pounding hard in his chest, as he noticed every problem and every potential in the house.

I would have created the home you couldn't wait to get back to.

She had been doing that for years, Ryder thought as he turned the ignition. Now it was his turn, and he couldn't wait.

CHAPTER NINETEEN

Katie lowered her head and winced as the music blared through the speakers. She felt the rhythm vibrate in the floor, through the soles of her feet, and invade her frail body. Her wrung-out heart pounded. It was building and building until it threatened to puncture through the weak armor of her skin.

"I can't believe you dragged me to this," Katie yelled over the music as she stood against the wall of the New Year's Eve party. She would usually try to drag her friends out of the darkened corner, but tonight she wanted to be invisible. She didn't want to pretend that she was having fun. She certainly wasn't going to reminisce or look forward.

One of her male coworkers walked by and smiled at her. Katie glowered back. Hmm, she might have dated that one once. She couldn't remember and she didn't care.

"Hey, you have no right to complain," Melissa decided, guzzling down a glass of champagne. "You dragged me to the Christmas Eve party."

"That was different."

"Hardly." Melissa wiped the back of her hand across her mouth. "You're even wearing the same outfit."

She looked down at the black turtleneck and leather skirt combo, complete with the black leather stiletto boots. Katie hadn't had a chance to return them, and when she saw them in her closet she felt they suited her mood perfectly. "If anyone asks, I'm in mourning."

"Fine, I will be, too." Melissa gestured at her outfit. The fitted black pantsuit was kind of cute. Sexy and sporty. It suited Melissa, emphasizing her athletic build and tomboyish style.

Katie felt old and dowdy next to her friend. She had no energy and just wanted to go back home and sleep until spring. Katie leaned her head against the wall and let out a long, whiny groan.

"I'm beginning to regret forcing you out of the house," Melissa said as she grabbed another plastic flute of champagne. "I really thought this would be a good idea. I'm sorry."

"Sure, now you say that." Where was the reprieve when she was under her warm covers, huddled in a ball, and all cried out? Melissa showed no mercy and had been adamant that Katie fulfill her obligations. And all this time Katie thought her friend had been a softie.

"You're obviously not ready to be out in public," Melissa said and took a big gulp from her glass, wrinkling her nose as the bubbles got to her. "I know you think I'm being hard on you, but the sooner you get back out in the world, the easier it will be."

"Remind me never to ask you to be my life coach," Katie said. "In case you haven't noticed, Melissa, I lost my dreams all in one day. And that day was *today*. I haven't even had twenty-four hours to come to terms with it. Give me a break."

"It only feels like you've lost." Melissa patted Katie's shoulder with bruising force. "It's really a setback."

"No, I ran out of time. Out of luck." Katie rubbed her shoulder.

"You know, I went after what I wanted, all cylinders firing. I did not hold back. I was so sure that if I gave it my all, I would achieve the impossible." She obviously had read too many articles on positive visualization.

"Why are you surprised?" Melissa said, trying to talk and drink champagne at the same time. "Okay, I get it with the house. I'm as surprised as everyone else that there was a buyer."

"Melissa, that house was a diamond in the rough!"

"If you say so." Melissa waved off the declaration with her hand. Unfortunately, it was the hand that was holding the champagne. The golden bubbly sloshed from the rim and Katie jumped out of the way.

"But Ryder?" Melissa asked and shook her head. "You knew he was leaving. The whole point was to get him into your bed before he left. You did that. Mission accomplished. Let's drink to it." She took another gulp from her glass.

Mission accomplished? It sounded so cold. Katie glared at Melissa. "My time with Ryder was more than that."

"I know. I hope that you'll be able to look back and appreciate what you had with Ryder, even though the outcome wasn't what you hoped for." The corners of Melissa's mouth turned down and trembled. She pressed her lips together and determinedly gave a small smile. "Let's focus on something more positive," she suggested as she raised her glass for a toast. "Let's hope that Hilary will be just as successful with her resolution."

"Hilary made a resolution?" Had she learned nothing from this past week? And all this time Katie had thought Hilary was the smart one out of them all.

"She learned that blondes really do have more fun," Melissa said as she watched the party around her. "And Jake prefers blondes, so guess what?"

Katie stared at her friend in shock. "Hilary went blonde? *Our* Hilary?" She looked in the crowded party, hoping to see that Melissa had gotten it wrong.

"Platinum, baby." She took another sip of champagne and smacked her lips. "She's probably stalking Jake now. You know how Hilary likes to get a head start on projects."

"I can't believe she's doing this. Not after . . ." Katie snapped her mouth shut. She had promised not to reveal Hilary's lowest moment. "Not after the mess I made with my resolution."

"But everything turned out fine. Ryder isn't mad at you anymore and you had your wild affair."

"But that's all I got and I wanted it all."

"There will be other houses and"—Melissa hesitated—"other men. Just wait and see."

She didn't want to think about other men. "You surprise me, Melissa. You kept saying that Ryder and I were made for each other. Now there are other men out there for me?"

"Well, Hilary wasn't the only one who learned a lesson this week." Melissa looked down at her champagne glass. "I finally realized that just because you're made for each other doesn't necessarily mean you get the fairy tale."

Katie knew that Melissa was trying to be comforting, but each word cut like a knife. And now her rosy outlook had taken a hit. Katie hated that. She wanted her friend to believe that love conquers all, especially when she was having trouble with it herself.

"Okay, no more champagne for me," Melissa said as she set her glass down on the floor. "And maybe we should let Hilary handle the pep talks from now on. Although I don't think I can take her seriously as a blonde."

"She'll just tell us to suck it up," Katie said as she tilted her head on the wall. "It's not as easy as she says."

"You're doing a good job," Melissa assured her. "You haven't cried at all."

"I'm all out of tears. And I know my mascara will run. The fear of looking like a raccoon is a great deterrent." Katie saw a gleam of gold from the corner of her eye and stiffened.

"Look who showed up, Sasha," Tatum said as she approached. "Katie Kramer."

Katie didn't move. She wasn't in the right frame of mind to deal with Tatum, but there was no getting out of it. If she walked away, they would just keep circling until they went in for the kill.

She eyed Tatum, who was wearing the gold freakum dress. The men couldn't keep their eyes off her. A few were starstruck and it was obvious that they would do anything to make it a very happy New Year for Tatum.

Tatum was acting as if it was her due. And why not? Both she and Sasha knew how to make the most out of their appearance. They practiced the skill until it became an art form.

And while Katie was envious of their talent, she knew she didn't want to be like Tatum or Sasha. She didn't feel it was necessary to have every man lust after her. She only wanted the power to attract Ryder and bring him to his knees.

"I'm surprised to see you, Katie," Sasha said as she jutted one hip to the side and visibly calculated the label and price of Katie's outfit.

"Why is that? I wouldn't miss this party for anything," Katie said as she took a sip of her virgin daiquiri. She might be down and out, but she had her pride.

"Happy New Year!" Melissa said cheerfully, searching for a conversation that wasn't fraught with minefields, but Tatum and Sasha ignored her as usual.

"Like my dress?" Tatum asked Katie. She rubbed her hands over her sides and hips.

"It's very nice," Katie said, refusing to rise to the bait. She didn't trust the mood she was in. She felt numb, but she knew it wouldn't take much for her to start crying. That was the last thing she wanted to do in front of these two.

"Didn't you wear that outfit at the last party?" Sasha asked Katie.

Katie crossed her arms. She knew the magazines said it was a defensive pose, but she didn't care what her body language was saying anymore. "Why do you ask? Are you dedicating a blog to my fashion sense?"

Sasha's laugh was brittle. "You're not that interesting."

"Apparently I am if you're keeping track of my every move."

"Katie," Melissa murmured in her ear, "are you sure that drink doesn't have any alcohol?"

"Yes, unfortunately." She twirled the daiquiri glass in her hand.

She gave Sasha and Tatum a nervous look before telling Katie, "I've never heard you talk like this."

"Really?" That surprised Katie.

"Well, in public."

"Hold on tight, Melissa. I have a feeling that it's only going to go downhill from here."

"Everyone thought you'd be at home," Sasha said with pseudo-sympathy, "drowning your sorrows in ice cream. You made a fool of yourself going after Ryder. Now look. He slipped right through your fingers."

Katie took a step closer and noted with grim satisfaction how Tatum and Sasha took a step back. "Here's a lesson, free of charge. I don't need a tight grip to keep Ryder. If I want him, all I have to do is snap my fingers."

She snapped her fingers in the women's faces and watched them flinch. As much as this was an act of bravura, Katie realized what she said was true. Ryder might be leaving, but he wasn't turning his back on her. She could still call him and e-mail him if she needed him. She was sure he would be there for her, especially after everything that had happened between them. And if she asked for help, Ryder would drop everything and give her whatever she needed. The question was, did she have the nerve to use that power?

Her instincts said no, and for one simple reason. She could stake her claim on him all she wanted, but she didn't have the right. Ryder loved her, but he wasn't in love with her, otherwise he would have stayed. That was a big difference in her opinion.

Tatum was having none of Katie's ramblings. "Come on, Sasha. Obviously Katie can't handle the fact that she couldn't keep Ryder's interest for long. Not even for a full week."

Okay, that hurt. Tatum's comment cut way too close to the bone. Katie gripped her drink so tightly that she was surprised the glassware didn't snap under her whitened fingers.

It was amazing that Tatum could zero in on her deepest fear with such accuracy. Katie had given her all to Ryder and he was still walking away. It hurt knowing that she had shed her inhibitions, opened her heart, and it wasn't enough.

She jumped, startled, when she felt a masculine, very familiar hand, clasp her wrist. It was only then that she realized she was about to toss her strawberry drink down the front of Tatum's dress.

"Careful, Katie," Ryder said as he removed the glass from her hand. "You almost spilled your drink."

Katie turned around in total shock. She couldn't believe Ryder was there. She had assumed he was halfway to the airport by now and would never come back to Crystal Bend again. She couldn't take her gaze off his face. "What are you doing here?"

"I thought I heard you snap."

Katie stared at him, noting the way his eyes gleamed with amusement. She felt the hot, red tide zoom up her neck and surge into her cheeks. How much had he heard?

"Hi, Ryder," Sasha said, tossing back her gorgeous mane of hair. "I didn't know you would be here."

"You're looking hot, Ryder," Tatum said, curling her hand on his arm.

Katie had to agree. Tonight he wore a dark black suit and a black shirt. He was sinfully handsome. He looked like he could have walked right off of the cover of a men's magazine. She thought he looked sexy in jeans and a T-shirt, but right now he was overloading her senses.

"Stop eating me with your eyes," Ryder cautioned Katie. "You're making everyone blush."

She didn't care. In fact, she wanted to make him blush. "Would you rather I turn my thoughts into actions?"

He flashed a wicked smile. "Yes . . . Yes, I would. Excuse us," he said to Melissa, ignoring the other women. "I need to drag Katie away."

"Why don't you just toss her over your shoulder?" Melissa suggested.

"I need to conserve my strength," Ryder said with a wink.

"As happy as I am to see you," Katie told Ryder as he led her away, "what are you doing here? I thought you were leaving."

"I'm not finished packing."

Her heart was beating hard, but she wasn't going to read anything into Ryder's unexpected appearance. She was hurting too badly to indulge in foolish hopes. "And the way to complete the job is to go out and party for a few hours? Or did you come here to recruit me because you know how much I love bubble wrap?"

"I couldn't stay away from you, Katie. I was thinking about what you said today."

She took another sip of her drink and decided she was really thirsty. Ryder took the drink from her hand and handed it to a guest walking by.

"Hey, I wasn't finished with that!" She reached for her drink but it was too late.

Ryder stood in front of her to gather all her attention. "I said that I was thinking about what you told me today."

"I said quite a few things and I don't regret a single one."

"Good to hear. I wanted to give you this." He reached into his jacket, removed a sheaf of papers, and handed them to her.

"These look official." She unfolded the document and glanced at them. She frowned as she caught a few key words and started reading it in earnest. "What is this?"

He watched her intently, but there was no expression in his face. "I put in an offer for the Merrill house."

He bought the Merrill house? That can't be. "But it was sold." She saw the sign herself.

"I bought it from the buyer."

He acted as if it had been the simplest thing to do, but she knew it must have been a battle. How had he managed to get the house? Why did he do it? "What did you have to offer?"

He gave a wry smile and shook his head. "You don't really want to know."

"Why did you make an offer for it?" Why would he do this for her? Was he trying to take care of her one last time, or was it something more? No, she wasn't going to get her hopes up high again. Katie ducked her head and covered her mouth with her hands. "Ryder . . . this is . . ."

"Did I get this all wrong?"

Katie glanced up and saw the vulnerability in his face. "No, not at all. I can't tell you how much this means to me, but I can't accept this." She handed him the papers.

He refused to take them. "Don't get all ladylike on me now. You're keeping the house."

She pressed the papers against his chest, determined that he take it all back. "You said I couldn't afford it."

He clasped his fingers around her wrist, trapping her hand against his chest. "We'll find a way."

"That it was too much house for me," she reminded him.

"You'll need a room just for your Christmas decorations."

"Ryder, I'm serious. I wanted the house because I thought it was the perfect place for you and me. As a couple. But since you're leaving, I really can't imagine living there."

Ryder closed his eyes and sighed. "I messed up."

"No, not at all." She cupped his cheek with her other hand. "It was a beautiful gesture."

"That's not what I meant," he said with a groan and opened his eyes. She felt the kick in her veins when she saw the determined glint in his eyes. "I'm getting the house because I'm staying."

"You're staying in Crystal Bend?" she asked. "In my dream house? How can *you* afford it?"

"I've been saving for my move for a while. Once I canceled my ticket to Dubai, all the money was enough for the down payment. I'm a carpenter, aren't I? I can do the renovations cheaply and turn it into a beautiful home. But I can't unless we do it together. I'm staying for you. With you."

Heat curled and melded in her blood as her pulse quickened. Did he mean what she thought he meant? "What exactly *are* you saying?"

"You are mine," he declared as he took a step closer until her hand was trapped between them. "I am yours."

She smiled and looked up in his eyes. "Tell me something I don't already know."

He rubbed his hand over her fingers. "I'm going to put a wedding ring on you so everyone knows we belong together."

Her heart started thumping. "Marriage?" The word came out in a croak.

"Yep." He took another step and guided them into the shadows. Her spine was against the wall, and the party around them faded into swirling colors and white noise. She felt like they were in their own little world.

"You don't have to," she said, and instantly wanted to kick herself. But she also didn't want him to feel pressured. "Everyone already knows we belong together."

"Do they know that you love me beyond distraction?" he asked with a smile.

"When did you figure it out?"

"I got the hint when you bound yourself to my bed. And I figured you knew I was crazy about you."

Her heart skipped a beat. "No, I didn't know that."

"Are you kidding me? I've been in love with you for so long. I don't know when it happened. It's like it suddenly sneaked up on me. One day we were in my truck, laughing over something. I looked over at you and the realization hit me so hard, I slammed on the brakes. I don't know what it was about that moment. Maybe because of the way you were smiling, or the way you were looking at me. All I knew was that at that moment I loved you and I wanted to be with you, always."

"You never said."

"I'm not good with words," he admitted. "But I thought you could tell. Why else would I look after you? Chase you and bring you home from that damn club? Why else would I leave town so you could find a family guy?"

She pulled her hand away and allowed the sheaf of papers to fall to the ground. Katie linked her hands over his shoulders. "I don't want anyone but you, Ryder."

"Come on, you guys. It's almost time for the countdown," Melissa called out as she walked past them and into the crowd.

Ryder didn't respond, his gaze never leaving Katie. "So are you going to marry me?"

"Was there ever any doubt?"

"Yes!" Ryder wrapped his arm around her waist and held her against him. "Why do you think I made sure I had the house documents before I asked?"

"I would have said yes no matter what," she confessed as she curled into him, her breasts pressed against his chest. "But what about the house? It's a big risk."

"We'll make it." He brushed his mouth against hers.

Where were the lists of reasons why she shouldn't have the house? "How can you be so confident?"

"I've seen you in action, Katie," he said over the crowd counting down. "You fight for what is yours."

"And so do you." She kissed him hard as the cheers exploded around them. Confetti and curls of ribbons rained down as balloons bumped against their heads and shoulders.

"Happy New Year, Ryder," she said against his mouth.

He lifted his head. "Hey, you were right."

"About what?" she asked dreamily as she raised her leg and curled it against his hip.

"You swore that I was going to wake up in your bed on New Year's Day."

She laughed and hooked her other leg over his lean hip so she was astride Ryder.

"Behave yourself, Katie," Ryder teased as he glided his hands down to her hips, fitting her snugly against him. "We're still in public. You don't want to scandalize the town with your wanton behavior."

Katie crossed her ankles, effectively caging him with her body. She had no intention of letting him go. "They'll have to get used to it."

EPILOGUE

December 31

TWO YEARS LATER

He was naked. Gloriously, beautifully, wonderfully naked.

Katie Kramer Scott's pulse skipped a beat. She knew it was bad manners to stand there and stare. The least she could do was cover Ryder's body with hers, breasts to chest, hip to hip, and share her body heat with his.

But she couldn't. Not yet, when she could watch and savor the moment quietly. Sprawled against the king-sized mattress, arms flung out, Ryder was in the exact position she had left him in when the sun rose. After she had rode him hard and long, and held him until he fell back to sleep.

Ryder had been a willing victim to her insatiable carnal need. Now he slept soundly, replete and satisfied. The thick, dark blue comforter had fallen on the floor at the foot of the bed, exposing his magnificent masculine beauty.

Her gaze hungrily traveled down Ryder's naked body. He was a glorious sight, and not just because the winter morning light shone on his muscular form. He was in her bed. *Their* bed.

Katie considered what would be the best way to wake him up. Should she smooth her hands along Ryder's golden brown chest,

letting her hands sink into the luxurious mat of hair before following the trail to his thick and aroused cock? Or should she greet him
in the morning by cupping his cock with both hands before pressing
her lips against the crown?

Decisions, decisions. She loved waking up with him, and she
enjoyed having the freedom to touch Ryder anytime, anywhere. It
had been worth the wait.

Katie shivered as she felt a curl of the winter morning cold.
Skimpy nighties and arctic winter mornings really didn't mix. Fortunately Ryder knew how to warm her up.

She gripped two hot coffee mugs and padded barefoot into the
master bedroom. This room was the first area they had renovated in
the Merrill house. She hadn't thought much about what she wanted
it to look like, but with Ryder's input, it had become a warm, sensual and inviting room that she never wanted to leave.

And, in the past two years, she had transformed herself into the
woman she'd always wanted to be. She was the confident, sensual
and powerful woman of her dreams. It was no longer a guise. Instead she had shed her insecurities, thanks to having Ryder at her
side. Katie hadn't been aware of her gradual transformation until
recently. It had happened so naturally.

Her clothes weren't so daring, at least outside of the bedroom,
and she'd been quick to return those leather stiletto boots, but it
didn't matter. Ryder had been right—what she'd thought were her
weaknesses were actually her strengths.

She was still curvy and soft, and she'd used her good-natured
traits to attract the man she had always wanted and captured him
for good. She no longer needed guidance from the celebrity magazines. She knew what she wanted out of life and she went after it
her way.

Katie froze when she heard the chime of the ankle bracelet she had worn since Ryder had given it to her a few days ago for Christmas. She looked down at the slender strand of gold with the jeweled heart charms and heard Ryder stir. She was beginning to wonder if he'd placed it on her ankle so he could hear her stealthy approach. More than once she had used the element of surprise to her advantage.

Ryder's eyes opened, his gaze colliding with hers. A silky heat curled deep in her belly. He immediately relaxed and stretched as he watched her set the coffee mugs on the bedside table.

"Good morning, Ryder," she said softly.

He reached for her. "Come back to bed." His voice was gruff with sleep.

She was tempted to fulfill his request, but once she got back under the covers, she knew she wouldn't leave for hours.

"I can't," she said with genuine regret. "We've got to get ready for the party." This was going to be their first big party now that the renovations on their house were complete. It was by no means finished. For now it offered the warmth, love and protection for her and Ryder. But Katie was sure that taking care of the Merrill house was a journey, adapting it to meet their needs once their family grew. She planned to be in this house with Ryder for the rest of her life.

"That won't be for hours," Ryder said. "Come lie with me."

She compromised and straddled his lean hips, his cock pressing against her. Katie moved forward and flattened her hands on his pillow, trapping Ryder. She leaned down, grinding her hips against him, as she placed a kiss on his lips.

"I love you, Ryder."

His eyes gleamed. "I know."

Katie scoffed and grabbed the pillow from his head. She got in a good whack before he rolled over, taking her with him. He tossed the pillow on the floor and pinned her to the mattress. She was well and truly caught. Katie wiggled her hips, not because she was trying to escape, but to torture Ryder.

"Tell me more," Ryder insisted as he kissed her lightly on the lips. "Tell me that you're mine."

"If you insist." She smiled slyly. "You are mine."

"I know." His eyes darkened.

She saw the trust and desire. She saw the love as clearly as if he had spoken it. He had made her feel loved and appreciated every day.

Ryder tilted his head to one side. "Why are you smiling like that?"

"Like what?" she asked innocently as she bucked her hips against his.

He closed his eyes and clenched his teeth, but her maneuver didn't distract him. "I know you, Katie. You're up to something."

"I'm smiling because I know something that you don't."

"What is it?" he asked as he kissed a trail down the curve of her throat.

"I took a home pregnancy test this morning."

Ryder froze. He looked up and stared at her with wide eyes. He swallowed hard, but said nothing. She saw the nervousness and hope flickering in his dark eyes. He moved slightly and rested his large hand against her stomach. Emotions welled up inside her at the protective gesture.

"That's right, Ryder." Katie draped her arms over his shoulders and drew him down for a kiss. "I'm pregnant."

ABOUT THE AUTHOR

Susanna Carr lives in the Pacific Northwest.
Visit her Web site at www.susannacarr.com.